M000085428

# The Willing

## By the Author

Not Broken

The Willing

**Visit us at www.boldstrokesbooks.com**

# The Willing

*by*

Lyn Hemphill

2022

**THE WILLING**



ISBN 13: 978-1-63679-083-1

This Trade Paperback Original Is Published By
Bold Strokes Books, Inc.
P.O. Box 249
Valley Falls, NY 12185

First Edition: February 2022



---

**Credits**
Editor: Barbara Ann Wright
Production Design: Stacia Seaman
Cover Design by Jeanine Henning

# Acknowledgments

Thank you to Red for helping me (again!) with Talia, and to Jenni and Vicky for letting me use their Oxford Uni experiences.

To freedom and found families.

# Chapter One

## *Talia*

As I walk along the pavement, my shoes soaking up the autumn rain, I wonder how easy it would be to die.

All it would take is a slip, a fall off this kerb. The cars whipping past on Woodstock Road aren't going fast, but the buses are heavy enough to get the kind of momentum I'd need. Or maybe I'd need somewhere higher, one of Oxford's many bridges.

It would be easy. Just one step. People do it all the time, don't they? All these lives jostling me as I lug my suitcase down the street, all of them so busy and careless and so much more important than anyone else. There are so many of them. But how many more have died? It must be easier than living.

I'm sweating by the time I get to my college. Check the address one last time on the front of the welcome pack, though I know it off by heart. I look at the towering facade of the college, wrinkling my nose against the rain, and I don't know why because I've seen it a million times before on Google Street View.

I'm up the stairs. There's no lift, just me and my suitcase and my new neighbours pushing up and down. The corridors smell of floor polish and age and ancient history. The students smell of sweat and too much Lynx body spray.

And then there's my room. It has a door, and right now, that's enough for me to love it. It has a bed, and just like that, I'm sold. I open my suitcase and pull out the duvet, already in its cover. Kick off my shoes and drop my coat on the floor, and I'm huddled under and out like a light.

A week later, I still feel like I just got here, and at the same time, I feel like it's been forever, and the thoughts clash in my head, jostling for position.

England is warm. It's well into October, and I'm sitting on the windowsill staring down into the quad. The sun's out, and that means the grass is peppered with study groups. Some of them have plaid blankets—that's never tartan—and I wouldn't be surprised if I saw someone with a picnic hamper. It's all so different to back home, but it's exactly the same.

I thought I would like the other people here. I thought there would be people like me, people who don't fit in. I guess, thinking back, I hoped that they'd look at me and beckon. Come into the fold, they'd say. We can see you belong here with us.

You're home now.

Stupid, I think, and I throw my apple core into the bin.

I thought a new place would bring me home, but maybe the problem's me. I've never had a home inside me, something like that.

I turn from the window and look at my blank walls. I wish I'd brought my posters. They wouldn't have taken much space, but then Ma didn't leave me much time to pack my things.

Stupid. I should have waited until I'd packed before telling her I wasn't coming home. "You're all high and mighty now, ya little English slut," she said. I ducked the ashtray she threw at me. "You take the best years of my life and leave with no thanks and no repayment for the roof I've put over your head for eighteen years. Well, fine, go! You always were a stuck-up little bitch."

It's funny, if you think about it. She's going around telling all her mates I'm taking tea with the Queen, all posh and that, but down here, they look at me like I'm speaking a foreign language. Some of *them* could take tea with the Queen, I bet. Their vowels could cut glass.

The long and the short of it is I packed a suitcase of clothes and a duvet. I've got a hoodie folded up as a pillow, and I'm going to have to spend some of my living allowance on socks soon because my one pair's soaked through again. I wish I'd grabbed my Doc Martens rather than my old trainers, but Ma threw one of them at me, and it went out the window. I couldn't risk going to find it and getting locked out, and then I was grabbing my bags, and it all went too fast. I just wanted to get away.

I could've gone to the synagogue, I know. And just like that, my bed looks more inviting than anywhere else in the world, and I can't resist the pull. I crawl under my duvet, the bare mattress scratchy under my palms, and bury my face in the makeshift pillow, covering myself from head to toe and wishing I was back there.

Such bitter irony that I found my home and my family just a little way down the road from the place where I grew up, but it took moving hundreds of miles to realise that. I try to breathe steady and slow and pretend I don't feel the tears seeping out and trickling down my nose. I see their faces, I can hear the melodic song of *hatefila*, and more than anything, I can feel the total focus.

It took me years to learn it. The words and the traditions, yes, but more than that, the trust. To learn that this specific warmth and smell and sound meant safety, meant that I could lose myself in the rhythm and the worship and believe in something greater than all the grey in my world.

I saw in colour when I prayed.

One more week goes by. I've got an essay due on Thursday, I tell myself as I grab my diary from the desk. Email it to Professor Yeo by midday Thursday. I hold the information in my head as I have done since I left the tutorial. I feel my muscles relax incrementally as I write it on my schedule. I'm angry with myself for forgetting my diary this morning, leaving it here when it should have been with me in my tutorial. I press the pen harder than necessary, tapping out a period at the end, an imperative. Then I scowl at the paper because Ma used to do that when she signed my permission slips for school, annoyed that I'd interrupted reruns of Jeremy Kyle on Dave or whatever.

I push the diary to the top of the desk, snap it shut like a warning. To myself or the diary? I don't know. Better to think of elementary optics instead. I open my laptop to start on the essay.

There's a red number one on my email icon, and my heart skips, then aches. I forget about my work and open Rabbi Morgan's message like a starving dog on a bone.

*Dear Talia,*

*It was so lovely to hear from you this weekend. We're all so proud of you for getting into such a prestigious university and on such a difficult course too! I'm glad you've settled in. I'm sure you'll be making friends in no time.*

*It's an awkward subject, Talia, but I want to be honest with you. Kenny from the Labour Club has a sister who lives over in Kennishead, and he seems to think your ma's kicked you out of the house? I don't like to gossip, but if that's true, I just wanted to extend all our love and support to you. It's always yours anyway, but the thought of you going all that way by yourself just breaks an old man's heart, and I hope you know there will always be a place for you here. You know Mrs. Jacobs would be thrilled to have you to stay. All the better to fuss over you.*

*I suppose what I'm saying is, I know the Shul can't possibly replace your family, but we're all very fond of you, and wanted to remind you of that.*

*I would also like to introduce you to Rabbi Daniel from the Oxford Synagogue. I've told him a little bit about you, no gossip, of course, just how bright and passionate you are, and he's keen to welcome you to Oxford. He's a young man too, so I'm sure you'll find him much easier to get along with than us. I've attached his details here, but he says you can just drop in any time too.*

*Yours affectionately,*
*Morgan*

I stare at the email for a long time, reread it again and again. I can hear his voice as if he's handing me a cup of tea after Shabbat service. My heart catches on mention of Mrs. Jacobs, and I think of her and the other ladies that used to fuss over me and tell me I'm too skinny, bring me home-baked challah and cupcakes. How could I get along with anyone better than them? How could I even try?

I close the email and blink my feelings back down inside where they're meant to be. Physics makes sense: particles and forces and waves that manage to be mysterious and absolute at the same time, that follow rules, if we can only find out what those rules are.

I've got an outline by the time the sun's going down on dinnertime. It's like pulling teeth, getting the ideas out of my head into a coherent structure, and I'm not satisfied with my work. It shouldn't have taken that long, and I stare out the window, throwing my legs up over the arm of the chair. I'm being moody, I know, but there's no one here to care.

The sky's a deep velvet blue at the top of my window, lightening to an artificial glow over the roof of the other side of the college, yellow lights reflecting off puddles and the damp in the very air, muddying up the clarity of night. I consider getting dinner for a moment, but the thought of other people and their conversations and their *chewing* noises and their heat…I can't bear it. But I also can't stay here.

Decision made, I'm all motion. The stamping of my feet into my shoes is satisfying, a tantrum without the judgement, of whom I don't know. I slam the door and throw my coat on in a spin. I can feel my body wanting to make loud noises and angry motions, but for now, the thump of my steps on the stairs echoing around the halls is enough.

I burst out into the night air and breathe in the cold. My eyes shut briefly, relief. Maybe I should have done this earlier. The endless balance of self-care and work. Work's more important. People actually care about work. They'll bug you for not finishing your work, while they don't give a shit if you've eaten today.

I tuck my hands in my pockets and walk aimlessly, and my body feels like it's uncoiling, falling into the air around me like onto a feather bed. I don't think of anything as I dodge people, lampposts, puddles. It's just me and my feet and the possibility of the road in front of me.

It's how I found the synagogue over three years ago. I'd been walking like this for miles, straight out of the school gates, not wanting to go back home to a flat that stank of cigarettes and stale breath and dirty dishes. Sometimes, I think my feet led me that way for a reason because even though I'd never been there before, they knew the way home.

I'm walking across a wide road near a shopping park when it happens. Maybe I've been walking too long, maybe I'm more tired than I thought, maybe I didn't pay enough attention, though I could have sworn I looked both ways. But I can't have because there's a scream—brakes? A person?—and something hits my legs out from under me, and then my hips, and then my back and my ribs and my head, and oh God…oh God.

I don't know if I'm hearing right. I don't know if what I'm seeing is real; there are blurring lights, and it hurts to breathe, to move. I'm scrabbling on the rough tarmac as bubbles pop out of my mouth, sharp and tangy and warm and so fucking painful. I'm crying. I would be begging, calling out for someone to hold me and take it away, take it all away, please, but I can't because I can't get the breath to speak.

When I wake up, I remember dying. I remember the lights, the fear, the all-encompassing pain. I remember not being ready to go.

That surprises me.

I sit up and look around. Nothing hurts. Nothing's even uncomfortable. I touch my ribs, hips, legs. Everything's where it should be, smooth and unblemished.

I stand. I've been lying on the ground. I suppose it's some sort of ground, though looking at it, finding out what it is, what it's made of, *where* it is, seems to be impossible. My eyes skate over it onto something else.

But what else? There's nothing here. The world I now inhabit is grey and formless, a mist with shadows moving just out of reach of my eyes.

"Hello?" I call. My voice doesn't echo. "Hello?"

I begin to walk.

# Chapter Two

## *Kitty*

Something sharp jabs into my ribs, and I sit straight up. "'M not sleepin', sir, honest," I call.

Then I blink. There's no manager staring down at me, no colleagues looking and judging me, just my best mate giggling his head off like the buffoon he is. "Ugh, Matt." I put my head back down on my arms.

"C'mon, sleepyhead," Matt says. "It's time to go. Dad'll be waiting."

I groan and act like I haven't heard him. Matt goes over to the counter of the café to flirt with Connor, so I take full advantage and get a bit more kip in. I hear his trainers squeak on the lino as he stops and stands over me. "Go chat more," I grumble.

"I did," he says, the smile evident in his voice. "I've been chatting for like five minutes, Kitty."

"Kids today. Don't take their time over a good conversation." I haul myself up and drag my backpack out from under our table. There's a little bit of my latte left, and I chug it with a grimace because it's cold.

"That thing's more hole than backpack," says Matt, fingering one frayed corner of my bag.

"Don't listen to him, Henry," I croon, stroking the black nylon. "He doesn't see you like I do."

"You named your backpack? You named it *Henry*?"

"Shh, you'll hurt his feelings."

"You are one odd girl, Kitty Wilson."

I stick my tongue out and swing Henry over one shoulder. "What's that say about you, then?"

We wave to Connor and push the door open, the bell above it ringing merrily. I dodge around an old lady with one of those wheelie shopping baskets and trot to catch up with Matt, who's tapping a ciggie out of its pack. I open my mouth to ask about Connor, and it turns into another massive yawn.

"Another rough night shift?" he asks, taking my bag.

"Nah. More...*before* the shift that sucked."

"Wanna talk about it?"

I chew the inside of my lip a little longer than is really polite, but Matt knows me. Bloody ought to after all these years. He just waits. I shrug at last. "Not much to say. There was a guy who wanted his daughter back, but it'd been too long. We couldn't find her."

He links his arm with mine and squeezes for a moment. We walk like that a little way, even though it's hard with our height difference.

"You okay?"

"Sure, I guess. I mean." I force a laugh. "No matter whether I can do anything for them or not, it always ends in death, you know?" He looks at me, serious and sad, and I shrug. "Stupid power, anyway, innit?"

"It's an odd one, that's for sure," he concedes.

"*You're* an odd one."

He snorts and stubs his cigarette out as we get to his street, throwing it into the wheelie bin outside his house. He trots down the wonky steps to the door, which grinds as he tries to push it open. "Bloody thing's stiff again," he says, giving it a kick. I reach out beside him to help push the rain-swollen wood.

"Is that you, Matthew?"

"Yes, Papa. Are you gonna sort this door out or what?"

"Mind your manners." Peter grins as he comes down the stairs into the hallway and gives me a kiss on the cheek. "Tea?"

"Please," I say like my coffee was hours ago, not a short walk back.

"How was work?" he asks over his shoulder as he leads

us into the kitchen. His accent curls around the words, adding diphthongs everywhere. Always makes me smile.

"Tiring," I say, rubbing my eyes. "At least I get the rest of the day off after a night shift."

"You are such a hardworking girl," he says, hugging me close and kissing my head. I grin and don't push him off like Matt would, like he'd feel he has to. Peter's lovely, all lanky limbs and turtlenecks and scruffy reddish hair. "If you need sleep, you tell me, I'll collect Sam from school today."

"Nah, Peter, you don't need to," I protest. "I'll get plenty of sleep this afternoon anyway, and you do enough for us picking him up when I have to work day shifts."

"It's my pleasure," he insists. "The Wilsons and the Wiśniewskis, we're family. Isn't that right, Maciek?"

"You know it," Matt says from the food cupboard and throws me a packet of crisps. I fumble and drop them because I'm a liability. Matt laughs because he's a git, then points at his dad. "You've got ink on your nose again. You been doing the accounts?"

Peter sighs and rubs his face. "Yes, when are you going to get your economics degree and take over for me?"

Matt rolls his eyes. "How about never?"

Peter shakes his head and looks at me, attempting puppy eyes. "Where did I go wrong with him? Aren't I a good father? But no, he wants to be a music producer and find new talent to bring joy to the world. Traitor." He ruffles Matt's hair and laughs at the glare he gets. "What about you, Kitty?" he asks, handing me a cup of lemon-flavoured tea. "You want to be an economist or accountant perhaps?"

"Leave Kitty alone, Dad. Why don't you pay someone to do it?"

"But I *can* do it myself. I just don't *like* it." He sounds like Matt when he whines like that, and I hide my smirk in my cup.

"Hard luck," Matt says.

"Are you sure you don't want a job as an accountant, Kitty?"

"I wouldn't trust my maths," I say sympathetically.

"I don't trust my own," he grumbles.

❖

I feel the pull under my ribs just as I've slipped into a proper deep sleep. It wakes me up with a jolt, like someone's inside me pulling this string that's attached to my solar plexus. Tug, tug, tug.

I groan and rub my eyes. They feel like they're made of sand. Two nights in a row is taking the piss, honestly.

The moonlight is casting an underwater glow across my room. If I had the energy, I'd take a minute to appreciate it because it's beautiful, but I know I'll fall asleep if I don't move now.

The pull comes again, and I roll my eyes. As if I could fall asleep with *that*. I groan and roll out of bed, tugging a dressing gown on. The storage heaters aren't giving off much warmth yet, and my duvet looks so good from this angle, I could…

*Tug tug tug.*

I sigh and cross the corridor to the bathroom, checking that Sam's door's shut and his light's off as I go. I shut the bathroom door behind me and lean against the sink, sighing at my own reflection in the mirror.

"Right," I say. "Let's do this."

I relax, staring into my own eyes until I can feel the magic bubble inside me. I feel it flow into my arms as I reach out and draw the symbols my mother taught me. My hands move almost instinctively into the right shapes, they always have, directing the power somehow so that it reaches out into space and time to find that call, that desperate person on the other end of the metaphorical line. The face in the mirror reflected back at me blurs at the edges, wobbles, and morphs into someone else.

He jerks back, and his jaw drops open. "I…how?"

I wave cheerfully and stifle a yawn. "Let me guess," I say. "You were staring into the mirror thinking about your loved one and how you'd do anything to get them back?"

He blinks at me. "Um."

I'll take that as a yes. I hold out my hand. "I'm Kitty," I say, and launch into my spiel. I could do it in my sleep, which is bad, as I might fall asleep while doing it one of these days. "I have the power to bring people back from the dead, but only if there's someone willing to take their place. I don't know how it happens, I don't know why, all I know is that when people are desperate enough, they come to me. Or I come to them. Either way. So who would you like to see?"

"Is this a joke?"

"I wish," I say. "It's, like, three a.m., and I got woken up last night with a really long case. I'm knackered." I bite my tongue to stop myself from telling him to hurry it up.

"So you really…" He points to me, then points out into the misty grey nothing that surrounds us. I look at his finger, then back at him, and raise an eyebrow. He looks around. "Where are we? Is this death? Are *you* death?"

"I doubt it," I say. "I think I'm just…" A numpty with shitty superpowers. "A messenger."

"Right," he says, heavy eyebrows bunching into a frown. "This is some sort of hallucination, isn't it?"

"You'd be surprised how many people think that."

"Really?" he says, his voice pitching almost into a squeak. "You're wearing a fluffy dressing gown and telling me you can bring my best mate back to life, and you think—"

"Jason?" Ah, right on cue. I turn my retail smile on the newcomer, a young guy with a buzzcut and army fatigues. The man who called me staggers backward.

"What are you doing here, Jase? Are you dead too?" The newcomer glances at me sympathetically. "And you?"

"Ah, no, I'm actually—"

The first guy, Jason, launches himself at the newcomer, grabbing him in a bear hug so hard, I swear I hear someone's spine clicking. "Harry, mate, you're okay!"

"Well, other than being dead, I feel fine," says Harry.

Jason stands back and holds Harry at arm's length, looking down at him. He swallows hard. "You look…"

Harry smiles and slaps Jason on the shoulder that way boys do. "It's okay, mate."

Jason looks like he's going to cry. "I held you when…I was there—"

"Yeah, I know. I remember."

"You do?" Jason looks horrified.

"It's okay, it doesn't hurt anymore." Harry holds out his arms like he's displaying them. "All fixed, see? No bits missing."

Jason looks a bit ill. "I could've got you back to base faster. They could've stitched you up."

"Nah, mate, I was a goner as soon as that thing went off. I knew it. But you, you're not dead too, are you?"

"Me? No, no I'm not, but listen. Kitty here says she can bring you back, would you like that?"

Harry glances at me a bit apprehensively. "Come back, what, with both legs and an arm missing?"

"It wouldn't be like that," I interject. "It's more like you'd swap places with Jason, like he would always have been the one to die."

Jason winces and glares at me. "Oh, what?" I say, crossing my arms. "You think I was going to trick him into letting you take his place? You both have to be willing. Ain't you never had the informed consent talk?"

He looks at me funny, and I roll my eyes, figure he probably never has had the talk, or it's never been called that to him. Or it's always been in the context of *don't force yourself on girls*. Honestly. Society.

Harry looks at Jason so sadly. "Mate," he says, and just like that, I know it's not going to happen. "I don't want anyone else to die for me."

"And I didn't want you to die for me," Jason blurts out, grief making his voice shrill. "I should've been the one, it should've been—"

"It shouldn't have," Harry says, holding Jason by both shoulders. "It shouldn't have been any of us, but I'd do it again."

"You've just got married, though," Jason says. He looks down, his shoulders starting to curl in. His battle against the tears starting to fail. "You have so much to live for."

"So do you," Harry says. He hugs him, and their quiet words are lost to me, muffled in a tight embrace. They cling to each other; they murmur. Jason nods.

When they step back, Jason can barely bring himself to let Harry's shirt go, his hand caught in a rictus around the material. Harry looks at me, gives me a smile and a nod. He looks at Jason again, makes sure he has his attention. "You can do this, mate," he says.

Jason sniffs. Harry's starting to fade, and Jason snaps off a smart salute, so straight and rigid, he's almost shaking with the tension. I think that's all that's holding him up right now. His face is white and his eyes distant when he turns back to me. "What now?"

"You'll go back home," I say. "And listen, you should look up some mental health support, yeah? I know the army's a bit shit for that, but you deserve it."

He snorts and rolls his eyes. "I don't need it."

"That doesn't matter," I say firmly. "You deserve it, and it'll make it easier. Trust me."

I don't know if he'll take my advice. All of a sudden, I remember how bone tired I am and how soon I've got to get up to go to work. I sigh and beckon his gaze to meet my eyes. "Relax," I say. I let the magic rise up again, golden sparkles more visible in this world than they ever are in the real world. He watches the tendrils snake out from my palm and swirl around him, and he's gone.

I know I can't stay much longer. I look around, turning full circle until she appears from the mist to my side. My face splits in a grin. "Hiya, Mum," I say.

She laughs and runs to me, picking me up in a hug. "God, you're getting big," she breathes, brushing my hair back. "I won't be able to pick you up soon."

She says this every time. I crinkle my nose at her. "As if, you're as strong as an ox," I say.

She curls her arm as if to show off her biceps. She looks like the better version of me: a little brighter, a little taller, a little stronger. It seems like when you die, you revert to the happiest you've ever been, and it gives me a deep relief that she looks exactly the same as the last time I saw her alive.

"How are you two doing?" she asks, cupping my cheeks with both hands. I lean into it and soak up the love and magic there.

"Sam won an award for reading," I say, diving straight into the good news. "He came first in the whole school. I'm not surprised, though. That boy's always got his nose in a book. We're going to go into town this weekend to spend his voucher."

Mum claps her hands. "Aw, he's such a clever boy. Both of you are. Did that sigil help when you came through this time?"

I nod. "It smoothed out the bumps nicely, thank you."

"Seems like your magic really clicks with those flowing symbols, more so than the angular ones." I try to hold back a yawn. It hurts and doesn't work anyway. Mum frowns. "You're not getting enough sleep. What time is it out there?"

I sigh. "Four a.m., I think."

Her face crumples. "Oh, darling, I'm so sorry. I'll try to think of something to hold back the pull, at least part of the time."

She's starting to fade. I clutch her hand, but I can feel it turning cold and hard. Her words drift into dreams, and she might even have given me an extra push out of there, sent with a wave of love. I take a gasp, and I'm back in my bathroom, staring at my own exhausted face in the mirror, my hand gripping the sink.

❖

I can smell carp and something with that pickled cabbage stuff Matt really likes when I knock on their door. Peter opens it and gives me a hug, as always. "How was work?" he asks as I follow him through.

"Good," I say. "You?"

He crinkles his nose up. "There was a woman whose boiler burst this morning, two inches of water all over her floor." I hiss sympathetically, and he nods. "Oh yes, but the worst thing is she has cats, and the litter box had not been cleaned out. Did you know, Kitty, that cat poo floats?"

I bite my lip to stop laughing. "I did not."

Sam's at the kitchen table already doing his homework. I give him a half hug, leaning over his shoulder to look at his fractions. "God, you're so diligent," I say, ruffling his hair. "Are you sure you're my brother?"

Sam grins and continues writing.

"Kitty, is that you?" Matt yells from upstairs.

"Yeah?"

"C'mere!"

I roll my eyes and pretend like I'm reluctant to go, which fools exactly no one. "What?" I yell as I'm halfway up the stairs.

Matt leans over the banister. "Come on, come here."

"I'm coming, Jeez."

He drags me into his room and shoves me onto his bed. "Right, here's the thing. I need you to invite me for a sleepover tomorrow night."

"What? I'm working late tomorrow night. I won't be back till, like, one a.m."

He bites his lip. "And I need a spare key so I can get in later."

I laugh. "Fun sleepover. I say again, *what*?"

"I have a date."

"Oh my God!" I kick my shoes off and wriggle onto the bed properly, crossing my legs and leaning my elbows on my knees like it's story time in reception class. "Okay, I'm comfortable, go on."

He looks at the mirror, then back at me, a grin nearly splitting his face, his fists clenched up to hold him still. "So you know how I've had a crush on Connor Mururi forever?"

"No way!" I squeal.

"Shh! Yes, I asked him out, and we're meeting up in town later. So will you help me?"

"Of course, you numpty. But why do you need me to have you over? Does your dad not let you date or what?"

Matt snorts. "Like I'm gonna tell him."

I frown. "You're not...Oh!" It dawns on me, and I stare

open-mouthed. "You haven't told him you're gay? Seriously? I thought you guys talked about everything."

"Yeah, but not *that*."

"You think he'd be weird about it?"

Matt shrugs and sits next to me heavily, picking at a loose thread on his duvet cover. "I dunno," he admits. "I don't…okay, look, this sounds stupid, but I don't want to risk it, you know? I mean, some of the things he says when we watch TV are a bit…I'm just worried. Like, I love my dad. What if he doesn't accept this?"

He glances up at me, uncertain in a way he never lets himself appear, and my heart hurts. I wriggle forward and squeeze his hand. "Okay," I say. "Yeah, I'll be your fairy godmother."

He waggles his eyebrows. "Nice. You're the godmother. I'm the fairy, right?"

"Shut up." I laugh and push him backward.

He jumps to his feet, his eyes sparkling once again. "Okay." he says. "Okay, God. This is actually happening. I'm going out with Connor. Actual *Connor*! I don't even know what I was thinking when I asked him out, you know? I swear I thought he was gonna turn out to be a homophobe and punch me, but he *blushed*, Kitty, my God, he's so freaking *cute*!"

I bounce up and down on his bed, tucking my fists under my chin. "That's so awesome, mate. Where are you going on your hot date?"

"He got his license last week, so he's taking me up to the cineplex to watch the new Avengers movie, and then…"

I waggle my eyebrows. "And then?"

"Shut up," he says and shoves me, his pale cheeks flushing pink. "What am I gonna wear, though?"

"Work it out now. I'll critique. Go on, make yourself pretty."

He rolls his eyes at me and strips his shirt off while I pick up his guitar from the bottom of the bed and sling the strap over my neck. "Sure you don't mind me staying?" he asks, fiddling with his hair in the mirror.

"Not if you're quiet when you come in. Sam and I probably won't even notice. You'll have to sleep on the sofa, though."

"Yeah, yeah. Leave a duvet out, won't you?"

"And a pillow," I nod, picking out an arpeggio. "I know you hate sleeping on them throw cushions."

"They're pointless. Why do you even have them? It's not like they're comfortable."

I laugh at him. "'Cos they're pretty and I like them."

"But they get in the way." He shakes his head. "Throw pillows are such a girl thing. I don't get it."

"Nan gave them to me every birthday for years, feels like," I say with a smile. I regret it when Matt shuts his mouth with a click. I never meant to make him feel guilty. I sigh and let it go and tighten up the D string a touch.

Matt tugs his T-shirt a bit and straightens the collar of his plaid button-down. "How do I look?"

"Like a bisexual. Gimme my plaid back, that's appropriation."

He makes a face and flips me the bird. "Seriously, do you think it looks stupid?"

"No, of course not. You look gorgeous as always. Connor's gonna fall in love the moment he sees you."

"Kitty, stop taking the piss."

I lean both arms on the curve of the guitar and smile at him. "I'm not. You look amazing, Matty, you got that whole blue-eyed, soulful white boy thing going on. Connor doesn't have a chance."

He blushes, and I laugh until he covers his face. "Shut up."

"Come on, then," I say, putting the guitar aside. "Let's go get Sam and tell your dad about the 'sleepover.'"

❖

I'm on school run duty today. Sam can probably get home by himself—he's nearly eleven—but after those little gits cornered him in an alley and ripped his clothes, I've been waiting for him round the corner and walking back with him.

Leaving him home alone is not as bad as letting him walk home alone. Here there're cars that can hit him or little shits that can hurt him, but at home, there's the main door buzzer to get into the block of flats as well as the lock on the front door. Peter keeps telling me Sam can stay over when I've got a night shift, but I can't. I can't square that with what they already do for us.

"Hey, Kit," Sam says, knocking his bag higher on his back as he runs up to me and squeezes me around the middle. I hug him back. Matt keeps saying he's gonna grow out of this sometime soon, and I've banned him from saying anything like that to Sam. I want to be cuddling my little brother till he's in his twenties.

He tells me about this project they've got to do about scientists, and he's been reading up about Rosalind Franklin. I bet even the teachers don't know jack about her, but here's my little bruv with his Great Women in Science books and his chin up, not giving a crap about what the others think of him. Sometimes he's so damn mature, and he's always so damn clever. But he's still *little*, and I worry.

I pull my key out as we get to the flat. A thick, claggy smell curls out of the door, and we both crinkle up our noses. "Ugh, Kitty," Sam groans. "You forgot to leave the cabbage out."

"Bugger," I say, rushing to see if I can salvage it.

Sam groans and pokes it with a spoon. "I dunno why you even buy cabbage, not like anyone likes it."

"It's nice if it's not overdone," I protest. It's also cheap and filling, but Sam doesn't need to think about that.

He raises an eyebrow at me. How come he can do that, and I can't? He starts opening cupboards and pulling out spices, smelling them and adding some to the stew. "All right there, Jamie Oliver, what're you turning it into?" I ask.

He grins. "Caviar sauce on top of a venison tortellini."

"Nice. Lemme guess, with a saffron jus?"

He giggles. "Jus," he repeats, drawing out the *oo* sound. "On square plates, obviously."

"Oh, obvs." I cross my arms and lean against the counter, watching him work. "Are you really gonna add jam to that? It's stew."

He stirs a massive spoonful of cheap strawberry jam into the steaming concoction. "Trust me, I'm a doctor."

"Why would I trust a doctor to cook me dinner?"

"Just…go be useful. Get the bowls out or something. Can we have toast?"

I peer into the bread bin and crinkle my nose up. "We can have one piece each if we cut the mouldy crusts off." I think about it. "Is it bread you're supposed to throw away if one bit is mouldy?"

"I thought that was yogurt? You're not supposed to pick the mould off yogurt and eat the rest."

"Ugh, definitely not. But bread?"

He shrugs. "I dunno, you're the adult."

I consider. "Screw it, I'm not that hungry anyway. You can have the non-mouldy piece, and I'll get some on my way back from work tomorrow."

"Okay, thanks," he says.

I wonder for the millionth time, while I serve up bowls of stew, what our relationship would've been like if we'd had an easy life. If me and Sam'd had fewer responsibilities, would we be more like typical siblings you see on the telly? Would we wind each other up on purpose, get each other into trouble, have endless petty rivalries?

"Oh, Kit," he says, not looking at me as he lays the cutlery out on the table. "I think I need new school shoes."

My stomach drops, and I swear up a storm inside my head. "Yeah?"

He nods. "My toes are getting a bit squished."

I force a laugh. "You grow way too fast. You'll be overtaking me soon, then I'll make you do thinks like change the lightbulbs and get things off high shelves." I think I can make it work if I get lucky on eBay. If necessary, I can always get some from the cheapo place in town, but I don't like to. They may be cheap, but it's like they freaking dissolve in the rain. I'm sure they're made of cardboard. And then I have to buy new ones anyway.

Sam snorts. "You already get me to fetch things off high shelves," he says, taking the bowl from me and taking a huge mouthful. He spits it straight back out. "Hot, hot, hot!"

I laugh. "Careful, it's hot."

He sticks his tongue out at me. I make a show of blowing over my own spoonful before eating it. The tang of the jam almost hides the flavour of the overcooked cabbage, and I think of the vitamins as I swallow.

# CHAPTER THREE

## *Talia*

I don't know how long I walk before I find her. Does time exist when all your ways of measuring it have gone? Heartbeat, tiredness, all of it seem to have faded into memory.

She's the first person I've seen sign of, a middle-aged Black lady crouching to draw on the floor with a piece of chalk. The mist rolls over her work, and she frowns at it. Then glances up at me and stands with a bright smile, a denim maxi skirt swishing obnoxiously around her ankles. "Hello," she says. "You're new."

"Am I?"

She smiles and holds out her hand. I shake it because why not? "I'm Madeline," she says.

"Talia. What is this place?"

"We call it the grey place."

"It's death, isn't it?"

She screws her face up. "Not exactly or not entirely. Most people move on at one time or another. Some stay longer than others. Those who aren't ready to move on."

"Move on? To what?"

She shrugs and laughs wryly. "As you can see, I'm not ready to know either."

I bite my lip and look down. What can you do with this sort of information? It all seems so pointless, so empty and…well. Fucking unfair.

She pats my shoulder. "Maybe Kitty will come for you," she says. "Maybe that's why I've met you."

"Kitty?" I frown at her. It'd be just my luck to be caught in limbo with a crazy cat lady.

"My daughter," she says. "She's a genius."

*So am I*, I don't say and feel bad about it anyway, doing my mother's job for her and yelling at myself for being arrogant even in the privacy of my own head.

"Come, sit down," Madeline offers. She makes a gesture with both hands, and red patterns appear briefly in the air before forming into a sofa. I gape, and Madeline laughs. "Magic," she says, wiggling her fingers.

I shrug. Of course it's magic. I'm dead and still conscious; why wouldn't there be magic? Might as well sit on the comfy looking sofa with the cat-lady-slash-proud-mum.

"So," she says, crossing her legs and clasping her hands in her lap. "How'd you die?"

I laugh so short and sharp, it may as well be a bark. "Hit by a car, I guess."

She nods sagely. "Car accidents are a common one, especially for young people."

I scramble for manners in this new world. "Uh, what about you?"

"Oh, I'm not sure. Something that hurt a lot at the time." Her flippancy is more shocking than the words themselves.

"I'm sorry."

"It was years ago," she says. "And as I'm sure you've figured, none of it hurts anymore."

"Yeah," I say slowly.

"It's one of the rules of the grey place, it seems," she says, counting them off on her fingers. "Nothing hurts. You go back to your favourite time of life, the time you felt most comfortable. And you can only get out by moving forward or going with Kitty."

This lady is definitely crazy. But then, I'm dead. Who am I to judge? I'm pretty sure she can't kill me again, and if nothing hurts, then, well, hopefully she's right about that. And maybe I have trust issues, but I'm not planning to take her at her word.

She turns like a voice has spoken in her ear; for all I know, that's exactly what happened. "'Scuse me, will you?"

"Sure," I say, waving awkwardly. She's gone so fast I gasp.

Then the sofa disappears from under my arse, and I land on the floor with a thump. Turns out, she's right. Nothing hurts here.

# CHAPTER FOUR

## *Kitty*

The bus ride home is a blessed relief to my aching feet. Sometimes, I miss the last one home after this shift, and I have to walk. It's not too far, but after eight hours of walking around the warehouse and lugging boxes, sitting down feels like heaven. I wriggle my feet in my boots. The steel toecaps always make them cold, even with thick socks, and they're heavy. But at least they're provided by the company. Yay for unions. I don't have to wear out the soles of my trainers.

The bus hits a pothole, and my head cracks sharply against the window. I wince and sit up properly. It wouldn't do to fall asleep and miss my stop. Though I know this driver pretty well; he'd probably give me a shout when we got there, bless him.

It's been raining all day, but by the time I get out at my stop, the clouds are starting to wisp away, and a couple of stars are peering through the light pollution. I take a sec to tip my head back and watch my breath puff out of my mouth like a dragon. It always makes me smile.

I shove my hands in my pockets and walk the last street home. This coat's huge on me, and I feel like a kid with it on; it's one of Peter's old ones. It's great. I can layer right up with two sweaters and a massive great scarf, and there's still plenty of space.

I'm looking forward to the embrace of my bed as I walk up the stairs of our block of flats. I'm opening my front door as quietly as I can so as not to wake Sam when it comes.

*Tug tug tug.*

"You are shitting me." I groan. I'm tempted to scream, but I don't want to wake Sam up. Well. I suppose it could be worse. The call could have come right after I'd fallen asleep or an hour before my alarm went off. I keep telling myself that in the hopes that it'll be reassuring, but nope. Still want to scream.

I dump my jacket and bag, shove off my boots, and take a few moments—interrupted by the bloody pull, of course—to put on my happy face. It's not the case's fault I'm tired. It's not their fault they're keeping me awake. Most of them don't even know how they're calling me.

It's still unfair.

I smile into the bathroom mirror and try to look past my tired face, greasy skin, messy hair. I reach out with my magic, write my mother's sigils in the air, and there he is.

"Jesus fucking Christ," he cries, and falls onto his bum, scrambling back. "Who the hell are you?"

"Hiya, sorry about that," I say. My smile's a little more real. You've got to get your comedy where you can sometimes. I refuse to feel bad about that. "I'm Kitty. I've got the power to bring people back from the dead as long as there's someone, you, willing to take their place."

He stares at me, stares around. "Really?" he says, his voice small.

I spread my arms. "Really. I don't know how or why. It just sort of happens." I hold out my hand, and he lets me pull him to his feet. He's in his early forties, maybe, with a full head of brown hair but a slight thickening around his belly. He wears a business suit, minus the tie, and his eyes are bloodshot, like he's been crying or drinking. Or probably, considering the circumstances, both.

"You're young," he says. "What are you, sixteen? Or are you some sort of angel? You know, ageless?"

"I'm nearly nineteen, actually," I say, indignant, then shake my head. "Not an angel, either, though that's kind of you to say. So who are we looking for?"

"I'm sorry," he stutters, "but shouldn't you be in university? Not doing this?"

It stings. It shouldn't. I tell myself this was always going to be my choice. "I don't need a degree," I say and realise my voice is a little too sharp. "I need to contribute to the household, not like death-dealing pays the bills."

The man's shoulders droop. "God, I'm sorry, I keep…that was rude." He sniffs. "I'm a teacher, for God's sake, I'm supposed to be *helping* young people, not…" He covers his mouth and gulps as tears start to fall.

Tears aren't hard for me. I've been well-acquainted with grief, and of all situations, this is pretty high up on the list of reasons to cry. "Hey, there, it's okay. Let it all out. Would you like to tell me how I can help you? Who were you thinking about when you stared into the mirror earlier?"

He gets his breathing under control and stares into the misty distance. "I hit someone. With my car. A young girl, uni student, they say." He sobs again. "She was in Oxford. A bloody scholarship kid. All that potential and I took it from her."

I keep patting him as he breaks into sobs again, barely able to hold himself up, but it's more distracted as I focus on the flow of magic through my fingertips. What he said should be enough, and sure enough, a figure starts coalescing out of the mist, staring around her with a faint furrow between her eyebrows.

"What's this?"

The teacher looks up sharply, then breaks into louder sobs when he sees the girl. A distractingly pretty girl, with reddish-blond hair, wide dark eyes, and a small mouth. Her hands are bunched into fists, white-knuckled, and I have an urge to touch her, to comfort and make her smile and realise that everything's okay. I stand up straight and hold out my hand. "Hi, I'm Kitty."

"Kitty?"

"Yeah, uh, Kitty Wilson? I bring people back?" Why am I saying it like a question? She doesn't know. I bite my tongue to stop talking.

"I'm sorry, Kitty? Really?" The girl scowls like I'm playing a cruel trick, and I drop my hand, flustered and irritated. Apparently, beauty and fantastic Glaswegian accents don't automatically make you friendly. Shocker.

"Yes, Kitty, is that all right with you?"

She blinks and hunches a little. "Aye, no, sorry, I just…" She gestures behind her. "Someone was telling me about you. I thought she was mad."

"Oh, you met my mum? That's great, how is she?"

"She's fine," the girl says. She's still wary, on guard, like she thinks at any moment I'm going to jump on her or bite or something. "She made a sofa."

I laugh. "Bless her, she likes to show off. What's your name?"

"Um. Talia?" It's not just me who makes statements sound like questions, it seems, but Talia seems to soften a little. There's the hint of a smile curling one lip. It's a *really* nice smile. I knew it would be.

I have to shake myself mentally. It's a damn good thing I *don't* get paid for this job. Flirting with the cases is surely inappropriate. "I didn't get your name, sorry," I say to the man, who's still staring at Talia like he's seen a celeb.

"You're her," he says.

Talia actually takes a step back, and I can't say I blame her. He looks like he might grab her and hug her or something. "Who're you?" she asks.

"I'm Mr. Bourne, I mean, I'm George. I was…" He gulps. "I was the one who hit you. With my car."

Talia raises her eyebrows, her lips forming a voiceless *oh*. George wipes more tears away. I can't help but try to fill the silence. "Mr. Bourne's here to offer his life for yours," I say. Honestly, there really has to be a better way to say things like this.

She lets out one loud *ha*. "He what now?"

"I want to take your place here," he says. He looks at her like she's his saviour.

"What? No! I don't want to kill you."

He starts crying again. Talia looks a lot less okay with this than I am, so I step forward and put my hand on the teacher's back once more, patting him. "This wouldn't be a revenge thing or whatever you're thinking. Mr. Bourne wants to do a straight swap. He'd exchange his life for yours, you'd wake up—"

"Wait, wait, *wait* a minute," she says, eyes widening. "What d'you mean, exchange your life?"

I give up on the standard speech and shrug instead. "That's how it works," I tell her. "Mr. Bourne here has to be willing to take your place, and you have to be willing to allow it, and that's really all there is to it."

"But how can you—"

"It's my fault you're dead," Mr. Bourne blurts, grabbing at the girl's hands. "I can't live with the guilt. I can't bear being the one who snuffed out someone's life. I'm so…I'm so *sorry.* Please let me make it right. Please let me take your place."

"But you're alive now. If you take my place, how is that better?" Her voice is shrill with confusion and panic, and I wince in sympathy. How many times is her life being turned on its head?

Mr. Bourne shakes his head. "Please, let me. I can't live like this anymore. I can't bear it. I'm not going to last much longer anyway, not like this."

She goes even paler, her eyes sparking with sudden anger. "Are you trying to manipulate me now because—"

"No, I'm trying to set things right. You can give the world so much more than I can."

"One life isn't more worthwhile than another."

"But it *is,*" he insists. "I'm a bloody wreck, barely functioning as an alcoholic even before the crash, and after…I couldn't return to work, I left my wife, I can't look my daughters in the eye and call myself their father after I took your life with my carelessness. I never can again. I look at them, and I see you."

He's standing straighter now, and I can already feel the threads of their lives aligning as the girl stares at him. "Please," he says. "They say you were a bright young woman, a scholarship student. What if you're the one to, I don't know, find the cure for cancer or solve the Middle East crisis or something?"

She laughs, thin and reedy. "No pressure, then."

"No, that's not what I meant. I won't come back and haunt you or anything if you don't, but the potential is there. Just, please, live well. Better than me."

There's silence, an elastic moment as they stare at each other. I can feel the moment the magic works, two lives slipping through my fingers, swapping places. Then Talia nods once. The man's face splits into a blinding smile, eyes shut in ecstasy. "Thank you."

She clears her throat and turns those big dark eyes on me, looking small in her uncertainty. "How do we do this, then?"

"It's already done," I say. Mr. Bourne's already starting to fade as he turns that beatific smile on me. I wave and send him off with a smile of my own. He'll be at peace now.

"It's already…but…" The girl stares at her hands as he fades into nothing. I can see the panic rising in her. "I don't know… how do I…"

"Here," I say, taking pity on her. "Look into my eyes, that's right. When you get back, it'll be like you never died. The teacher will always be the one who died in the accident."

I have more to say, but the words and air are gone, like I've been punched under the ribs without pain. I gasp fresh air back in and fall forward. Talia catches me, strong hands wrapped around my biceps, and I straighten, meeting her gaze. We stare at each other for a moment, and in that moment, something else jars in me. Not like I've been punched this time, but like I've been caught. Like I've been falling, falling for so long, I'd forgotten I was. It feels familiar and new. It tastes of roses.

I clear my throat. "Sorry," I say. It's barely a whisper.

"Are you okay?" Her eyes search me, her hands flexing around my arms like she's afraid to let me go. I swallow my hope down. I just fell on her. No wonder she's fussing.

I nod and muster up a smile. She smiles back, just a flicker before she can stop it. Really, *really* pretty smile.

"Here," I say. I form the sigils in the air between us. She stares at it in wonder, lifting up one hand to touch the sparks with a fingertip. I feel a hollow, hopeless kind of ache that she's one more case I'll never see again. It's how it's supposed to be. It's for the best.

The mist around us is starting to solidify as she looks back at me and meets my gaze. I stare into her eyes, trying to find answers when I don't even know what I'd be asking. In my peripheral vision, I can see her room appearing, surprisingly bare. A desk, an old laptop, a bed with a bare duvet, and for a fraction of a second, that looks like Matt sitting there.

❖

I groan when my alarm goes off way too early and thump it with my index finger until, by chance, it switches to snooze. I hear Sam chuckle. "You're such a teenager."

"What gave it away?" I mumble, pushing my face into the pillow.

"C'mon, get up, dopey."

"*No*." I moan as Sam strips my duvet off. I clutch my pillow. "Don't tear me away from my one true love."

Sam jumps onto my back, burying his evil little hands in my hair, pulling my head up. I can see his grin out of the corner of my eye. "You're the spawn of Satan," I growl.

"You're my sister, so what're you saying about yourself?"

"Get off me, Sam."

"You getting up?"

"Yes, you little git, now get off."

Sam gives my hair one last tug, then climbs off with a cackle. I drag myself up and pull jeans and a long-sleeved khaki T-shirt out of the drawer under my bed. I spray anti-tangle on my curls and comb them out as I walk, yawning, down the hall to the living room.

Strange. Matt's nowhere to be seen. I didn't think he'd have stayed out with Connor all night. The duvet's still folded up on the foot of the sofa, so it's not like he's got up early. As if he would.

I pour hot water over instant coffee granules. There's not

much milk left. Hardly surprising, I think, as I look at Sam's cereal bowl, cornflakes practically swimming in the stuff. I've been tempted to use the dregs for my coffee in the past.

Okay, I'll admit it. I've *used* the dregs for my coffee in the past.

I cradle the cup and yawn, my jaw popping. "You brushed your teeth?" I ask, checking my watch.

"Damn it," I hear him mutter. "I was about to do it," he yells from somewhere down the hall.

I hear the bathroom door and smirk to myself. "Hurry up, you haven't even finished breakfast. You'll be late."

"I can walk myself, you know," he says, appearing again, his nose in a book. "It'd be faster. Plenty of year fives do it."

"They live closer," I mutter. I don't want to stop walking him, not this soon. Secondary school's coming up fast, and then I really won't be able to cling on.

Sam sits in front of his cereal and spoons it in his mouth mechanically, eyes fixed on his Percy Jackson book. "So," he says, glancing over at me with an exaggerated eyebrow wiggle. "Matt didn't get in last night."

I hum.

"Do you think he got lucky?" Sam asks.

"Do you even know what that means?" He looks up at me and shrugs. I grin and check my watch. "You ready to go?"

Sam raises his eyebrows and leans back, putting his book facedown on the table. "I am, but you're not. Eat some breakfast."

"I'm fine. I can't be bothered with cereal."

"I'll make you some toast, then," he says, dumping his bowl in the sink and filling it with water so that the cornflake crumbs swell up and scatter. I crinkle my nose up and sip my coffee. Things like that don't help my sorry appetite early in the morning.

Sam smears a thick layer of butter and a thin scraping of marmite over two slices of toast from a new loaf. "Now, eat."

"Yes, boss."

"Hey, two can play at the *patronise your sibling* game," he says, pulling his shoes on without untying the laces.

"I don't mean to be patronising."

Sam sighs. "I know. But I'm old enough to walk ten minutes along quiet roads by myself, and you only got, like, five hours of sleep last night. It's silly."

"There's that busy road by the co-op you have to cross over." Not to mention the little twats who cornered him that one time, but I don't want to remind either of us of that.

"Which has a *crossing*, Kitty," he says, rolling his eyes. "Look, I know you remember Mum *and* Dad dying, and that must've been horrible, but I'm not going to get hit by a car in a damn twenty zone."

"How do you know?" I snap. "Everyone thinks it can't possibly happen to them, we're all so bloody complacent, you can't *know*."

My adrenaline's spiked from negative numbers into full fight-or-flight. Sam's frozen, staring at me with wide, cautious eyes. My stomach feels like lead, and I bang my plate on the counter. I stalk to the front door to get my shoes, my nerves twitching in my arms, fingers shaking as I try to tie the laces of my Converse knock-offs until I'm swearing and slapping my hand against the wall.

The air seems to freeze while I fight the tears that prickle behind my eyelids. I try to force back the images of last night and Mr. Bourne and Talia, how it must've felt to die like that. To see something like that, right there.

Finally, I slip down the wall, rest my forehead on my knees, and take deep breaths.

"Kitty," Sam said, small hand touching my shoulder, hesitating before he squeezes. "Hey, I'm sorry. You can walk me to school."

I feel warmth seep through the denim over my knees where I've got my eyes pressed. Sam puts both arms around my shoulders and presses his face into my bicep, squeezing tight. After a moment, I hug him back. "I'm sorry," I whisper. "You're right, and I don't want to baby you."

Sam lets go and sits on the floor against the opposite wall. "It's okay," he shrugs. "I can put up with you tagging along like an emo puppy."

I laugh damply and sniff, wiping my face. "Come on, then," I say, finishing my laces. "Or you'll be late."

The sky's a dank grey, the leaves piled in soggy heaps or rotting into a slippery mush on the pavement. Sam talks about the upcoming residential, and I feign excitement and try not to mentally list all the things that could kill my little brother on a school camping trip.

At the crossing, I take a deep breath and pat Sam on the shoulder. "I'll leave you here, okay?"

"Sure?" asks Sam.

I nod firmly. "I can't keep you safe all the time," I say, trying to sound dry and unconcerned. "You have to take responsibility for yourself at some point."

Sam rolls his eyes but gives me a tight half hug. "Have a good day, Miaow."

"You too, kiddo."

I can't quite resist watching until Sam's crossed the road and caught up with a round kid on a bicycle. Even after that, I keep throwing glances toward my little brother, moving away on the other side of the road while I head for the railway bridge and the little corner shop for some milk.

I text Matt. He doesn't reply, doesn't read his messages. I text him again on my way home. I sleep for hours, and when I wake up, the messages to Matt still don't have the "read" ticks.

I call him, and there's no reply.

I walk through the rest of the day in a haze of sharpening panic. I tell myself every few minutes that I didn't see him in the grey place or in Talia's room after. He and Connor had got stuck over in Todminster last night and would be back soon. Peter would be disappointed, but what's he gonna do, ground him? Matt's a legal adult; he can do what he wants. And anyway, Peter would be kind. He's always kind. He loves Matt so much.

Oh God.

My phone rings, buzzing in my back pocket as I walk to the bus stop for work. I almost don't answer. Almost have another few hours of my world appearing to function, of blissful ignorance.

"Peter," I say, ducking out of someone's way with an apologetic nod. "Is everything okay?"

There's no answer, just a shuddering breath. I stand still, my blood feeling like it's got ice crystals piercing my heart. "Peter?"

"He's dead, Kitty," Peter says. I almost can't recognise his voice, stuffed with tears and grief. "There was…he was with a boy and he's…"

"No," I say, my voice distant and calm, like I'm correcting him. "No, that's not…"

"He's dead. I saw him. Oh God. Oh God."

I can't feel my body and slump against the side of the bus shelter, sliding to my knees. "He can't. He can't be. He was meant to…"

He's meant to be with me. He's meant to be telling me all about Connor Mururi and how good he looks. We're meant to be talking about coming out to his dad. We're meant to be thinking about how to avoid lying again.

I've lied. I've lied to Peter, and now his son is dead.

Peter's crying so hard he can't breathe. Voices come distantly over the phone, the speaker crackles, and the line goes dead.

I stare into nothing and wonder if I can crumble into ash.

# CHAPTER FIVE

## *Talia*

I stand in front of the mirror in my bedroom for a long time, staring at my own face after the girl…after Kitty's face disappears.

I'm breathing. I'm standing on my own feet, and I'm alive. I can tell because things hurt again. I'm frantic, rushing over to my desk. Everything's as I always keep it, files in the same order, laptop still battered, still has that sticker on the back that's scratched to oblivion. My phone's charging like it always is at night, and I pick it up with trembling hands.

The date reads November twentieth.

I remember the day I died. October twenty-first, weeks after arriving. I'd been wearing my Han Solo jacket and walking like I used to back in Glasgow when things were bad with Ma.

*It'll be like you never died*, she said. What have I missed? What's happened in those five missing weeks? I drop my phone and stumble back onto my bed and scream.

The ghost sitting on my bed screams too.

"What the actual *hell*?" I yell, standing up again, my blood singing and my hands balled into fists.

"You sat on me!"

"You were *on my bed*!"

"Well, I didn't bloody want to be, did I?" he snaps, standing and facing me in a mirror of my own pose.

I clutch at my hair and turn away. "This isn't happening. You're a figment of my imagination. This is all some freaky dream."

The ghost is silent. No, he's not a ghost. I'm not going to have some breakdown, not now. There is no ghost in my room. I am alone. There is no bloody hallucination, no missing time, no temporary death or whatever. It's October, I've come back from a long walk, and now I'm going to go to bed.

I start stripping off my clothes and pulling on my pyjamas. The not-really-there boy squeaks. "What are you doing?"

"You're not really here."

"I *am* here, and I don't want to see your skinny butt, thank you."

"Then leave," I say, whirling around wildly. "Get out of my room, go back to whatever dimension or repressed memory or wherever you came from."

"Don't you think I would if I could?" he demands. "Do you think I'm here by choice? I can't leave. I can't!"

"Well then," I snarl. "I'll leave."

I walk out of my room in my pyjamas and march to the shared kitchen. Thump my cupboard door open, slap at the kettle to turn it on, turn around to get the milk, and nearly jump out of my skin.

The ghost is standing in front of the fridge, glaring flatly at me. "I meant," he says through gritted teeth. "I think I can't leave *you*."

I throw up my hands. "Why? Why are you attached to me? I don't even know you."

"I don't know," he says, his lip curled up in a snarl. "I can't go anywhere."

"Have you tried?"

He snorts and crosses his arms. "Have I tried, she asks. Of course I've bloody tried. What do you think I was doing when you were staring gormlessly at your desk? There I was, yelling at you, having my own little breakdown, which, by the way, I think I'm owed seeing as how I've just *bloody died*, and you don't even hear me until you sit on my lap? Which, by the way, not welcome. I'm gay."

"What?"

He frowns at me. "*What* what? Which part of that speech was problematic for you? Swear to God, if I've got myself attached to a homophobe—"

I wave him away like the annoying little gnat he is. "I couldn't hear you until I sat on you?"

"Oh. No." He glances away. "You're not homophobic, are you?"

I roll my eyes. "No, idiot, I'm a lesbian." Strange. It still makes my heart hammer to say it, though I know he won't react the way Ma did.

"Oh. Well, good. Wow, that would have been horrible."

I snort at that. "More or less horrible than being dead?"

He slumps his shoulders, and I can't help a twinge of guilt. I squash it ruthlessly. He started it, after all. But he leans against the counter, the picture of the boy hard done by, with his shoulders sagging and an actual pout on his lips. I sigh and get the milk out of the fridge.

There's silence for a long moment save for the sound of the spoon against the ceramic. I turn around and sip my tea. "So what's your name?"

"Matt," he says. "Matt Wiśniewski."

"I'm Talia McGregor."

He huffs a laugh. "You really couldn't be more Scottish if you tried, could you?"

I narrow my eyes and try to will the blush away, all sympathy evaporating in an instant. "No need to be an arse." I'm just glad I hadn't told him my birth name's Morag.

He cackles. "Oh, say *arse* again, it sounds brilliant. Nah, say *och aye*."

Little shit. I thump the rest of my tea on the counter and go to bed.

❖

I open my eyes to soft rain on the window and snuggle deeper under my duvet, goose bumps prickling over my skin. Like this, I can almost pretend I'm back in Glasgow, before scholarships and tutorials and snotty English boys who look down on me because Daddy didn't send me to Eton or wherever it is that snotty English girls go. I can imagine the person shuffling around outside is Ma, making the arduous journey from her bed to the sitting room to watch some shite telly. I can promise myself that soon, Ma will fall asleep again, and I'll slip out on my bike, cycle down to Shul. Be with my *real* family.

An obnoxious fake cough shatters my dream. "Are you going to get up or not? I'm bored stuck in here."

I'm in Oxford. I've got a tutorial in two days that I don't know if I've prepared for because I've died and got better, and all I've got to show for it is five weeks' worth of amnesia and a snippy little ghost attached to me for whatever reason.

I open my eyes only to glare at the wall and count backward from ten.

"I can tell you're awake," he calls in a singsong.

I throw my duvet off. It slithers onto the floor and tangles in my feet as I stomp over to the wardrobe to snatch out some clothes.

"Yay, you're awake," Matt crows.

I ignore him grimly, pack my satchel, and leave the room.

"Aw, come on, don't be like that," he says, skipping sideways alongside me as I murder-stride through the halls and out into the quad. "Jeez," he yelps. "Did you see that? That girl walked straight through me." He shakes his head. "Weird."

I grind my teeth and pick up speed. Hopefully, a lecture on quantum mechanics at nine a.m. will get rid of him.

It does not. Instead, I have to sit in the lecture theatre, my leg jogging furiously and my fingers tangled in her hair, while a *teenage boy* sits on the floor and whines about how boring this is. I've barely managed to take any notes, and I have no idea what the professor's going on about because I've missed a whole month.

By the time everyone's packing up, I'm ready to cry. I sit with my head in my hands and pray that I still have all the notes and essays on my laptop that I've hopefully written while also dead, and how, how is this my life?

Maybe I can still get this week's work done and catch

up on everything I've missed. Maybe pigs will turn out to be aerodynamically stable after all.

"Um," says the ghost. I drop my hands and glare at him. He actually looks quite contrite. "Are you okay?"

"No," I snap. "I've missed so much work, I have no idea how I'll ever catch up, nobody will believe me because I've apparently also been here the whole time, handing in my essays and actually learning stuff, and either I've gone insane *well* before the norm for an Oxford uni student, or I am actually being followed by an obnoxious invisible boy. And honestly, I'm not sure which is worse."

Matt hunches his shoulders and picks at a loose threat on his trainers. "I'm sorry," he mumbles.

I sigh and stare into the space of the empty lecture theatre. "It's fine."

We sit there for a long time. Then I get to my feet slowly and pack my things away into my bag.

Once we're out into the drizzle of the morning, which still hasn't let up, I'm desperate to get back home and check my laptop for hints of what I've missed. I kick myself mentally for not doing so last night. I dodge the groups of chattering students and take the long way around to avoid that second year girl who seems to think it's her life's work to integrate all of us and make us into a community. It's always a relief to get into the little bubble of my room. I can hear life going on outside the door as I lean against it and take a moment, but I don't have to take part. I don't have to make people like me.

I push everything to one side and start my laptop, my knee jogging impatiently as it spends what seems like hours loading. "When did you get that?" Matt asks. "2003?"

I hold up my middle finger and grit my teeth. So much for leaving judgement and other people on the other side of the door. I concentrate on clicking on my notes folder, my lip clamped between my front teeth and a constant litany of *please, please, please let it all be there.*

"Yes!" I whoop. I'm not often pleased with myself, but right now I'm appreciating my compulsion to organise all my files just so. This is fine. I can do this. I've got notes and references and links to all the papers alive-me has had to read. I've got tutorials arranged by date and nearly ten thousand words of essays to read.

This is fine.

I also have another two-thousand-word essay due on Wednesday, and I'm not even sure I understand the title. I fold my arms on the desk and press my forehead down on them.

"Hey, don't cry," says Matt.

"I'm not crying," I grind out. "I'm despairing."

"Well…don't despair?"

"Why not?"

"Well, for starters, you're still alive."

I lift my head and glare at him, but he's frowning, looking off to the side, and it's wasted on him. "You were dead, though," he asks. "Weren't you? For a bit?"

I tilt my head to one side. "Yeah." I hadn't realised this was new information to him.

He pinches his lip, deep in thought. "It was a grey place, wasn't it? Where you were?"

"Yeah," I say again. "I didn't see you, though."

He shakes his head. "I was only there for a moment, and then…it was Kitty, wasn't it?"

"What do you know about her?" I ask, my attention sharpening. "Is she, like, famous around dead people?"

"No, well, I don't know. But I know her because she's my best friend. And I know what she can do."

"What exactly *can* she do?"

He rolls his eyes and focuses on me rather than staring off into the middle distance. "Duh. She brings people back from the dead. Well, as long as there's someone willing to take their place."

I squirm around on my chair to face him properly. "But that's just the thing, how can she do that? How come we've never heard about things like this happening? *How* does it happen? It's physically and biologically impossible, you're talking time travel and…and—"

"Magic, obviously."

I shake my head. "I'm a scientist. That doesn't cut it."

"A scientist who's also religious, though, aren't you?"

I narrow my eyes but stay quiet.

He points at my necklace. "Star of David. I know Judaism is a culture as well, but you've also got a book in…is that Hebrew?"

I glance at the siddur he's pointing at and nod, surprised. "Yeah, it is." I turn back to him. "It's my prayer book. It's in Hebrew and English. I'm not fluent yet." I force myself to stop talking. I don't owe him an explanation.

Matt shrugs, oblivious. "Surely, you can find some room between your science and faith to believe in a bit of magic? Especially now you've witnessed it too."

I think for a moment. If there's anyone who would be able to navigate this no-man's land, it's Morgan. But there's a little part of me that worries as I scroll through my emails, a little niggling guilt that knows me too well. What if I didn't bother replying to his first email while I was dead? Not-dead? Temporarily un-alive? What even am I anymore? I know the other-me was as diligent about work as I am, but what if she was just a placeholder? A robot that filled in the space in the past where I should have been, that didn't know what was important to me? The only thing that's important to me.

I can't help but let out a triumphant little *ha* when I find the email thread. There. She—or I, or whatever term is correct when thinking about a time-travelling alternative version of oneself—had emailed him, and he'd emailed back.

I feel my heart warm as I read his words. In the quietest part of my mind, I wonder if this is what some people feel like when they speak to their parent. Having him write to me with such kindness, the same affection always as clear in his written voice as it is in his spoken voice, means more to me than I want to admit.

*Dear Talia,*

*I'm glad to hear that your studies are going well and that you were able to find the information you were so worried about a couple of weeks ago. You are such a clever lass. I can't understand what you're telling me about, and googling it only seems to confuse me more. But you seem to be diving into this difficult subject in another country with such energy and drive, it exhausts me even to think about it.*

*I do hope that you're getting enough rest and looking after yourself as well. We are all very proud of you. Mrs. Jacobs and Mrs. Sadowitz both want me to tell you that they hope you'll be home for the holidays so they can have the pleasure of your company for Hanukah, especially after your near miss with that drunk driver last month. You can't blame them for wanting to look after you after such a scare.*

*I wonder if you've considered going to meet Rabbi Daniel again? I know it's difficult to put your faith in other people, and I know that you've been let down in the past, but I believe wholeheartedly that not everyone is going to hurt you. Open your heart if you can manage it. It's such a big, kind heart. I'm not sure even you realise how much love is in there to share with the world.*

*I don't mean to nag you, but I want to make sure you've got someone looking out for you in a non-academic way. There's more to life than quantum physics, I promise!*

*Yours affectionately,*
*Morgan*

Rabbi Daniel. I remember the first time Morgan mentioned him, and with a chill down my spine, I realise it was back on the twenty-first, the day I died. Or for all they know, the day I had a near miss with a drunk driver. I think of the man—the teacher, Kitty had said—begging me to take his place, and I shudder, closing my eyes a moment.

I click on the link in Morgan's email, for a lack of anything better to do, which opens up the Oxford Synagogue contact page. There's a picture of a thin man with dark black skin and kind eyes. He has a smile that looks both gentle and mischievous, and I wish I'd never looked at the picture because I'm only getting my hopes up. Nobody could ever fill the gap that Morgan and the others had left, and it's unfair to get my hopes up like this.

"Are you going to go?"

I jump violently. I'd forgotten Matt was there. "Don't read over my shoulder."

He snorts and steps back. "As if I can read any other way. Intangible, remember? I can't turn pages or click on emails."

"That's no excuse to be nosey."

He shrugs, unrepentant. "So are you going to go? I could do with some fresh air."

"You don't have lungs, what do you care?"

He rolls his eyes and makes a *blah-blah-blah* gesture with his fingers and thumbs. "Your rabbi told you to go. Aren't you, like, meant to do what he says?"

"Fuck you. No. Jewish people are allowed to think for themselves, unlike some people."

He makes a pensive face and still looks distressingly unoffended. "Nice. Catholics could use a bit of that. I'm atheist, though, for what it's worth, so I don't have any, like, central authority figures to drone at me. Anymore."

My lips twitch against my will, and I look back at the picture on the screen. "Yeah. I used to be Catholic too. In name, anyway, never went to anything more than Midnight Mass."

He jumps onto the desk next to me. It doesn't shift under his weight at all. "Come on, let's go meet your new rabbi," he wheedles. "I'm bored, and you need, like, spiritual guidance."

"I do not." I sigh. I blatantly do. But I also have an essay due in two days and an absolute busload of work to read through and understand even before I start writing it. I shake my head. "Maybe later," I say and leave it at that. Matt groans dramatically and leans back against the wall, and I do not think about the fact that he seems to be able to select what walls he passes through. I can't exactly write an essay on *that*, can I?

I push everything else out of my mind, box it up, and keep it safe and hidden and open the first file of notes.

❖

"I've been thinking," Matt says the moment I open my eyes, and I groan and stuff my head under my pillow. "Don't give me that." He's pouting, I know he is. I can hear it in his voice.

"You thinking is dangerous," I mumble into my bed. My beloved bed. Sleep, why hast thou forsaken me?

"Har har," he says flatly. "I was *thinking*, we should go and see Kitty."

Kitty with her sweet smile and her amazing magical power that makes no sense and her warm brown eyes? "No."

"Hear me out. She brings people back from the dead, right? She could bring *me* back, right?"

A part of me perks up, but I shove my head deeper under the pillow. "Why hasn't she done it already?"

He's quiet for a moment longer than usual. "I don't know," he says flippantly. "There's probably a waiting list."

"Right, of course," I say and succumb to the day, throwing off the duvet and slouching to the bathroom. "There's a waiting list for people who want to come back from the dead, aye, of course there is. There's also a postcode lottery, and if you've died in a particular way, you're more likely to get seen ahead of time because there's also a dead-person triage, isn't there? I bet there's a right outcry when a famous person gets brought back to life because he was all on drugs, and that when he was alive."

A girl with frizzy brown hair looks at me nervously. I give her my best fake smile, and she scurries away. Matt smirks at me in the mirror. "Talking to yourself again, Talia?" He says my name in an annoying way, drawing out the first *a* into an *aah*. I bare my teeth at him.

"I'm serious," he says when I'm out in the sharp sunlight, throwing my bag over my shoulder and wondering if I've got time for a quick coffee on the way. I glance at my watch. Time, yes; money, no. I need a job.

"Are you even listening to me?"

"No," I say. "I thought that was obvious by now."

He sticks his tongue out. "Come on," he whines. "We live really close. Well. Kitty lives really close." He frowns for a moment, breaking his stride. "There's a bus from Oxford to Leithfield every two hours, and it only takes twenty minutes to get there. Come on, Talia, what have you got to lose?"

"I'm not having this conversation with a ghost," I snap. "Or a hallucination or whatever you are. Look, going crazy is a staple of the Oxford experience. I'm just doing it early. Now shut up because I need to study."

He narrows his eyes ever so slightly, and perhaps I should take the warning. But I don't. I push the door of the library open and enter the solid hush of it, the cushioned floors, the great stacks that allow no echo. I have a plan. I have my laptop and a notepad, and I'm going to work through all I've missed because I'm not wasting this opportunity. I am not.

"What are you going to do if I don't shut up?" Matt yells, and I turn like a startled wolf, hissing at him.

The students nearest me look up and frown. At me. Because, of course, they can't see him, he's not real. He smirks, and I should not be this angry, but I am. I glare at him and picture him bursting into flames. If he's a product of my warped imagination, he really ought to be bursting into flames right now.

"What are you looking at?" Matt asks me loudly. "Talia, what are you looking at? I'm not really here am I, *Taahlia*, just a hallucination, aren't I?" I glare at him. My teeth ache from how hard I'm gritting them. "Well? Go on, then. Do your work," he says with a shit-eating grin, gesturing to the stacks. "I'll be over here, doing hallucination stuff."

I'm so angry I could burst into flames myself, and I can feel the adrenaline pumping through my veins like acid. I practically throw my bag onto the table and then panic because my laptop's in there. A girl glances up at me, a frown between her eyebrows, but she quirks a smile and goes back to her work.

I take a deep breath and let it out slowly. Matt is dancing in the aisles between the shelves, singing "New York, New York," of all things. I open my laptop and tell myself I can ignore him.

It's not like I've never blocked out noise to work before.

Ma's always got the telly blaring, and there's a couple next door who scream at each other most nights. Sometimes, a plate hits the wall adjoining mine and makes me jump out of my skin, but I've learned to focus through it. The siren call of Oxford and freedom and success dragged me through, and now the new song of graduation and a job, maybe in the ESA or Boeing, something to do with fluid dynamics, will call me through this.

I've got a good page and a half of notes when my pen slips, scratching across the page and off onto the table. I freeze and stare at the paper now marked with a deep gouge that has torn through at points. Matt gets in my face. "Hey, Talia, guess what? I can move pens."

I can feel my heart pounding in my throat. I squeeze my fist around the pen, then pick up the thread of my last thought. My writing is shaky. Matt pokes my hair, curls the longest strand around to tickle my ear, and I twitch, but I can ignore him. He's not here.

And then he pokes at the mole at the back of my neck, the one right on my hairline, and he's Sharon Mulvey back in school, trying to distract me when I'm doing the extra work, and I've always wanted to stab her in the eye with my pen, and I'm on my feet, screaming and swearing, "I hate you, I hate you, I hate you!" And my arms are flailing and not connecting, and I'm tearing at my hair, and I can't breathe, everyone's looking at me, the shocked gasps because I'm the one causing a fuss, can't you see, *Morag*, you're the one making the noise here, Sharon was quietly getting on with her work.

The library is silent, every face pale and staring at me. Some of them have grabbed their stuff and are backing away toward the door. My heart beats so fast I can't hear through it, and I run.

There's a gap between some of the shelves right at the back of the periodicals section, between Plant Sciences and Zoology reprints, and I cram my way into it, pressing my back to the wall and putting my hands up by my ears so maybe I won't hear the terrible gasping, whimpering sound of my own breathing. All it does is intensify it, trap me in there with only the mocking noises of my own weakness, and I squeeze my eyes shut, rock back and forth and cry.

There's a sensation more than a sound, a knowledge that someone else is nearby, a witness to my breaking. I wrap my arms right around over my face and the back of my head, hiding. I can't see you, therefore, you can't see me. But of course, I've brought my own hallucination with me, and how long before he torments me more?

Someone clears their throat, and it's not Matt at all. I flinch and peer out at them, her. The girl with the dark hair. I think I've seen her before, before the library, I mean. She smiles and holds out my bag, and I take it like a squirrel, all quick movements and darting back into my safe place.

"You do physics as well, don't you?" she asks.

I nod.

"Third year," she says, pointing to herself. "Are you okay?"

I don't know what to say, and she huffs a laugh and sits cross-legged, pushing her glasses up her nose. "None of us are, really. Part of the environment, you know?"

"'We're all mad here,'" I quote, and sniffle.

She laughs. "Exactly. Hey, look, don't worry about that out there."

"I made a fool of myself."

"Yeah, and? Not much you can do about it now, is there? Everyone has moments like that here, and anyone who says they don't is either a rich Tory boy who already survived Eton, or they haven't got there yet. Or both." She shrugs. "It's Oxford. You either come out of this as suicidal or a member of the government."

I laugh, and it's wet and disgusting, but it's a laugh. She smiles like she's won a prize, then stands and holds out her hand. "Now, do you want to stay there a bit longer, or do you want a hug?"

I know I look suspicious. My masks are shot all to hell right now. I can't hide it. I don't know what it is that makes me put my hand out and let her tug me up before she wraps her arms around me and is rubbing my back. It feels…alien. I'm not sure I've ever had a hug from a person my own age before. The only people who ever hugged me have been Morgan and the old ladies back at Shul. I want to hold her closer, and I want to push her away, and I'm relieved when it's obvious that she's pulling back so I don't make even more of a fool of myself.

"Thanks," I say, hunching my shoulders and looking at the thick carpet.

"Pay it forward." She shrugs, pats my arm, and goes.

"I'm sorry," Matt says from behind her, and of course he's here. Of bloody course. I wipe my eyes. Matt bites his fingernails. Why? Why bother? "I really am sorry, Talia." He looks on the verge of tears. I'm so damn *tired*. "I promise I won't do it again," he says, and I swear his lower lip is wobbling.

I need help, I think. I don't think I can do this alone.

## CHAPTER SIX

### *Talia*

The synagogue isn't far from the B78 bus route, and I find myself standing outside the three-storey building, staring up at the bland facade, the icy grey of the sky an ominous backdrop against it.

"I think you have to go in," Matt says into my ear.

"Shut up," I mutter and stomp up the stairs, pushing the door open.

The building's well-heated, and I strip my coat off, stuffing the gloves into the pockets and throwing it over my arm. There's the possibility that Rabbi Daniel isn't in at all. If so, there's the further possibility that I'll take it as some sort of sign and never come back. I know myself, for better or worse.

I take a deep breath and go through the next door out of the anteroom. It leads straight into a wide hall, with various doors coming off each side, and a large set of double doors straight ahead that I assume leads to the main sanctuary. I turn slightly, looking around at the room with its community board, folding tables, and kids' corner with bulging drawers of craft and play materials. I'm considering whether to call out or make a run for it when a door opens to the left.

"I thought I heard someone come in," says a soft, deep voice, and I spin to see Rabbi Daniel poking his head through, a smile on his gaunt face.

"I'm sorry," I say and frown at myself. "I mean, I should have phoned."

He comes out into the hall properly, all long limbs and

punky combat boots. "Not at all, everyone's welcome. I'm Rabbi Daniel, what can I do for you today?"

I take his hand and shake it. "I'm Talia, I…well, I should've come a while ago when term started but…anyway. My rabbi from back home encouraged me."

He frowns and cocks his head. "Talia from Glasgow, right? Morgan sent me the first email about you months ago. I hope you don't mind, but he told me about your accident, I'm sorry. Are you okay?"

I nod jerkily and can't help glancing at Matt. "Yeah, I'm actually…" I take a deep breath. "I was wondering…"

His forehead crinkles in sympathy. "Would you like to talk?"

I nod, swallowing hard.

He gives me a half-smile and gestures toward the sofas in one corner of the room. I walk toward them quickly, letting out a long breath and clutching my jacket so tightly that my fingers hurt. Daniel sits opposite me and laces his hands, leaning forward with his elbows on his knees and a patented Open Paternal Smile™ on his face. He doesn't say anything.

I feel the first tendrils of panic rise up my throat, and I want to stand and run. Then I sense rather than feel Matt sit next to me, and I spare him a quick glance. He looks quiet and concerned. What does he have to be concerned about? He's dead. Do I look that bad? Am I falling apart that obviously?

"I think I died," I blurt out.

Daniel's eyebrows arch, and he blinks at me. I squeeze my eyes shut and press my hands against my face. "I, no, I know I did. Either that or I'm crazy, and I need someone to know."

There's a pause. "Okay," says Daniel slowly. "Can you explain further, do you think?"

I let out a long breath and drop my hands, but I can't look at him again. I keep my gaze firmly on the carpet with its faded geometrical patterns. "I…it's complicated. And I don't think you'll believe me, but…well."

It's safer than telling Morgan, I tell myself. If *Morgan* thinks I'm crazy, I don't know what I'll do.

"Okay," I say and sit up straight, facing it head-on. "You

know, I had a…well, to you it was a near miss, right? A car nearly hit me and crashed into a lamppost instead, and the driver died?" Daniel nods. "Well, I remember that differently. To me, I died. I remember the pain, the fear. And then I woke up in this grey *place*. It was mist and nothing else, until some woman came and had a chat with me. She made a sofa," I say because I might as well sound fully mad. "And then there was a girl. Kitty. I didn't find her, exactly, she just appeared, along with a crying man, and…she swapped our lives."

I bite my lip and look up at Daniel. He's staring at me, open-mouthed. "You don't believe me," I say, clenching my jaw.

"No, wait, it's just a lot to take in, really. I mean, of course, for you even more so, but…" He takes a deep breath and huffs a laugh. "I'm sorry. I'm new at this, I only qualified last year, and…wow."

I can't help quirking a smile. "What do the scriptures say about this, then?"

He laughs, and I can feel my smile widen. Daniel shakes his head. "Oh, dear. I have no idea what to say. I'm so sorry you've been through this. Has it taken you this long to find someone to talk to?"

"Well…no. I was in that grey place for over a month, but when Kitty brought me back, she told me it would be like I'd never died. Now I have all these notes and essays that I've apparently written in the last few weeks but no memory of them at all. The news reports all say the driver died, when in my… timeline, I guess, it was just me."

"Tell him about me," Matt whispers, and I glare at him without thinking because it's not like Daniel can *hear* him. He doesn't have to whisper.

Daniel frowns and follows my gaze into what must be empty air to him. He doesn't say anything. I sigh and roll my eyes. "I seem to have come back with a parasite," I say.

Daniel raises a single eyebrow and looks wary. I smack my hand on my head. "I didn't mean that," I say, my cheeks heating up. "I meant a ghost."

The other eyebrow shoots up. "A ghost?"

I sigh again. "I know. I sound like a crazy person, and you think it's all in my head."

Daniel shrugs. "Well, just because I've never experienced it doesn't mean it's not true. And just if something's all in your head doesn't mean it's not real."

"Did you quote Dumbledore there?"

He smiles. "I paraphrased." He leans back with a thoughtful frown. "I'm not here to tell you what's real and what isn't. I'm here to help you with your experience as much as I can, particularly your spiritual experience, of course. Now, there's nothing in the Torah that talks of ghosts per se. The Talmud prohibits things like trying to contact the dead—"

"But I'm not trying," I protest, and it's a little like I'm trying to protest to God as well. "I don't want him here. He just hangs around."

"Hey, I don't exactly have much of a choice in this situation either," Matt snaps.

"He says he can't leave," I relate to Daniel.

"No," Daniel says slowly. "I didn't think that was the case." He frowns and taps a finger against his lips, staring into the distance. Then he leans forward again. "I have to ask, Talia, have you spoken to a therapist? This may all be the symptoms of something serious, a mental health condition, unresolved trauma. It wouldn't surprise me."

I shake my head, but it's a fair question. "Nothing like this has ever happened to me before. And it's not like I've got gaps in my memory. It's like I remember something completely different to what everyone else remembers of the last few weeks."

"Are you sure? I can recommend an excellent trauma specialist."

"Look," says Matt. "Let's go and find Kitty. She can explain everything. This is real. It's not a hallucination, I swear."

"That sounds like something a hallucination would say," I snort. Daniel raises an eyebrow and chuckles.

"No, really," Matt insists, like he hasn't gone over this constantly for the last twenty-four hours. "Look, you don't know Kitty's address, right? You can't possibly know it. Come on a road trip with me. She only lives in Leithfield, and that's like twenty miles away from Oxford. What have you got to lose?"

"Uh, let's see, my self-respect, my petrol money, and my sanity?"

Daniel looks pained. "What's he saying?" he blurts at last. His cheeks flush, and he shrugs ruefully. "Sorry, curiosity killed the cat."

"But satisfaction brought it back," I reply without thinking.

Daniel bursts out laughing. "Very good," he says. "Is that what brought you back, then, satisfaction?"

I grin. "Nope, just a girl called Kitty."

Daniel cracks up with surprisingly high-pitched, infectious giggles. "Well, at least you seem to have a sense of humour about it all."

I shrug. "Well, it's either that or cry, and I've done that. Only gives you a headache."

"If you don't mind, what was he asking?"

I tilt my head. "Do you really believe in him?"

"I believe that *you* believe in him, and that's good enough for me. The language we use for things isn't always important."

I hum thoughtfully and glance up at Matt, who makes a *go on* gesture. "He was saying I should go and see Kitty."

"The girl who brought you back. How would you know where to find her?" asks Daniel, leaning forward in genuine interest now.

"That's the thing. Matt was her best friend when he was alive. He says he'll tell me the address."

Daniel taps his lips. "I have to agree, this might be the best course of action for you, mostly because it's the only way you'll know whether this is…hmm, let's say an external thing or an internal one."

"You mean, whether it's real or not?" I say. "You can say it, you know. I won't get upset."

He shakes his head. "But I don't mean that at all. As I said, Matt is obviously very real *to you*. Whether or not I can perceive him is irrelevant to the question of his reality. The question is only whether or not he is a hallucination, and in which case,

I'll help you source the mental healthcare that you need to deal with the situation, or, well, he's a ghost. And you actually died." He frowns at his hands. "I'm honestly not sure which of those situations is the one I'd hope for. Either way, you've got a hard time ahead of you."

I look back at Matt, who's staring at Daniel intently. Daniel looks up. "I hope that, no matter what situation you find yourself in, you know you've got a place to come for support. I don't have all the answers, of course, and as I said, this is breaking new ground for me, but I'll do whatever I can to help."

I smile, and there's something under my ribs that feels like it's uncoiling. "Thank you, Daniel, I really appreciate that."

"Are we going, then?" Matt asks, his expression sharp and intense. "What are we waiting for?"

I ignore him, stand, and take Daniel's outstretched hand. He clasps it and gives me a warm smile, his cheeks crinkling up into brackets around his mouth. "You're welcome any time, Talia. Go safely, won't you?"

"Come on," Matt grumbles. I make a point of being in no rush whatsoever. Matt bounces around in front of me when we get back out of the synagogue. "Can we go now?"

"It's four in the afternoon. We're going on Saturday."

"Ugh, you're so slow!"

I bite down on a smile and march back to the bus stop, my head held high. He's very easy to annoy.

## Chapter Seven

### *Kitty*

I can't say it's the first time I've thought of finding a dead person for myself. I can't say it's the first time I've tried by myself. There are so many people I want to find, yet all I can do is find them for others.

I stand in front of the mirror in my bedroom. Sam's at school. He went by himself this morning, and I let him. It didn't feel like quite such a big deal, letting him walk in. I don't think anything will feel like such a big deal anymore. He tiptoed around me this morning as I lay in bed wishing everything would just end. Wishing I could *not be.*

Wishing it had been me instead.

My eyes are puffy and red-rimmed, my nose swollen with tears, and I slap the glass with both hands, leaning in and glaring at my own face. I must have drawn the symbols twenty times. I can't seem to pull myself into the grey place.

I just want to see him. I want to see Mum and Nan, even my stepdad. But I can't call myself in. I need someone else.

❖

The world feels devoid of colour. I thought I could handle death through losing my parents, through my magic. But this… how does it get harder?

Sam and I are practically living at Peter's. Anytime we're

not at work or school, we're slipping into his house—*his and Matt's, let it be his and Matt's again, give him back*—and putting things into the dishwasher or cooking for Peter.

Peter fluctuates between blank immobility and frantic motion, manic smiles and rushing around like a blue-arsed fly, cleaning and telling us all about the family members who're coming over from Poland or up from Southampton for the funeral.

I feel like I'm walking through treacle. Every movement feels impossible. My arms weigh a tonne.

"Did you know?" Peter asks me one morning. I've come straight from a night shift. He's already up. Has he even gone to bed?

"Did I know?" I frown, foggy with grief and sleep deprivation.

"That he was gay," Peter says. He puts his mug on the counter and presses one hand over his mouth, staring down at the white knuckles of the other.

I nod.

He swallows hard enough for me to hear. Tears well up in his eyes and somewhere, distantly, some instinct is telling me that's good. He's processing his emotions. "Did he think I wouldn't accept him?" he asks, his voice plaintive. "Is that why he lied? He felt like he had to?"

I shake my head. "He didn't want to disappoint you," I whisper. My voice can't come through the band clamped around my chest.

Peter almost howls in pain, bending over the counter and sobbing. My face feels cold, and I raise one hand to touch my cheek. It's wet. "I didn't tell him enough." He gasps. "I didn't tell him how much he meant. I didn't let him know…he could have done anything. There is nothing he could have done that would have disappointed me, nothing. He was my everything. I loved him so much, Kitty, I loved him."

I pull him into a hug and stare at the colourless world over his shoulder.

❖

My eyes are still swollen and puffy when I get home and go through the motions of dinner and bedtime with Sam. He hugs me extra tight that night, and I cling back to him, feeling his little body shudder with grief through his fluffy pyjamas. "You okay?" I ask, my voice barely strong enough to raise above a whisper.

He nods. "I miss Matt." His chin wobbles, and more tears trickle down his cheeks. He's still so little.

I sit up a bit longer after he's gone to bed, staring out over town with a cup of decaf and a blanket draped over me as I lean on the windowsill. And that's when the call comes, the pull under my ribs.

I let my head drop against the window and grit my teeth to hold back a scream. This isn't fair at all. Why should anyone else get relief from their pain when I can't even help myself with my own?

In the end, it's more the thought of seeing Mum that drives me to my feet and over to the mirror. Not the pull that has becoming almost unbearable. What's one more unbearable thing, after all?

I sigh and watch my own face in the mirror disappear, leaving an older woman's face to take its place. She gasps as she steps back, but I can barely raise the energy to be sympathetic. "Hi, I'm Kitty," I say, my affect flat. "I've got the power to swap lives, who are you wanting to bring back?"

She's doomed to disappointment. I'm ashamed to say I don't remember anything about her; the moment she tells me anything, it's gone from my memory. The person she's looking for has gone, passed on to whatever comes after this. I do remember her disappointment. The emptiness in her eyes that's a reflection of my own.

When she's gone and Mum appears, I start crying and fall into her arms. She knows. Of course she knows, she's *here*. We fall to the floor, the mist-rolled ground that's somehow solid and not there all at the same time. I bury my face in her shoulder and cry like a little girl who's lost nearly everyone important in the world. For a moment, even the important things that I do still have, even Sam and Peter and all my friends in town, they don't matter as much as everything that's gone from me.

At last, I've cried myself dry. I always think, *this* time, I've cried all the tears I can possibly cry; there can't be any tears in my future. I'm always wrong. There are always more tears in there somewhere. I sit back and wipe my face.

"I'm sorry, darling," she says, brushing the hair back from my face. I smile a little. Her hand on my cheek reminds me of my own hand on Sam's cheek, and my life seems a bit less empty.

"Is he here?" I ask. I don't know if I hope he is or not. I want him to be at peace and move on, but selfishly, I also want to see him again.

She shakes her head. "Honestly, I thought I'd managed to send him back out," she says and laughs.

I frown. "What do you mean? I didn't think you could do that from here."

She bites her lip and glances at me, a little shifty. "Yeah, I guess I can't."

I narrow my eyes at her. "What did you try?"

"You know that girl you brought back, the hit-and-run girl?"

"Yeah, Talia."

She blinks and looks taken aback. "Oh. Well, Matt turned up here that same night."

"Yeah," I say, drawing it out. I've got a rising sense of foreboding, and I don't want to listen to it.

"Well, Matt died in a car accident too, so I thought it might work if I swapped them right as you were sending that girl back."

"Mum!"

"I'm sorry, love, I thought it had worked. I had to act quickly, he turned up, and then you took Talia away. I should have prepared for this in advance, but—"

"You were going to swap his life for some other girl, not get permission from either of them?" The horror and disgust hurts right down to my core. "You can't do that, Mum."

She frowns a little. "But it still keeps the balance, one life for another. They're a similar age. The universe would be fine with it."

"Well, I'm not bloody fine with it!" I cry. "I can't believe you think that's okay. They have to be *willing*, to know what they're getting into."

"Now, Kitty—"

"How could you even think of this?"

"I was trying to fix things for you, Kitty, because I know Matt's your best friend."

"That doesn't matter, I…" I can't get the words right in my mouth, I can't *breathe* with how wrong it feels down in the magic of me. For the first time in my life, I don't want to be with my mum.

And just like that, I'm not. I'm sitting on my bum on the cold floor of my bathroom, with nothing but a bad taste in my mouth and that bottomless well of tears full again, ready to get back to work.

# CHAPTER EIGHT

## *Talia*

I dump my bag in the footwell of the passenger side of my car and frown at Matt, who's standing and staring at the car like it's some sort of spaceship. "Come on, get in," I say, winding down the window. Yes, it is actually that old.

He shakes his head, startling himself out of whatever daze a ghost can go into and walks through me to sit on the seat. I wrinkle my nose at him. "Arse."

He shrugs. "Got to be some advantages to being dead, surely."

I snort and start the car up. She may be old, but she's reliable. She got me all the way here from Glasgow, after all, and she's got enough space in the back that I can sleep there. I got her off one of Morgan's friends. He's got a farm near Loch Lomond and agreed to sell her to me cheap. She's not a typical student car, but I love her.

Matt, on the other hand, doesn't seem that keen. "Where are we going?" I prompt him as we start to get out toward Kidlington.

He doesn't answer, and I turn to frown at him. He's staring out the window, his fists clenched in his lap. "Hey, Matt."

He jumps, sucking in air like he actually needs to breathe. "What? No need to shout."

"Which way?"

He points to the third exit, and I indicate, pulling out to circle the roundabout. "You'll have to give me a bit more warning than that if you don't want to end up down in Worcester," I say, my hand resting on the vibrating gear stick.

He's quiet, and it's nice at first, but it's moments before I'm realising that quiet and Matt don't go together. I glance at him again when we're on a straight stretch of road, Oxfordshire opening up into farmland around us. "You all right?"

He doesn't look all right. He looks pale, and yes, I know he's a ghost, but it's not right. My heart speeds up to see the staring blank eyes, the grey cast to him. There's a layby, and I'm in it before I can think, cutting the engine and leaning over, hands hovering over him because I can't touch him, can't shake him, can't physically knock him out of this trance he's in, and I never meant to do this to him. I don't want him in my life but I don't want this.

"Matt," I snap. "What the…*Matt*!"

He gulps air, and there are tears making their way down his ashen cheeks, but he's staring out the window like there's a monster out there, and he's the rabbit in the headlights. "I couldn't move," he says, his voice just above a whisper. "I couldn't…it hurt so much, and I couldn't move. I could see Connor, and it was dark, and there was so much blood, his head was cut, but he could move, and I *couldn't*, and I was afraid. I was so afraid."

I look out the window at the bright morning, the cars rushing along the A road, and I bite my lip. "It was a car crash, wasn't it?"

When he inhales, it's juddering, and his face is shiny with tears. I want to hold him right now. I want to give the kind of comfort I'm sure I'm no good for, but it hurts in my chest to see him like this, so afraid. I feel useless.

"Do you want to go back?" I ask, awkward and asinine.

He shakes his head, closing his eyes tight and starting to cry properly, body shaking with sobs rather than just leaking tears. "Matt," I say, and I try to put my hand at the start of where his shoulder would be, try to give some comfort. "I'm sorry." Pointless. What does he care? What does it do?

He cries, and I sit there, wondering if there's some sort of set amount of time that one should sit and look at a crying person. Have I already passed it? Should I drive on? I suppose if there is a time limit, I've long passed it, so I continue sitting and looking and feeling like a chocolate teapot.

He turns and hunches his shoulders after a while, wiping his face and placing his back firmly toward me. "Just drive," he says, and it's like a gift, knowing what to do. I concentrate on pulling out and not getting Matt into another car accident.

He directs me down this road and that into a small, nondescript town. "Up there," he says, and his voice is almost clear, the stuffed-sinus tone almost back to normal when he tells me to park on a narrow, tree-lined road. "That's hers," he says in the quiet of the car, jerking his head toward a small block of flats.

I look at him a moment and wish I was the sort of person for whom comfort comes naturally. Instead, I nod and push the door open, tugging my beanie on against the chill wind.

When I look up, she's walking toward me. I recognise her instantly and freeze because holy shit, how can she possibly know I'm here? What's she going to say? Is she going to see Matt right there, standing next to me?

Is any of this even real?

But she's walking past my car, her head hanging low, a young boy beside her.

"That's her," says Matt, and he's grinning wildly. "Talia, go on, that's her. You recognise her, don't you? See? I *told* you I'm real."

She's crossing the road now, and I'm startled into motion, looking both ways before following her down the hill. I frown as I get moving. I don't want to rush up to her while she's with what I assume is her family and tell her I've come with a message from beyond the grave. I don't think that's going to go down well.

However, what I am doing right now is stalking her, and that's pretty creepy. I stop.

"What are you doing? Come on, there she is." Matt gestures to her and stops.

The two are standing in front of another house. It looks like there's a party happening, cars lining the road, people converging on the door, which stands open.

Everyone's wearing black.

"You are shitting me," I say.

"What's going on?" asks Matt, and if he was corporeal, I'd hit him because he's being infantile now.

"What do you think? It's your bloody funeral." I laugh and press the heels of my hands to my eyes. "I cannot bloody believe this, what are the chances of turning up for your *bloody* funeral?"

He walks closer, stopping just before he gets to the next road and putting his hand up as if against an invisible wall.

"What are you doing?" I sigh.

"I can't go closer," he says, quietly, wondering.

I roll my eyes and walk the ten feet or so to stand next to him. "Try now."

He frowns in confusion, and I jerk my head that way. He takes a step forward and looks up in surprise.

"It's me, idiot," I say. "You just can't go far from me."

He laughs, and there's something hysterical in it. "Jesus, I thought it was because my dad's such a staunch Catholic."

"Such a dumbass," I say. "Look, do you want to come back another day?"

He shakes his head, and his eyes are still fixed on the house. "Could we…for a moment…"

"You want to go to your own funeral?" I say, aghast.

"I want to see my dad."

I stare at him another moment, then slump in surrender. "Fine," I say. "Fine, but I swear, you are damn lucky there's no Jewish hell because I'm pretty sure crashing a funeral is a Bad Thing."

"You're not crashing it. I'm inviting you." He grins and runs ahead of me across the road.

"I don't think that counts," I mutter, and shove my hands deep in my pockets.

The house is packed with people, and I hunch my head right down, not bothering to take my beanie off as I squeeze in. I don't know how Matt can stand it, people walking through him left and right, but he's looking at faces, open-mouthed in a tragic kind of amazement as he recognises relatives and friends and what might be his grandmother, her lined face weeping silently behind a black veil.

He stops at the entrance to the kitchen and staggers to the side, leaning against the wall and covering his face as grief overwhelms him. I stand beside him, awkwardly guarding him from the press of bodies.

There's a tall, slim man in there, cooking frantically, bustling around the kitchen, hounded by hysteria. He's offering canapes with a shaking hand and eyes that beg people to keep him busy, keep him moving, don't let him rest, don't let him remember. It's a moment before I notice Kitty off to the side with the little boy, staring at the tall man in a kind of empty horror.

The boy walks forward slowly and joins the man at the kitchen counter, picking up a small knife to slice spring onions. An old lady comes up and strokes the man's back a moment, then takes a plate of pierogi to hand around the mourners. She offers me one, and I smile and shake my head, then wish I hadn't smiled, and turn it into a sort of grimace. God, that's worse.

"Peter," says Kitty gently as the tall man starts washing plates. "Peter, won't you let me do that?"

"No, no, Kitty, this is my role as host. It's no trouble at all. Thank you for all your help, and you too, Sam, my little sous chef." He gives a smile to the little boy, who tries to flicker one back, and just watching, I can barely hold the tears back.

"Peter," says Kitty more firmly. "Stop, c'mon, sit down or you'll drop."

"I can't," he says, and like that, the strings holding him upright snap, and he leans heavily on the sink. "I can't, or I will think."

Kitty puts her hand on his upper arm and looks at him with kind brown eyes, so gently that I nearly cry to see it. "I know."

"I can't believe he's gone," he says. It comes out strained, like it's forced through a tight space. The first tears fall, landing in the sink, sending out ripples, and Matt cries out aloud, his hand over his mouth. He's reaching out for Peter, and I want to hold him back, want to wrap myself around him, turn back time, and take him away from here.

"I know," Kitty says again, her own voice low and grief-soaked.

"He was everything to me." He covers his mouth with a wet hand. "What am I without my baby, Kitty?"

"Dad," sobs Matt. "Papa. I'm sorry. I'm so sorry."

"Don't say that," Kitty whispers, wiping tears away from her own eyes.

Peter shakes his head. "It's the truth. You know this as well as I do. But then, you have Sam. I have no one left. No one worth living for."

"Don't you say that," she sobs aloud. The little boy, Sam, whimpers, and Kitty grabs him, pulling him close. She's got her fingers white-knuckled in Peter's jumper, pressing her face against his shoulder. Matt is standing in front of Peter now, trying to grab his hands, trying to touch his face, and it's awful, I can't stop crying myself, an intruder to their grief and pain.

Peter turns to face Kitty and Sam fully, away from Matt. "I'm sorry," he says, touching Sam's head. "No, don't listen to me. I didn't mean to upset you."

Sam turns and flings himself at Peter, sobbing against Peter's chest, his arms wrapping right around Peter's waist. "Oh, *kochanie*," Peter says, and wraps long arms around Kitty and Sam, locking Matt out of their comfort.

I want to call out to him, call him back to me. I want to help in some way because he's broken. They're all so broken, and he's right there and yet not there at all, other than to me. I jump when I feel a hand on my shoulder and look down at the little old lady with the pierogis. For a moment, I had forgotten I was visible.

"Would you like a hug, dear?" she asks. She's wearing a clerical collar, and I remember Matt saying he was once Catholic.

I feel the old, ingrained guilt digging in. I shake my head and wipe my eyes fiercely. "I'm sorry," I say. "I shouldn't be here."

"Nonsense. Everyone's welcome. Did you know Matt from school?" Her hand is gentle, rubbing up and down my bicep, squeezing just that right amount.

"I…no. I was…" I glance at Matt, but he's no help, of course. He's barely holding himself together. "I knew him through the internet," I say, hoping.

She nods, but that's when Kitty looks up.

I see the moment she recognises me. I see the possibilities and the paranoia run through her mind. I see the fear in her eyes, and I turn, murmuring my apologies to the priest, stumbling out, bumping into people and almost certainly dragging Matt kicking and screaming behind me. My heart's beating hard when I get out into the cold autumn air, and the tears sting on my cheeks as the wind hits them. I wipe them away fiercely, marching hard, trying to get away from that place, away from feelings, from danger.

"Hey," I hear, and I speed up. "Hey!"

She's on me in a moment, hand around my upper arm and dragging me around to face her. I can feel my jaw tensing, my shoulders hunching, watching every shift of limbs to work out where the slap will come from, if she'll have a weapon in her hand this time, if—

"What the hell are you doing here?" she demands in a furious whisper. "How'd you find me?"

I open my mouth and shut it again, centre myself, refocus. I glance around for Matt, and she shakes my arm again. "How did you find me?" she demands, her words staccato.

"You're Kitty," I say stupidly. Of course she's Kitty, we've established that.

"I'll call the police if you don't tell me how you found me." She stands back a step and takes her phone out. "Three. Two."

"Matt brought me," I blurt. It's a mistake. Her eyes narrow, and she lifts her phone to her ear. "I'm serious," I say. "Matt, tell her…shit."

Matt's on his knees facing his house. I really have been dragging him all this way. I run past Kitty and crouch by him. "Matt…" But that's where my comforting abilities end, and I'm squatting there awkwardly by the open air. "C'mon, Matt, you need to get up." I hesitate, bite my lip. "I need your help."

He rises to his feet slowly, and I follow carefully. It's like any sudden movement could make him splinter, drift away on the wind. I clear my throat and look back at Kitty. "We didn't know it was his funeral."

"This is sick," Kitty says, her voice low and trembling with grief or fury or both. "I don't know who you are, or how you found me, but—"

"Oh, come on, you can't tell me the girl who brings people back from the dead doesn't believe in ghosts," I snap.

She hisses and looks around her wildly, like someone might be listening in. "I don't…what are you talking about?"

"Sure you don't." I sneer.

"Her real name is Katrina," Matt says. He sounds hollowed out, and I bite back the sarcastic comment about how I could have guessed that. "She calls herself Kitty because people used to call her Hurricane in primary school."

"Hurricane Katrina." I roll my eyes. "Of course they did."

"How d'you know about that?" Kitty asks, grabbing my arm again.

I shake her off and take a step back. "I told you," I snap. "Matt."

"But…" She looks desperately to the side, just off where Matt's standing. "But that's not how it works."

I shrug. "All I know is he was sitting in my room when you sent me back. And he can't go farther than a couple of metres from me."

"Kitty, can you bring me back? Please?" Matt goes right up to her, desperate. "You saw Dad. I can't leave him. Please, I'll do anything."

Kitty doesn't respond. She's looking at me again or glancing to the side as if she'll catch a glimpse of him but never meeting his eyes. I clear my throat awkwardly. "He wants to know if you can bring him back."

Something ignites in her eyes, the faintest flicker of manic hope. "Come with me," she says.

I have to scramble to keep up with her, this ball of fierce energy. She walks back up the hill, past Matt and Peter's house and into the block of flats. "Up here," she says unnecessarily, leading me into a small flat. I hover awkwardly as she rummages through her room, muttering to herself.

Matt follows her. "What are you looking for?" he asks, and he's not even raising his voice, just poking around at stuff that he *knows* he can barely interact with. I grit my teeth. I'm not going to state the obvious.

Then he sniffs and wipes his face roughly. His shoulders are sloped, and he looks small and insubstantial, which should be expected for a ghost. Somehow, it feels wrong to me. I sigh. "He wants to know what you're looking for," I mutter, just loud enough for Kitty to hear.

She stands, eyes wide and blinking, like she'd forgotten I was there. I cross my arms and lean against the wall. I think the wrong one of us is invisible.

I shrug. "Just thought you might want to know."

"Uh, a magnifying glass," she says. She glances around the room, her eyes flickering back to me, then away, but she's got no hints as to where Matt's standing. I take pity on her and jerk my chin toward him. Kitty flashes me a smile, and I shrink more into myself. Kitty turns toward Matt. Her focus is still off; it's like she's doing one of those thousand-yard stares, looking through him, ignoring him. The opposite of what she wants. "I'm gonna try to turn it into a revealing spell of some sort."

"You can do that?" I ask.

She gives me a flicker of a smile. "I hope so," she says, then drops to her knees to search under her bed, dragging boxes out and flinging the lids off. "I've got a sigil I can use for seeing magic. It was one of the first ones Mum taught me when I was a kid, but I reckon if I make a tweak to the downsweep, I can change it so that it'll help me see something invisible rather than something with a certain kind of energy."

"That makes no sense," says Matt, crinkling his nose.

I snort. "He disapproves."

She laughs, distracted and short. "Yeah, he usually does." She scrabbles through a box of tat and pounces on something with a *ha!* She holds up a pink magnifying glass, the logo for the

Natural History Museum clear on the handle. "I knew I had it somewhere."

The door bangs open, and I'm rigid once more, slamming my back against the wall as Kitty's brother comes in. "Kitty, are you…oh, hi," he says, throwing a puzzled glance at me. "Kitty, what are you doing? You said we had to stay for Peter, and now you're bailing?"

"I know, I know," she says, the magnifying glass slipped smoothly into the pocket of her hoodie. "I'm sorry, I'll be back in a min, promise."

He looks at me, giving me a proper once-over, and I bristle at it and have to remind myself that he's only a wee thing. "Who's she?" he says.

"This is Talia," says Kitty. "Talia, this is my little brother, Sam."

"Hey," I say flatly, holding up my hand.

"Cool," he says. "But who *is* she?"

Kitty laughs even though all the warning signs are going off in my mind. Be invisible, be unnoticed. This is not invisible. "Look, she's one of Matt's friends. Can we please…" Kitty makes a *shoo* gesture.

He rolls his eyes and turns away from staring me down. "Fine," he says, dragging out the vowel. "But if you're not back in fifteen minutes and I have to walk in on you two making out, I *will* make you pay for therapy."

I can't hold back a laugh as Kitty blushes bright pink and hisses, "Sam!" after him. She glances at me and tucks her hair behind her ear as Sam slams the door. "Sorry about him," she says.

And maybe I can forgive the little brat if his sister glances at me again like that, through her lashes, the blood flushed to her cheeks, looking like a little Disney princess.

"Hey," says Matt *right* next to my ear, and I leap out of my skin.

"Jeez—*fuck*!"

"You were going to say Jesus Christ, weren't you?" Matt says with a smirk. "Bad Jew."

"What, Matt? What do you want?"

"Well, it would be nice if you could save the googly eyes for my best mate *after* she brings me back to life. I'm dreaming big here."

It's my turn to blush violently, shoulders coming up around my ears so strands of hair will cover my face and maybe hide my embarrassment. I force myself to straighten and spin on my heel, marching into what I hope is the living room. "Are we doing this or what?" I snap.

"What did you say to her?" Kitty whispers behind me. Matt mutters something quietly enough that I can't hear to translate, thankfully. I stand awkwardly in the centre of the room and do a slow turn as I realise I've just walked into someone else's space, and I don't know if it's appropriate to sit or stand in a corner or what. Luckily, Kitty doesn't seem to have noticed my angst and is rummaging through the clutter on a coffee table.

"What're you looking for now?" Matt sighs. "You need to tidy up, Kit."

I roll my eyes and don't translate.

"There should be a Sharpie here somewhere," Kitty mutters to herself. "Ah!" She stands with a triumphant grin, and I can't help smiling back. "Right," she says. "If I draw the sigil on the handle here, I should be able to make it reveal magic, but if I change *this* line a bit and do *this*, I should be able to…"

She clips the lid back on the pen and closes her eyes. It almost looks like she's praying. All the humour sinks from her face, and she looks tired and desperate. She opens her eyes, nods to herself, holds her hand over the sigil she's written, and it fucking *glows* under her hand. I gape at it.

Kitty looks at me. "Where is he?" I gesture to Matt, standing tense against the bookshelf. She lifts the magnifying glass, her hand shaking. Then she cries out and clamps her hand over her mouth. "Matt!"

"Hey, Kitty," Matt says, his voice tremulous. He waves and offers a shaky smile.

"Oh God. Oh, Matt, I'm sorry. I'm so, so sorry."

"Wow, it really works," Matt says, and I can hear the smile in his voice. "You can really see me? Hear me?"

"What? I can't…oh, Matt." She puts her hands over her nose and mouth and starts crying. I look up in horror. What does one do with crying girls anyway? But Matt's already there. He can't touch her still, but he's curling his body around her, patting her on the back or just above the back, going through the motions of comfort as best he can.

"I miss you so much," Kitty manages through her sobs.

"I miss you too," Matt says, his voice wobbling with tears as well. I stare off into the corner of the room.

At last, she gets herself under control and sits up, wiping her eyes. She holds the magnifying glass up again. "I'm going to get you back," she says firmly.

Matt breaks into a wide grin, but he tries to hide it. "Do you think you can?"

Kitty glances at me. "I can't hear him," she says apologetically. "Can you…"

"He asked if you think you can," I say.

It sounds weird and flat in my voice, but she doesn't seem to care. She turns back in delight, nodding. "I know I can. I have to."

He frowns. "I don't want anyone else to die for me, though."

I translate for them.

"Don't worry about a thing," she says, and there's that manic gleam in her eye. "It's not like I'm going to tell Peter or anything."

He sits back on his haunches. "How is Dad?"

Kitty sighs. "He's struggling. He, uh, he was worried…" She trails off and wipes fresh tears from her face. "He was worried you thought he wouldn't accept you."

Matt slumps. "Being gay?"

Kitty nods, and her chin wobbles. "He said…what was it, uh…there's nothing in the world you could have done that would have disappointed him."

Matt seems to become smaller, hunching down and covering his face as he cries. "I should've…"

"I know," Kitty says through her tears. I don't even need

to translate. Kitty bends down in front of him, and they crouch there, curled toward each other in their grief.

I feel like an intruder, as much of a weird necessary go-between as I was when no one else could see Matt. And the whole thing is too depressing. To have a parent who actually cares and be taken away from them? Morgan always did say God must have a strange sense of humour, and I don't expect to understand it.

At last, they stand. Kitty wipes her eyes with the back of her hands and holds up the magnifying glass again to smile at Matt. "I better get back to..." She waves her hand in the direction of Matt's house.

"To my funeral," he says with a snort.

She shakes her head. "What even is our life?"

"Well..." He gestures to his intangible self.

"Shut up," she says with a giggle. She looks at him, then puts her head on one side. "What's that?"

Matt looks at himself and tugs at his plaid shirt. "This? Kitty, I've told you, just because you're bisexual—"

"No, no, the red thing. Wait." She circles him, looking through the magnifying glass, then drops it onto the sofa. She holds out one hand and says *something*. The words are strange; they slip from my mind and memory like oil, but where she gestures, I can see the faintest glimmer of red.

"What's that?" I say, and almost recoil when I look down and realise that the glimmer leads right to me.

Kitty closes her eyes. "Fuck."

It's so surprising to hear this soft, cheerful girl swear that my first reaction is to laugh. It's only afterward that it occurs to me to be worried. "What?"

"Ah...that's my mum's magic."

"Your mum?" It takes me a moment to remember the woman in the grey place, and I step back. "Why did she—"

"I'm sorry," Kitty says, holding her hands up. "I'll talk to her. She didn't mean any harm...well..."

"Kitty," I snap, and Kitty shuts her mouth quickly. "What

the fuck is this? What's it doing to my chest? Is this why I'm the only one who can see Matt?"

"Will you sit down?"

"Is it going to kill me again?" And it shocks me that I really don't want that. I'll fight for this life. My heart's beating hard, and I'm tempted to claw at the glittering red haze like it's a physical thing.

"No, nothing like that," she says. She looks so earnest. I shouldn't trust her, this girl I don't know with this power I don't understand. But it soothes me anyway. She steps closer like I'm a cornered animal. "Look, I'm really sorry. She should never have done this."

"I still don't know what *this* is." I'm furious with myself for being close to tears.

"She tried to swap you and Matt when I sent you back. I'm sorry. I was so angry with her when she told me."

"You knew?"

"No, we thought it hadn't worked. She told me when I saw her again last night. I was furious with her."

My shoulders relax. Kitty flops into the sofa, and I perch on the other end. "Why?"

"She thought it would make me happy," Kitty says, blinking at me, looking miserable.

"No," I say. "Why were you mad with her?"

"Well, because it's wrong! You can't go making decisions like that for other people. You can't just switch lives without permission from every party. Surely, that's obvious, right?"

She looks up at Matt through her magnifying glass, as if inviting him to agree with her. He shrugs. "Kit, you're the only person who can even do that. I mean, yeah, I'm glad you always ask for permission from everyone, but I don't think I'd call it obvious."

"Sounds like God knew what he was doing giving you this power," I say. Kitty smiles slow and sweet, and I have to look at my hands so I don't spontaneously combust.

"Thanks," she says softly.

"Right," says Matt. He's leaning against the doorjamb with

his arms crossed, looking awkward. "Do you think you can get me out of here?"

I pass the message on. Kitty sighs and leans her elbows on her knees. "I don't know," she says. "I'll try, though. Gimme a few days. Maybe I can talk to Mum again." She grimaces. "I didn't exactly leave on good terms with her."

"Everything okay?" I ask. "You don't have to go back there if she'll be mad with you."

Kitty laughs and shakes her head. "Nothing like that. We need to clear the air. But she might know what to do. Or have some suggestions at least." She checks her watch. "Do you think you could come back soon? I'm sorry, I have to get back to the funeral, but I want to see Matt. Or I could catch the bus over to you instead if it's more convenient. It's no trouble—"

"No, it's fine," I say quickly. Something warm ignites inside my chest, and I press it down. This is not about me. This is about doing the right thing.

# CHAPTER NINE

## *Kitty*

For ages after Talia drives off with my best friend, the ghost, in her passenger seat, I'm twitchy and irritable. I'm sure sod's law will make it so I can't see my mum right when I need to ask her something. But it's less than forty-eight hours before I get the call again. I guess grief can't be stopped by the all-powerful spite of the universe.

I do not bring my A-game to the case, but it doesn't seem to matter. All the time that this man's talking to his big brother who died years ago in a house fire, I'm glancing around, looking for Mum.

I think the guy gets closure. His brother certainly refuses to change places with him, and maybe he's been sitting around here like Mum has, not ready to move on because his loved ones won't be wherever it is we go after the grey place. When he says good-bye, it seems like he glows a little bit brighter. I wonder if, once he's gone from my sight, he'll move on. It makes a lump harden in my throat. I kind of want that for Mum, and I kind of really, really don't.

I force myself to concentrate on the tearful, smiling man as I send him back. And then I look around again. There's a part of me that's terrified that because we argued last time, Mum won't be here. Maybe I've pushed her too far away, and she can't get back to me.

But there she is. She's got her hands clasped under her chin, looking as worried as I'm sure I do. The first thing I do is run and hug her tight. She lets out a long breath. "I'm sorry, Kitty. I'm really sorry."

"I'm sorry too."

"No, you were right. I wasn't thinking about that Talia girl at all, I was being selfish." She pulls back and cups my cheek, smiling ruefully down at me. "My little moral compass."

I laugh at her. The world is almost perfect for that minute, and then I remember. "Mum, Matt did come back, though. He's a ghost."

She frowns. "I didn't think ghosts were real. Otherwise, we'd all be out there."

I shrug. "I dunno, but he's bonded to Talia with your magic, so maybe not a *ghost* per se, but he's there. Only Talia could see him, so I did some fiddling around with some of those reveal sigils, and there he was."

I drop my head on her shoulder, overwhelmed again by the memory of seeing him so insubstantial, but so *Matt*, all the most important parts of him right there for only the two of us to see. Mum hugs me tight as tears come like a surprise, shaking my body with grief and painful hope.

Mum murmurs some magical words and sits me on a plush sofa, wrapping her arms around me tight. I'm practically sitting on her lap, shamelessly childish.

"Sometimes," I admit when I can, "I wanted to come here for him. I wanted to exchange my life for his. I miss him so much."

Mum closes her eyes in grief but doesn't argue. She knows.

"He would hate it, though. He even said he doesn't want anyone else to take his place."

She hums a wordless response and seems like she's trying to pretend she's not relieved. I sigh. "I don't know what to do, Mum. He's stuck to Talia, he can't go much more than a few feet away from her, and that's no life for either of them. Well." I frown. "You know what I mean."

She taps her lips, staring out in thought. I shuffle back to give her a bit more space, squidge myself into the plush cushions a bit more, and play with the tassels on one. "I don't know what to suggest," she says at last. "The spell I laid on him was…well, it wasn't very well thought out. I recognised him when he arrived, but he was in shock still. I can't talk to them at that point. And then before I could really think, you were there dealing with Talia and I…well."

"What spell is it, exactly?"

She draws it out on my hand, singing the alphabet song as she does. Intent is everything in magic, and she wants to teach this to me, not cast it. So she sings a teaching song. "It's like a lasso, I suppose," she says as the sigil glows for a moment on my palm. I follow the shapes of the symbols with my finger, feeling the magic talk to me. It does indeed feel like a rope, like capturing something in a hurry. But it also feels like love. I know my mum only wanted to do something nice for me, though I don't agree with how she did it.

"I think I'll be able to undo this," I say. The answer is in the back of my mind, tickling at me, and I just need a little while, but the fatigue is getting to me, pulling me out of the grey place.

"You're so smart," Mum says, shaking her head. "The way your mind works, making links between things, it's amazing. But you need to go now, love. You've been here too long."

"I don't want to go."

She hugs me and chuckles. "You'll regret it if you don't. Your magic may be strong, but it uses up a lot of energy. And you're skinny enough as it is."

"I'm not skinny," I protest.

"Go on," Mum says anyway, not distracted. "Sleep well, my darling. Leave some problems for tomorrow."

❖

Putting things right with Mum makes a big difference. Though I'm tired the next day, especially after my shift at the warehouse, I feel less heavy. Less like I'm walking through syrup, like any moment, I'm going to get my knees knocked out from under me and fall, and I won't be able to keep my head above water this time.

I'm on the bus home when I see them. If they're trying to be stealthy, the posh white guy's not doing a very good job of it. He's even got one of them slim black brollies with the curved wooden handle; he looks like he's just missing a bowler hat. He and a skinny South Asian–looking guy sit on the seats in the front, the ones that tip back like cinema seats when you stand.

Then they stare right at me.

I pretend not to notice, of course. I lean my head against the window and let the vibrations blur my eyesight, make my face go a little bit numb like I usually do. But every time I glance up, they're still staring at me openly.

Nobody else notices. Why would they? It's eight o'clock on a Wednesday night, and we're all heading home after another drudge at work. Who's paying attention to anyone else? I try to ignore them. I'm sure it's nothing. But I look at the reflection in the dark windows, and they're staring, staring.

I fiddle with my phone as childhood fears of vampires start to trickle up from my memory. I wish it wasn't so late. I wish I could walk that last little way in the light. I can imagine myself getting out and them following me, as crazy as that sounds. Fuck it. I bring people back from the dead, so I think I'm allowed a little crazy.

The bus pulls up a few stops before mine, and I'm so busy gnawing on my lower lip that I almost don't realise they've left. They must've slipped off with the couple of people who disembarked on Leith Hill. I slump in exhaustion and relief, and my heart beats hard, like it's been keeping quiet up until now. My hands are shaking, and before I can think about it, I'm texting Talia, of all people: *Thought I was followed just now lol. I think I'm getting paranoid in my old age.*

I regret it as soon as I click send, and I'm jabbing at the message, trying to see if I can delete it after the fact, when the dots come up that show she's writing back.

And now my heart's beating hard again for a different reason.

*You all right?*

*Yeah,* I reply. I can't stop myself smiling. She's sweet under all that grumpy. *I'm on the bus. They got off a few stops before me. Being paranoid, like I said.*

*Okay, but be safe, yeah? Can you call me when you get home?*

*It's fine. I do this trip all the time, and they're gone.*

*Even so. How long does it take?*

I feel a little guilty now but kinda fond, I suppose. It's not like I'm unfamiliar with people looking out for me or anything, but this feels sort of safe and warm.

*I'm coming up to my stop. Five mins walk, no problem.*

She replies, but I can't check it. I have to ring the bell, pull myself up, and lurch down the aisle. I call out thank you to the driver and wrap my jacket tight around myself as I step into the biting cold, the ground already starting to glitter with frost. I struggle to pull my gloves out of my bag.

"Miss Wilson?"

His voice is posh and relaxed, used to getting its own way, and my blood seems to freeze with the adrenaline dumped into it. He's standing in front of me like fucking Mycroft Holmes, one hand on the umbrella that's resting on the pavement.

I should throw a curse at him. Mum taught me one years ago when she was still alive. It was one of the first pieces of magic she ever taught me, and what does that say about us? Thing is, she also told me never to start a fight.

"I see your research was correct, Shivam," says the posh man, and gestures at my hand. My bare hand which is now glowing with indecisive magic.

"Well, yes, sir," says Shivam. The "obviously" goes unsaid, but it's written all over his face. He looks sulky and awkward. Still shifty as hell, both of them.

"The name's Anderson," says posh man. "You'll forgive me if I don't offer to shake your hand. I imagine I'd lose it if I tried."

I snatch my hand behind my back like a naughty schoolgirl. "Sorry," I say and imagine Mum groaning and shaking her head at me. *You don't have to be so polite, Kitty*, she'd say. *You have to be safe.* I am safe, I think. I hope.

“I imagine you’re wondering why I’ve sought you out,” Anderson says.

“I was actually wondering how you know my name,” I say because it’s abundantly obvious he wants me for my magic.

Anderson raises his eyebrows, just a flicker, and inclines his head. “I have my ways, as you have yours.” He holds out his own hand, and above it, blue-green sparks shimmer and coalesce into a column of flickering lights, rising up in rows like something out of the Matrix.

My jaw drops. “There’re more of us?”

Anderson smiles. “Oh, yes, Miss Wilson. Usually, the gifted such as yourself would be detected and offered assistance as soon as possible, but I must admit, you slipped through the net. Shivam and I have come to rectify that.”

“Rectify…”

“We’d like to offer you employment at the Society. Powers such as ours should not be wasted on menial labour.”

“You’re offering me a job?”

He looks slightly pained. Shivam’s the one who answers. “They pay well. Twice what you’re earning now and only five hours a night.”

Anderson shoots him a poisonous look. Shivam ignores him. “Indeed,” says Anderson. “We wouldn’t want you to overwork your fledgeling powers.”

“And there’re more like us?”

“Oh yes,” Anderson says, waving a hand airily. “As I said, I don’t know how you slipped through the net.”

I bite my lip. It sounds too good to be true, but I want it so bad, to have someone understand the daily exhaustion and the raw ache in my soul when I can’t help them. “I can’t move, though, so if it’s all based in London or something…”

Anderson snorts, impatient or derisive, I’m not sure. “Miss Wilson, we’re magic users. A little thing such as location doesn’t matter. All we need is a doorway. Shivam?”

“You got Google Maps on your phone?” he asks, stepping forward. I consider giggling at the incongruity of it. Location doesn’t matter, but we still need Google Maps, apparently.

"Okay, here's the street address. This old warehouse, it'll be your portal."

I look down at the street view. I know the place, the concrete cracked out front and growing wild with buddleia in the summer. "So I go in there, and it'll take me to you guys?"

"To the Society, yes," Shivam says, glancing back at Anderson.

Anderson checks an expensive-looking watch. "It's settled, then. Come to the warehouse at eight p.m. on Wednesday, and we'll give you your orientation."

They disappear right in front of me, and I'm left standing in the cold, my jaw hanging open and my phone screen slowly dimming.

## Chapter Ten

### *Talia*

I'm trying to concentrate on my work, a paper that's due in three days, but my mind keeps going back to Kitty and the men who might or might not have been following her. She hasn't replied to my last text, and I'm *this* close to asking Matt to reassure me, but what if he doesn't? What if I've made a terrible mistake?

My phone rings, and I jump out of my skin, snatching it up. "Hello?"

"Hey," Kitty says, and my heart beats funny. "I was texting you back, but I've got too much to tell you."

I frown. "What happened?"

Matt appears at my desk almost lightning fast. "Is that Kitty? Put her on speaker." I don't even bother rolling my eyes, just put the phone on my desk faceup.

"You know those guys I texted you about? They were following me."

"What?" Matt and I yell at the same time.

"No, no, don't worry," she says quickly. She laughs breathlessly. "It's fine, really. They're like me." She drops her voice to near a whisper. "They can do magic."

Matt and I share a look. "How do you know?" I say.

"They showed me. I didn't know there was anyone else out there who could do this stuff. Mum never talks about anyone else. I mean, I suppose I should've guessed, but I never…and they said there's a whole society of them! I'm going there for orientation on Wednesday."

"Fuck's sake, Kitty." Matt groans and slaps his forehead.

"Are you sure about this?" I ask. Never would have thought I'd be the more diplomatic one. "How did they find you?"

"I dunno," Kitty says, still sounding too giddy to be taking this seriously. "Magic, I guess."

"Oh great," Matt says. "And why now? Why didn't they find her earlier?"

"Is this safe?" I ask. "How do you really know who they are?"

She sighs. "I don't know," she admits. "I…this is the first time I've ever met someone like me, you know? Other than Mum. I need to find out more about, I dunno, everything. My heritage, I guess."

Matt groans out loud. I manage to keep it back. "Yeah," I say at last. "I get that."

"Fine," says Matt. "But I'm going in with her."

"You're what?"

"What?" Kitty says.

"Sorry. It's Matt, he says he's going with you. Matt, have you forgotten all this?" I gesture between us, trying to encompass this ridiculous, impossible situation.

Kitty laughs. "Matt, you can't, you're a ghost."

"Oh shit, you're both right, what would I do without you?" Matt deadpans. "Look, being a ghost is perfect for this. Nobody else can see me."

"But they can see *me*, and you can't go anywhere without me."

"Well, Kitty's going to have to separate us, isn't she?" Matt says, tilting his chin up like the arrogant little twat he is.

Kitty gives a little awkward chuckle. "What are you guys saying?"

I grit my teeth. "Matt wants you to separate us so he can go with you, keep an eye on you."

"I'm trying," she says. "I'm sorry I haven't worked it out yet, I—"

"No, Kitty, it's not your fault. You don't have to apologise. Matt's just being an arse."

"Och, *arse*," Matt teases. I hiss at him.

Kitty hums to herself. "I think...would you be able to come here before this weekend, Talia? I think I'll be able to see Mum again and ask her for some help, then maybe I really can separate you? Or even..."

My mind races through schedules and timetables. If I get up a couple of hours early tomorrow, I can get my essay done. "I don't have lessons on Wednesday afternoon," I suggest.

"Really? Oh, that would be perfect. Are you sure you don't mind?"

"No, it's fine," I say, and try to remind the heart hammering in my chest that this is not a date.

I've always been a good liar. To everyone else, at least. Inside my mind, the voice that sounds too much like my mother roots out the most secret parts of me and throws them broken at my feet. "You've got a crush on a girl you just met? A girl you've seen face-to-face for less than a day, and that was at a funeral? The girl who only asked you over because you're inconveniently stuck to the ghost of her best friend? You're pathetic, Talia. Laughable."

It's a poisonous rhythm that pulses through me along with the beat of my heart as I drive to Kitty's house once more, Matt tense in the passenger seat. I open the creaky car door, by now almost dreading it, but then *she* runs out of the block and stops in front of me, bouncing up and down. For a wild moment, I think she might hug me. The thought terrifies and intrigues me all at once.

"Talia," she says, beaming. "Thank you so much for coming. Did you have a good drive?"

"Uh, yeah, it was fine."

"Come on inside. I've done some digging and found some of Mum's old stuff. There's this book I remember from when I was a kid, and I'd forgotten I even had it, you know how it is. Anyway, there are some really interesting suggestions in there that I think I can use. I dunno if it's going to work, but even if it doesn't, I was thinking maybe we could ask someone at the Society."

She rambles on, and in the effort to keep up with her stream of consciousness and the impossible new ideas she's coming up with, the cruel little voice in my mind slips away unheard.

Kitty unlocks the door to her flat, ushering me in. It's warm in here, a little stuffy for it, but it doesn't smell of cigarette smoke and old takeaway. The living room is bathed in weak winter sun, and I tuck myself to the side, tugging off my jacket.

"D'you want a cuppa, Talia?" Kitty asks, following me, picking up a hoodie from the sofa and semi-folding it, snatching up a little pile of crumpled tissues from the side table and trying to hide them behind her back as she steps into the kitchenette. The bin lid clangs.

"I'm fine, thanks."

"You sure? I'm gonna have some tea. I need the sugar. I think I've got some biscuits around here somewhere."

I hesitate. "Okay, tea please."

She pops her head around the wall to bestow a sweet, dimpled grin at me. I can't help quirking a smile back. It relaxes me.

Matt flops onto the sofa and laces his fingers under his chin, looking at me with a worryingly thoughtful smirk. I tear my eyes away and look around instead. Snooping without being too obvious, I hope. Last time I was here, I was a bit distracted.

There's a shabby but clean air to it that I can't help but like. A dining table with stacks of homework and envelopes shoved to one side, a couple of mug rings marked into the varnish. The sofa looks like one of those lumpy ones that folds out into an equally uncomfortable bed, and it's covered in a random assortment of homemade pillows.

Most alien of all is the pot plants. They're everywhere, hanging from the balcony, on the windowsill, and the shelves. One particularly venerable spider plant has its own little table, runners cascading off it with young clones sprouting off at all angles.

"Here you go," says Kitty, and I turn to see her holding out a mug with a little smile on her face. She has this openness about her that's too bright for me, makes me want to turn away, lay my gaze somewhere else.

I sip my tea to fill my hands and my time. "I like your plants," I mutter when the silence drags.

"Oh, thanks." Her face lights up. "I love them. We can't have pets here. I spend so much time dealing with dead things, a bit of life is just what I need some days." She giggles at her dark joke. Then clears her throat. "Where's Matt right now?"

"Hey, she remembered me," Matt says. "I was beginning to feel like the third wheel on a date."

I glare at him and gesture toward the seat he's occupying. Kitty's smile widens, and she holds up her magical magnifying glass and waves. He smiles fondly and waves back. "Hey, Kit. You going to separate me and Talia, then?"

"He says hi. And asks if you're going to separate us."

She makes a face. "Not exactly. I'm sorry, I was hoping to see Mum again and ask for suggestions, but sod's law, I haven't had a case. I think, though, I might be able to make Matt permanently visible to me. I know it's not much."

"It's a good start," I say. I'm not sure if I'm disappointed or relieved that I'll have to stick around.

"Would you mind sitting on the floor?" she asks.

"Yeah, sure, whatever you need."

"Great," she says, relieved, like it mattered what I felt about things. "I was gonna do it on the table but we, um, we need to hold hands, and sitting opposite each other would be uncomfortable 'cos of the distance, but sitting beside each other would be, like, at a weird angle, so…" She trails off.

"You want to start, then?"

"Yes. Um, if you wouldn't mind?" She ushers me backward off the rug, then rolls it up to reveal a set of scribbles in white chalk, various symbols and a circle split into three.

"Wow," I say. "I wasn't expecting it to be this stereotypically magic-looking."

"I know what you mean," she says with a grin. "Most of the stereotypical stuff you see in movies is just for show, but there are a few important parts like the symbols themselves. I could make these look a lot fancier if I wanted, even add a pentagram or two, but I don't need it. Maybe some people do. I guess I'll find out at the Society."

"Makes no difference to me. Not like I thought magic existed until a week ago."

"Yeah, sorry about that." She guides me to sit between two of the lines, then sits cross-legged right on the longest one, opposite me. She leans over to grab a few mismatched tea-lights and a lighter, and fiddles with it for a while, swearing as the flame licks over her thumb.

"You want me to do it?" I say at last.

"If you can. The wick's really short."

I take the candle and turn it almost upside down over the lighter so the short wick catches. Kitty sighs and slaps her forehead. "I feel dumb now."

I laugh, and she stares at me. "What?"

"Nuffin'." Her cheeks darken with embarrassment. "Just… that's the first time you've laughed."

"I've known you for days, and for literally the whole time, we've been thinking about your dead friend," I protest, my own pale skin surely showing my blush far clearer.

"Yeah, I know," she says, her face falling, and I regret everything.

She takes the candles, placing them in some obviously important positions around us. I fidget with the fraying heels of my jeans until she holds her hands out for mine.

They're gentle, the skin of her palms firm and a little calloused but very warm. My own bony fingers seem abnormally long next to her hands, almost blue against the warm brown of her skin.

I don't know if I'm meant to close my eyes when she does, but I find I can't. As she starts chanting—almost singing—softly in a rising-falling cadence, I stare captivated at the fine skin over her eyes, delicate as a petal. The curve of her cheek, the tight curls of her hair following the shape of her skull, they all seem to stand out against the darkness of the room, darkness that grows with her chant.

I know I'm staring. I know this is the time I'd usually turn away both physically and emotionally before I'm caught, but somehow, the growing dark and the music, and I guess the magic, seem to put me into a calm state I can't remember ever feeling. I notice there's a smile on my face. I didn't even realise that was happening, but there it is, and I don't hurry to brush it away. It's all so peaceful.

"Kitty?" says Matt, and Kitty and I startle.

"Matt," Kitty breathes and drops my hands. The dark and the magic that I've started feeling in the very air remain, but the warmth is gone with her touch, and I drop my gaze to the centre of the ritual circle. I don't know if I'm needed anymore, but I'm not moving. I won't be the reason she loses her best friend again.

"It worked," Matt says, a wide grin obvious in his voice. "That was awesome, Kitty."

"Oh my God, Matt," she says and bursts into tears again.

"Ah, Kitty," he says and bends down with her.

"I'm sorry," she sobs. My hands itch to reach out to her and comfort or *something*. "It's…hearing your voice again, seeing you without the glass. I miss you so much."

"I miss you too," he says, his voice rough.

"I'm gonna get you back, Matt," she says, wiping her face. "I have to. There's got to be something I can do. There'll be someone at the Society, I know it."

Matt and I glance at each other and away. He pats her shoulder. His hand sinks too low into her, a jarring sight I can't tear my eyes away from. "I know you will, Kit," he says. "You'll rock it."

She smiles up at him and blows her nose. "I wish I'd been able to speak to Mum again, find a way to separate you two at least."

"Don't worry about that," I say quickly. "I was thinking about it earlier. What if I drive you to the Society—"

"Which, by the way, sounds Illuminati as fuck," Matt adds. Kitty shrugs.

"And if they won't let me in with you, at least I can sit outside while Matt goes with you as far as he can."

Kitty looks up at Matt, who nods. "Won't it be weird, though?" she says. "You don't take someone with you when you're starting a new job."

"This isn't exactly shifts at Tesco," Matt says. "Two creepy guys come out and solicit you on a dark creepy street? I'd say you'd be crazy to go alone."

"If they're not okay with you having someone there with you, to support you and keep you safe, then they're dodgy," I point out.

She sighs. "Yeah, I guess. I just want it to be real so bad. I don't want to do anything to mess it up, you know?"

"You won't," I say firmly. I can't imagine her messing anything up.

"Thanks," she says, gifting me one of her sweet, sweet smiles. I wish my smile was nice enough to return it. She takes a deep breath. "Okay, we'd better get going, hadn't we?"

The warehouse she directs me to looks like it hasn't been used in years, but Kitty assures me that this is a gateway to the real Society building or dimension or whatever magic bullshit they've fed her. I park right up against the door and get out with her, scuffing broken glass and litter out of the way as we walk up in the dying light.

The door creaks open as we get closer, and a skinny Asian guy looks out. He catches sight of me, and his face hardens in anger and fear, a subtle shift, but it's noticeable. "Who's this?" he asks Kitty.

"This is Talia. Talia, this is Shivam, he's one of the—"

"I thought we told you to come alone."

"Um, I don't think you did, actually," she says, and I'm proud of her for not sounding apologetic. She just sounds like she's searching her memory and checking her version of events.

"Fuck," says Shivam under his breath.

"I'm only looking out for her," I say. I want it to sound firm, but it comes out sullen, teenager. "A girl going alone to meet two guys? It's a bit—"

"Yeah, yeah, I know, I know," he says, flapping at me and

muttering. I'm about to say that I'll wait outside when he glances back to the warehouse and back to me. "You stay silent, you hear me? I can't mask sounds, so you trip, you fuck us all, okay?"

"Uh, yeah?"

He glares at Kitty like it's all her fault, then says something, gestures at me. Green lights like old computer graphics flow from his hand over me, and all I can see is sparkling lights for a moment. I squeeze my eyes shut. When I open them, Kitty is staring at me in amazement. "Oh my God, that's so cool! Can you teach me that, Shivam?"

"No, your magic won't do it. Now come on, we've got to go."

"Holy shit," Matt says right by my ear. "She's invisible."

"What?" I hiss.

Kitty gropes for my arm like she's blind, smiling and grabbing it when she bumps me by accident. "Come on," she says. "Keep quiet, stay close." She looks back at Shivam. "Thank you."

"Yeah, yeah, come on. And keep your pet ghost out of the computers too."

"What?" Kitty squeaks as Matt's jaw drops. "You can see him?"

I glance at my arm as Kitty lets go to chase Shivam, bubbling over with questions. I'm relieved I can still see myself, but there's a sheen over my skin, a green mirrored effect, subtle. My hair prickles as I remember even Matt can't see me, and I stumble to catch up with them.

Shivam glares at my feet. "Walk quieter."

I make a face at him, and he rolls his eyes. It's a weird relief to know he can see me, at least. I feel a sudden kinship with Matt, who's been visible to only me for days. I've got a new respect for him. If it had been me, I'd be freaking out. He's just been an annoying, sarcastic bastard.

I slip off my shoes as I follow them into the warehouse, my feet silent on the cold floor. I creep closer to Kitty, almost glad she can't see me doing so. Shivam leads us through a corridor with a faint glow on the walls. The glow increases until it's almost blinding, all of us but Shivam squinting through it so we don't fall over our own feet…and then suddenly, we're out.

"Holy shit," Kitty breathes and laughs softly.

"Bloody Illuminati," mutters Matt. He's not wrong. The place looks like something out of a James Bond movie, all industrial steel and white, with metal stairs and gangways lining the walls around a vast central floor. Below us, people bustle from door to desk, passing papers to each other, calling out instructions I can't make out over the general noise of feet on metal stairs and whirring fans in the corner.

"Kitty, come on," Shivam calls, and we turn to see he's waiting near a nondescript white door like all the others around the atrium. "In here."

Kitty rushes over, almost skipping. Her face falls when the room is mostly a regular office, a desk with a PC in one corner, another empty desk across from it. The only unusual feature is a mirror taking up most of one wall.

"This is going to be our room," Shivam says, sitting at the desk behind the computer. "You'll be working with me, mostly, but Anderson says he wants to give you some of the training, see where your limits are." His eyes flick up to her and away.

"What is it we actually do here?" Kitty asks.

"A variety of things," Shivam says, distracted by passwords on the computer. Matt peers over his shoulder until Shivam holds his middle finger up right in front of his eyes. "It really depends on your skill set."

Kitty sits in the chair across from Shivam, a little deflated. Then she stands straight back up again like a child for the headmaster when the door opens, and in comes a middle-aged man who looks like he stepped right off the Monopoly board.

"Ah, Miss Wilson," he says, and of course he sounds like *that*. "Ready for your first shift, I see?"

"Yes, Mr. Anderson," she says, her face lighting up with that smile. "Though I don't yet know what it is I need to do."

"That all depends on your magic. Tell me, Miss Wilson, what is it you *can* do?"

"Well," she says, tangling her fingers together and glancing up at Matt briefly. "I mostly bring people back from the dead."

There's a beat of silence, like the whole place just took a breath. Shivam looks straight up to Anderson, eyes wide. In fear, maybe?

"A reaper," says Anderson. His voice sounds bored, but every nerve in my back is twanging, all my hackles up. I may not be a magic user, but I've learned from eighteen years of living with a woman whose mood can change at the slightest provocation that you do not ignore the signals. I want the wall at my back because I can feel threat in every pore, and I can't look in all directions. This man is anything but bored.

"I guess," says Kitty, shrugging, still with that sweet, almost apologetic smile. Even Matt doesn't look like he's picked up on this, still poking at Shivam's computer, his finger going right through the screen. Kitty continues. "I didn't really know there were types of magic, if I'm honest."

"Well, of course," Anderson says, moving farther into the room and placing his umbrella and black leather gloves on Shivam's desk. "Shivam here is a seeker. He can find anything lost or yet to be found."

"Cool," Kitty says, smiling at Shivam. "That's how you found me, then, I guess. What about you, sir?"

Anderson looks pleased to be asked. "I create," he says with entirely too much drama. "My magic allows me to change time and space."

"So you made this place, right? That's how it fits into the warehouse?"

"Not a bad guess," he says. "In fact, I simply created pathways from the various entrances to this central location. You are no longer in Leithfield."

I slip my phone out of my pocket and bring up Google Maps because I'd love to prove this smug bastard wrong. No signal, though. Which could be due to the massive warehouse we walked into or okay, Lord Anderson's magic dimension or whatever.

"This is freaking cool," Kitty says, her eyes bright with excitement, glancing between Shivam and Anderson. "My mum never told me about this kind of stuff. She taught me whatever spell we needed, and we didn't talk about the theory of it much. Kinda made it up as we went along."

Anderson sniffs like he smells something nasty. "Hedge witchery. I suppose there's not much we can do about that."

"Was there something wrong with it?" Kitty says, and the way she's deflated makes me want to puff up and stand in front of her. How dare they do that to her?

"It sounds like your mother didn't have much magic herself," Anderson says, and he sounds sympathetic, but even Matt's side-eyeing him now. "It's possible that's why you didn't show up on our radar until now. Your powers may not be very strong."

"Oh," Kitty says like she believes him, the idiot.

"Wait, that's bollocks," Matt says, loudly enough to make Kitty, Shivam, and I jump. "She's been bringing people back to life for years. How can she possibly be weak?"

I nod vigorously, though nobody except Shivam can see. Kitty does a grand job of pretending everything's totally normal, ducking her head like a scolded schoolgirl to hide her grin. Anderson seems oblivious, thankfully.

"These two are talking out their arses, Kit, don't listen to them," Matt says, walking almost through me to stand next to her, and I'm grateful to him. I can't do that. I'd like to think I would if I wasn't under some sort of invisibility spell, but I've always been a coward, and I still don't know what these guys can do.

"Never mind, Miss Wilson," Anderson says. "Any magic is useful magic. It just means you might be working one on one with Shivam to complete your tasks, rather than joining the rest of the reapers for big jobs."

"There are other reapers?" Kitty says, and she looks like she might jump at him and shake him for information. "Can I talk to them?"

"Not now," he says, checking his watch. "I must warn you, we're not exactly a 'meet up for drinks after a shift' sort of group. Magic users are a solitary breed, from necessity. One gets used to one's own company after keeping secrets so long."

"A society that isn't very social," Matt snarks. "Sounds perfectly sensible and not a load of bollocks at all."

"Now, if you'll excuse me," Anderson says, "I'll leave you in Shivam's tender care. Good luck, Miss Wilson."

He dips his head in a little bow, pauses a moment like he's studying Kitty's face, then leaves in a bustle of self-importance.

There's silence for a moment. Shivam seems to slump slightly. "Right," he says. "Let's see what you can do, shall we?" He shoots daggers at Matt, then glances at me and jerks his head to the side. I take a few steps back and lift myself onto the second desk, which creaks. Kitty's head snaps right to me, and she smiles in my direction before turning back to Shivam.

Now I've got over the existential dread of being invisible, I don't mind it. I'm glad Shivam hasn't taken this glamour off me the moment Anderson left. It would be just my luck to have him walk right back in the room for some reason. I'm good at moving quietly. In fact, if I had control over this power, it would have made my life a whole lot easier. While Matt's wandering about, already bored, I'm settling in to watch Kitty's first magic lesson.

"The sigils you use, which ones are they? Who taught you?" Shivam asks.

"My mum taught me," Kitty says. "She taught me everything I know about magic. Well, and then I made some stuff up too."

"You made it up?" he asks, frowning.

"Yeah, I mean, magic's all about your will, right? I linked a couple of things together and you know, decided they were going to work."

Shivam stares at her. "And…they did?"

"Yeah, well enough," she says with a shrug. I try to catch Matt's eye, but he's poking his head right through the wall.

"Right," Shivam says. "Well, you're going to have to stick to the script here." He seems to recover his composure and walks her to the big mirror. "I'll be finding the cases for you from now on. We can't have just anyone getting to you. They've got to go through the proper channels."

"What do you mean?"

He gives her a jaded look. "Where do you think you're going to get your pay from?"

Her eyebrows shoot up. "What, you mean we're charging people to bring their loved ones back? That's not right."

"Why not?" he asks, an edge of defensiveness creeping in. "Haven't you ever heard of the expression 'cross my hand with silver'? Magic should be paid for."

"But why? We can help them, so why are we charging them?"

"Doctors help people, but you don't bat an eyelid when they earn fifty grand a year, do you?"

"Yeah, but the NHS—"

"When was the last time you had a good night's sleep, Kitty?" He crosses his arms and raises his eyebrows when she looks away. "You've been working all sorts of shifts for fuck-all money, then getting up at all hours to bring people back. How long do you think you can keep doing this? Wouldn't it be better to actually get a regular sleep schedule, take care of your health, be paid enough to do this for longer?"

And well, when he puts it like that, I'm angry on Kitty's behalf that she's been left to deal with this situation on her own for so long. I'm almost grateful to these guys for finding her and giving her what she deserves.

It's still sketchy as hell, of course.

"Come on," says Shivam. "Show me these sigils you use." He takes out a whiteboard marker and sketches a square onto the mirror, putting some little scribbles in the corners.

"What's that?" Kitty asks.

"It's to keep your magic contained, of course, so you can make the sigils for demonstration purposes. How did your mum teach you without a demo box?"

"She'd draw them in the air and sing the alphabet so her intent was to teach, not to cast," Kitty says. "What's this from? What language?"

"It's modified from Khudabadi," he says. "You won't recognise it. My family's from Pakistan, so that's what they've always used. What does your mum use?"

She laughs. "I think Mum and I are both magical magpies. All sorts of different ones. All I know is that the flowing ones work better for me." She bites her lip. "Is that bad?"

Shivam hesitates. "Honestly, I don't know. I don't know many other magical families. I don't know if it's different for other people."

"Really?" she says with a frown. "What about all the other reapers?"

He blinks rapidly. "Oh, well, yeah. I mean, there's loads of them. From all over the place. But fair warning, they're stuck up, okay? Maybe best not to try to talk to them. They aren't very friendly."

Kitty smiles. "That's fine, I'm friendly enough for both of us. And I've talked to snobby people before. I can handle 'em. It'll be worth it to learn a little more about magic."

Shivam bites his lip. "I really don't think you'll get much of a chance to talk. They're always really busy and rushing about."

"But surely you have *some* free time, right?"

"We don't spend it here," he says quickly. "We leave straightaway, and we don't come to work early or anything like that. It's not like any of the shifts go through mealtimes. So, no, there's no socialising really."

"That's…sad," Kitty says.

"That's bullshit," Matt says. I nod.

"Just is what it is," Shivam says. "Now, let's do a dry run, I'll see what you can do, and then we'll call it a night." He bustles Kitty to the mirror to do her thing and doesn't give her a chance to bring the subject back up.

# Chapter Eleven

## *Kitty*

Shivam shoos me out of the Society building after my shift's over. He says he wants to get home, and I'm not allowed in there without him, so I guess I really won't be getting too much of a chance to explore. I try to tell myself I'm not disappointed. He glances back at the door before casting the counter spell over Talia and bringing her back into sight. I can't help grinning when I see her.

"What did you think?" I ask her and Matt when we're sitting in the car.

They glance at each other. "You realise there's something weird going on with the whole thing, right?" Matt says.

"Other than it being a secret magical society," Talia adds.

I frown and sit back. I can't help but feel a bit deflated. "It's just new, that's all," I say, and I resist the urge to pout.

"Yeah, no," Matt says with a snort. "New is learning all the rules about who buys coffee, which fridge you put your lunch in, and where the loos are. *This* place is sus."

"I will learn those rules too, and things are bound to be different in a magic place, after all. It's not like getting a job at a supermarket."

"Come on, Kit," Matt says, and I hate when he gets so patronising. "I know you're naive, but—"

"But you also know I'm not an idiot," I snap. "Give me some bloody credit."

There's silence in the car. I lean my elbow against the window, and Matt huffs and throws his hands up.

There's a creak that pulls my attention round. Talia's hands are white-knuckled around the steering wheel, a muscle twitching in her jaw. Her eyes are wide and glazed, fixed on the road ahead. "You all right?" I ask, distracted from Matt. He leans forward too.

"Yeah," she says quickly, nodding. "Yeah, of course."

She's obviously not, but I sit back. Her shoulders have dropped a little, at least. They were almost up around her ears. "You think it's dodgy too, don't you?"

"I don't. I mean, I think whatever you guys think. It's all fine."

Matt laughs. "What's wrong with you?"

"Nothing," she snaps. Her face flushes pink, a little blotchy. "I'm fine."

I sigh again and cross my arms, leaning my head against the window. I'd wanted it all to be perfect. I'd wanted it to solve all my problems like it was already solving money and the pulls that came at any time of night.

"I'm not dumb," I say quietly. I turn to give Matt the puppy eyes. "Am I?"

"Of course not," he says promptly. "I'm sorry. I know I can be a bit…"

"Of a twat?" I finish with a grin.

"Patronising," he says, narrowing his eyes. "I didn't mean to imply that you were dumb. I'd never think that. You just like people too much. You want everyone to be as good as you are, and they're not. Nobody is."

I grin. "And I think you have too little faith in humanity. I'm looking at two pretty good people right now." Matt and Talia give me twin sceptical looks, and I roll my eyes at them. "Look, I'm not as trusting as you think I am. No, really," I say when Matt opens his mouth. "I'm not blind. I know there's something off. But it's the closest I've come to an answer, isn't it? I haven't seen Mum in days, and I've read all her books. What if they've got a library there? What if Shivam knows something that can help bring you back? It's worth a try, right?"

"It's not worth it if you're in danger," Matt says.

I smile at him fondly. He's wrong, of course. He's worth much more danger than this.

# CHAPTER TWELVE

## *Talia*

When my phone rings the next day I'm concentrating on a research paper about the nonexponential decay of quantum tunnelling, and I don't notice straight away.

"Talia," Matt says. I ignore him at first, and he puts his hand *in* my head like the little poltergeist bastard he is.

"What the fuck?"

"Kitty's calling," he says, pointing at the phone.

I rub my face, muttering oaths at him, and tap *answer*. "Uh, hello?"

"Talia?" Kitty says. I frown. Her voice sounds little over the phone, and something protective rises in me.

"Aye, it's me, you all right?"

"Is Matt there?"

I put the phone back down on the bed and flick it to speaker. "He's here," I say. "Can you hear him?"

"Kitty?" he says obediently.

"Matt?" Kitty says. "I, uh…" She swallows audibly. "I saw Connor today."

Matt sits on the bed like his strings've been cut. He's silent, and I rack my brain for something helpful to say. "Is he okay?" I manage eventually.

Kitty sniffles. "He's…yeah, I guess. He's been in hospital after the crash and all. He's, uh, he's on crutches, but he's fine. Well. No. He's sad, Matt. I wanted to…I don't know why, but I thought you'd want to know. He misses you so much."

Matt's staring into space. I slowly pick the phone up and turn it off speaker. "He's processing, Kitty," I explain.

She sniffs again, and I squeeze my eyes shut. Too far away to offer comfort to her, too alive to offer comfort to him. "You sure you're okay?"

"Yeah, yeah," she says, and somehow, I can visualise her waving, dismissing concern for herself. "God. I wasn't sure if it was the best thing to do, you know?" she says. She pronounces it *fing*, her accent more London than Oxfordshire, and I find it endearing. "I want to tell Connor that Matt's okay. I want to tell him I can see him, you know? But no way that'd go down well."

"No, I doubt it."

She sighs, and there's a rustling over the line, like she's rubbing her head, moving in some way that rubs the mic. "S'weird, that's all, I guess. He's here, but he's not here. I mean, I thought my relationship with death was weird enough what with what I do. Anyway. Sorry, I wanted him to know. Sorry."

"You don't have to apologise," I say.

"Sure," she says. "Thanks, I'll, uh, I'll leave ya to it, okay? I…sorry."

Before I can remind her not to apologise, she hangs up. I put the phone down and look at Matt. He's crying silently, and I bite my lip.

"You all right?"

He shakes his head. I scratch my head, tug at my hair. "Sorry." I frown at myself. Too many apologies all over the place.

Matt wipes his face and sniffs. "It's not fair," he says in a whisper. "It's not fair."

"Aye, I know."

"Do you think…" He glances at me. "Do you think I was too happy?"

"What?" I cock my head.

"I, uh. I was so happy. So lucky. And I don't think…I don't think I appreciated it enough, you know? Do you think I was punished?"

He looks at me like my opinion matters, like I can make

a difference, and it's scary, but it's also bullshit. I put my hand right over his and look at him hard. "No, I don't," I say. "I think life and death, they're random bastards, and it's *shit*, and I'm so, so sorry that you're dead, but no, I don't think you're being punished."

"You think?"

I nod firmly. "It's hard enough to find happiness, but when you find it, you hold on to it, okay? For as long as it lasts."

He wipes his eyes. "Not very fucking long, that's the thing," he says softly.

"I know." I nod. "I know."

It's only an hour or so later when the phone rings again. That's what gets me. That's why I screw up. I assume it's Kitty again. I don't check the caller ID.

I regret it instantly.

"Morag?"

It's Ma's voice, and I sit up, my eyes widening, my heartrate rising. "Uh, yeah?"

Matt, sitting on the windowsill with a leg hanging over the drop, turns with a quizzical look. I shake my head, forgetting she can't hear him.

"It's me, your mam."

"Yeah, yeah, I know." I clear my throat. "How are you?"

"Aye, not bad, lass," she says, and there's this treacherous part of my heart that goes *she loves you really, she can say nice things.* "How's Oxford?"

"It's good, Ma. Thanks. Um. Difficult but I'm enjoying it."

"Good, good," she says. She trails off. I can tell something's coming. "Love, I don't suppose you can send me some cash till the end of the month, could you? Your auld Ma's a bit skint."

I bite my lip and grimace wide. Matt's eyebrows shoot up, and he's over on the bed in a blink. "I can't, Ma. I don't have any spare cash."

"But you're down there in England in your fancy school, and you're not even getting a loan for it with that scholarship of yours."

"That's not how it works." I sigh. I don't know why I think explaining again will work. "The scholarship's only part of the fee. You signed off on the student loan paperwork, you know."

"And you don't have a job yet?" she says, and how, how does she manage to make me feel guilty about that when she's not had a job since April, when she lost the Working Men's club gig? "Don't play me like that, Morag, I know you. You'd get one as soon as you could."

"I'm not," I insist. "I'm working too hard at my studies for a job." But I could get one, my mind whispers. I'm sure I could spare a few hours a week.

"How're you getting food, then, hmm?" Ma asks.

"I get an allowance," I say before I can rein it in.

It's like a match thrown into a puddle of petrol. "Oh, she gets an 'allowance,'" says Ma, and she puts on a mocking accent which I suppose is meant to be English. "You get an allowance from the bloody Tories to party all night long, not having to do a day's honest work in your life, and you won't share with your ma?"

"No, it's—"

"You always were a selfish little bitch, and now you've gone off to that posh school, and you're putting on airs, too good for me now, aren't you? Fucking ungrateful little bitch, after I gave you everything I had. I gave up my life for you! I put a roof over your head and you repay me by walking out on me an' buggering off to England to be all hoity-toity with your spoilt brat friends."

I feel like I'm fusing to the bed, like my body has lost all life. It's draining out through any point of contact with the mattress, dripping down into the carpet and spreading through the building. Soon the floorboards will sprout leaves because I'll be nothing but an empty husk, holding the phone to my ear as my mother spews poison into me.

And then I drop the phone. It lands on the bed, faceup, Ma's voice tinny with distance. Matt bends his messy head over it, yells "Ey, fuck you, Talia's mum," screws up his face and *presses* the cancel button.

"What the…how did you…"

He looks flushed, almost breathless, considering he's a ghost and can't breathe. "Told you I could move stuff."

I stare at him, then look back at the dark screen. "Why did you do that?" I ask, my voice croaky.

"I figured she didn't have anything useful to say after she started calling you a bitch," he says with a shrug. It seems calculated to look unconcerned, but he's tense and still glaring daggers at the phone.

My hand drops to my lap at last. I still feel like I've been hollowed out. "I should send her—"

"No, you shouldn't," he says. "Unless that sentence was gonna be 'I should send her a text filled with the middle finger emoji,' the answer is no. And if you send her any money, I will use my awesome ghost powers to cancel it." He pokes at my phone again and gives it a glare when it doesn't light up on the first try.

I look at him. I want to ask…I want to beg…I don't know what I want so badly, but I want it. I stare at him.

Matt looks up again, his face softening. "You're not a bitch," he says firmly, holding my gaze. "She is."

The first tears take me by surprise. I curl up, wrapping my arms tightly around my knees, and breathe slowly, controlling the trembling of my lungs, forcing the tears back down. "You don't think I'm ungrateful? After all she—"

Matt snorts and sits in front of me, facing away, for which I'm pathetically grateful. "What, she put a roof over your head? Great, she did the bare minimum. That's literally what parents are *supposed* to do, innit? You don't owe her shit."

My mind brings up all the arguments, how she never wanted me, but she kept me and didn't get an abortion. I should be grateful for that because I'm alive. How she lost her chance to graduate because of me. I caused her life to fall apart just by existing. How it wasn't all bad. She smiled sometimes, we had a laugh sometimes, she did my hair, and she took me to the park as a little kid, and one year, she bought me a bike for my birthday.

I cry so hard it hurts. Matt spends half an hour blocking her number from my phone, and I think I should stop him, but I don't.

❖

"Isn't it Friday?" Matt asks.

I look up from my notes, my mind still buzzing with Schrödinger's equation. "What?"

"Friday," he says, jerking his chin toward the calendar. "Don't you go to the synagogue on Fridays?"

I lean my chin on my knee and frown at the pages spread over the bed. "I, well, Friday night or Saturday morning, I guess, but—"

"And you met the rabbi. He was nice, wasn't he?"

"What's this about?" I say.

"I'm *bored*," he moans, throwing himself onto my bed. "Talia, you spend all your time in this bedroom or in your tutorials or the library. You're so freaking boring. I'm begging you, please, let's do something involving other people."

I snort a laugh, and I see the mischief spark in his eyes. He crawls off the bed and over to me, clasping his hands. "I'm not even asking you to take me to a nightclub, although *that* is something you could totally do with, you know. Just saying."

"Does that really look like my scene?" I ask, raising an eyebrow.

"Haven't I been good?" he wheedles. "I've been sitting in your bloody lectures for *weeks*—"

"It's been one week."

"—and I haven't made a peep, please, Talia. I'm an extrovert. I need people."

"Fine. God." I shake my head and laugh, putting my work aside. I was at a good stopping place anyway, and he's right. He has behaved himself. "I'm surprised you didn't ask to go to a café or something."

"I know your limits." He grins. He's standing by the door, and I'm reminded of a dog that needs walking. "Anyway, your rabbi is cute."

I throw a shoe at him. It passes through his shoulders, and he shrieks. I laugh and forget to be nervous.

Of course, sitting on the bus and having to ignore Matt's constant chatting, my nerves come back, and it's all I can do to get off at our stop, force my legs to respond.

Morgan would be disappointed if he knew I'd been missing Shabbat. Probably. I mean, I'm disappointed in myself, so it would make sense. And I've even missed Sukkot and even Yom Kippur and *everything* in October. I squeeze my eyes shut against the wave of shame.

What if Daniel is irritated that I didn't come back for service last week after I met him? What if he realises I've been in Oxford all this time, and I haven't done *anything*. I've barely even been managing my prayers once a day.

My heart beats faster and faster, my feet move slower, and I think now I'll turn around, now I'll give up and go back to my dorm room.

And then we're there, up the steps, into the building. I shed my coat and hat, my tallit around my shoulders a comfort. Through the double doors that open to the sanctuary, gestured in with *shabbat shalom*. I find a seat in the corner, look up to the podium, and breathe.

When the service is over, the peace I've regained lasts long enough for me to follow the congregation out of the sanctuary and into a long room that smells of floor polish and challah. Matt's wandering around between people, listening to conversations and pretending to be a contributing part. He sees me watching and puts on a thoughtful face, answering the question one woman is posing to another. I have to bite my lip to stop from laughing. God knows I look strange enough as it is when wandering around alone.

I'm not the only young person here. That's the first thing that makes me notice how different this shul is to my own back in Glasgow. It makes sense. Most of the Glasgow uni students would have gone to the central synagogue, might have had services on campus even. Here, it seems like half the congregation is my age.

I miss my home. I find a hidden corner and cross my arms and wonder if I'll ever go back. On the one hand, it would mean being in the same city as my mother once more, and I seem to have burnt that bridge. I don't regret it. I should feel bereft, but there's nothing but peace when I consider a future without her in it.

On the other hand, the thought of never seeing Morgan or Mrs. Jacobs or Frank or Ruth or any of the rest of them, the people who gave me a family when I didn't know the meaning of the word…I can't bear it.

"Talia?" says Rabbi Daniel, and I startle violently, jerking my elbow out of his hand where he's lightly touched it. He steps back and holds his hands up. "Sorry. Are you okay?"

I rub my forehead and nod. "Aye, sorry. Thank you for the service tonight."

He smiles. "Thank you for coming along. It's good to see you." He seems to waver a moment. "So last weekend…"

I chuckle. "I met Kitty Wilson," I nod. "And she can do magic."

He raises his eyebrows, incredulity sparking through his eyes. "Really?"

I nod. "Yeah, we turned up during Matt's funeral. It was… awkward."

He huffs a laugh. "I honestly don't know what to say to that."

"I didn't either." I wonder if he believes me. If he's talked himself out of any belief he had last week, if he's writing me off as delusional even now. Part of me is offended and wants to bring Kitty to him, but I'm tired. It all feels pointless. I wonder if Morgan would have been able to believe me if I'd still been in Glasgow when this whole thing started. I wonder if he would have believed that the "near miss" had caused temporary insanity and would have had me institutionalised or something. I don't want to believe him capable of that, not without my say-so.

I cross my arms again and sigh. I feel heavy, like any movement, even breathing, is an effort not worth the results. Matt is flitting from group to group and seems to barely register when people walk through him anymore.

Daniel shifts restlessly. "How are your studies going?"

I nod. "I'm catching up at last. I hope." Thinking about it

exhausts me even more. "I have to catch up," I admit. "I need to find time to work too, need petrol money."

He tilts his head a little. "What kind of work would you apply for?"

"I don't know. Anything, I guess." My heart sinks. "Not that I'll get anything. I've barely got any time to spare."

"Can you touch-type?"

"Aye, of course."

"I can't," he says. "I've been looking for someone to do a couple of hours a week for me, mostly on Sundays and Wednesday evenings—"

"I'm not a charity case," I snap.

He smiles serenely and points to a noticeboard to my left. *Help Wanted!!!* it says, and my first thought is that I really must introduce him to Terry Pratchett's opinions on the dangers of overusing exclamation marks. "You're really looking," I say.

"I am." He nods. "Hazell, who does most of the admin, has just had her first baby, and though she still comes in when she can, it's not so easy to juggle anymore. Do you think it's something you could do?"

I bite my lip and study the flier. It really is too good to be true, and I'm deeply suspicious that he's only doing this to be nice or to manipulate me into continuing to come or…but there are phone number tabs at the bottom, and a couple are missing.

My fear swings the other way, and I'm panicking that I'm not good enough, that the others who took the tabs will be better, that this is the only hope I have for a job, that I've still got to save up for the holidays because my allowance doesn't cover those.

I take a deep breath. "I think so," I say. My eyes want to go everywhere but at him, but I glance up. He's smiling, but he seems to do that a lot.

"Excellent," he says. "Do you think you'll be able to come next Wednesday, see what the setup is, and whether it's something you're familiar with?"

"I don't…what about the others?"

He shrugs. "I was excited when I saw the tabs missing, but

I haven't had any calls. I suppose if they call between now and Wednesday, we'll have to have some sort of interview process." He frowns at the flier and rubs his chin, then brightens again. "Let's cross that bridge when we come to it, shall we? What time can you make it on Wednesday?"

## Chapter Thirteen

### *Kitty*

Peter sits me down and interrogates me about my new job on Sunday morning after church. I feel awful lying to him again. I can't help thinking about the last time I lied, what might have happened if I'd refused, if Matt had come out to his dad before it all happened. Connor's drawn face keeps rising in my mind and Matt's intangibility. But what can I tell him? He wouldn't believe the truth, not this time.

"I'm so proud of you, Kitty," he says, and I want to cry. "You've worked hard for you and Sam. I know you don't like asking for help, but won't you consider letting Sam sleep over when you have the late shifts?"

I bite my lip. "You already do so much for us, Peter."

"I don't," he says firmly. "It's not much at all. And it helps. Having you around."

"Oh, Peter."

He laughs, but I can see the tears threatening. "It's stupid, I know. But it makes me feel like I am still a father. I know I'm not yours, and I would never want to take that place for you—"

I cut him off with a tight hug, tears already sliding down my own face. "You are still a father," I whisper fiercely in his ear.

He chuckles softly and hugs me back. When I sit back down, we laugh at each other for being so wet. "Are you sure it's not too much to ask?" I say.

"It's never too much to ask," he says.

I smile, and some of the concern I've had over leaving Sam

every night drains away. At least at the warehouse, it varied, but the Society wants me on eight to one or eleven to four. There are no day shifts. "Thank you," I say.

It's a late one on Monday night. I catch the last bus down to the warehouse and kick my heels until eleven, when Shivam pushes the door open from the inside. "How long've you been waiting?" he asks with a frown.

"Not long," I lie, hurrying in and blowing on my hands. "What's on the agenda today?"

He bustles back with me through the long corridors, talking about how they've got a *client* lined up already. A young woman walks past, her hair up in a professional bun and heels clicking. I wave, but she doesn't spare me a glance. It's like I don't even exist. She pushes a door open, and I scurry to catch up with Shivam. It's worth it, I tell myself. This is my only chance to find out more about magic and bring Matt back.

I've only been here a few days, but I'm almost beginning to settle in. Work at the Society means minutes of breathless chaos when a "case" comes through, followed by hours of boredom, kicking my heels on the other desk while Shivam casts spells, muttering to himself, or types away at the computer, ignoring me. I fluctuate between relief that I don't have to do anything but recover in between—these new spells I'm learning seem to take it right out of me—and wishing I'd learned how to knit when Nan tried to teach me as a kid.

"Can I do something?" I ask when the seconds seem to have slowed to a glacial pace.

"Hmm?" Shivam says, barely turning his head.

"You seem busy," I say. "And I'm not. Isn't there some menial stuff I could do to take the load off you? Data entry? Filing? Envelope stuffing?" What do people in offices even do?

"No," he says, distracted. "It'd take me longer to teach you than to get it done."

And he's off into a world of digital magic. I suppose. Might be digital normalcy for all I know. After all, it would *take too long to teach me.*

"Mind if I take a break?" I ask.

He frowns, dragging his eyes away from the screen. "What?"

"I won't be long. You won't even notice I'm gone."

"You're not supposed to go anywhere without me," he says, his eyes flickering back to the screen.

"I need to go to the loo, Shiv," I say. Bloody hell. He's going to offer to chaperone me there, I can tell. Time to play dirty. "That time of the month, you know." I shift on the chair uncomfortably. "Need to change every couple of hours."

He recoils almost invisibly, and I have to bite my lips to hold back a grin. Clearly, he hasn't got any AFAB sibs or a girlfriend or anything. Men like that are so predictable. "Okay, yeah, yeah, down the main corridor, back the way we come in, and it's the third door on the left. And don't go anywhere else, you hear? Just there and back."

I'm off before he can change his mind, shutting the door behind me on his last syllable. I take a deep breath. It feels almost like freedom. Trouble with freedom, though, is the lack of any plan.

I figure I might as well find the loos first anyway. I walk along the main corridor, the great atrium to my right echoing with quick, garbled words from below and footsteps along the metal corridor above. Another woman walks from door to door right across from me. I'm sure it's the one I saw earlier, the proper businesswoman with the heels. How does she manage to not get those things stuck in the holes all over these industrial steel gangplank corridors? Should I be wearing a business suit? I brush the thought off because nobody said anything to that effect, and I'm not keen on giving them ideas or on spending money on uncomfortable clothes.

The loo is easy to find, but they surprise me. I was expecting a large room full of cubicles, something that can handle the number of people I've glimpsed working here, but it's only one in a room by itself, a small basin on the wall. I've used the manager's loo in the warehouse once, when I had my annual review, and it reminds me of that. Has Shivam sent me to the wrong one? One thing's for sure, I won't be meeting many other employees for a chat over the sinks if I don't find the main bathrooms.

I try to work out what to do next. It took some doing to get Shivam to let me out, so I don't want to waste time, but I'm thrown. I don't know where to start.

I take a deep breath and grab the handle of the next door over. Locked. I stay still and listen out for anyone who might be on the other side, who might come out and ask me what I want, but there's silence other than the distant echo of the atrium. I try the next door, the next, the next, and they're all locked.

I'm almost running now, snatching at handles frantically because how can they all be locked? I've seen that other lady walking into one, which was it? Why are they all locked?

"Miss Wilson?" says Anderson behind me, and I just about jump out of my skin. I turn to see him frowning at me, not angry, just quizzical. "What *are* you doing here? Aren't you meant to be on a case?"

"I was, uh, I was looking for the loo," I say.

Anderson raises an eyebrow and gestures to the open door beside him.

I laugh. "Silly me," I say and dart inside to see if I can flush myself down.

But the worst is yet to come because when I finally come out, having washed my face in cold water to get rid of the burn of embarrassment, Anderson is still standing there. He gives me a flicker of a smile. "Thought I'd take you back in case you lost your way again," he says.

"Ah ha ha," I say. "Thanks." Because this night actually can get more humiliating.

"Tell me about your family, Miss Wilson," he says as I fall into step beside him.

"Well, my mum's the one who taught me magic," I say, remembering what Shivam said about families and magic systems. "Her parents were originally from Barbados, but she used magic from all over."

"And your father?"

I snort. "I dunno who he is, honestly," I say. "Mum never told me much about him." Beyond saying I was better off not knowing him, but that's a bit too much overshare for my boss, I guess.

"Interesting," he says. "So you don't know anything about his magic?"

I tilt my head to one side. "I never thought about him having magic. I guess I've thought it was just me and Mum for so long. I mean, even Sam doesn't have it."

"Sam?"

"My little brother. Half-brother, really."

Anderson stops, and it takes me a step or two to realise. When I turn, I think I finally understand the expression *blood runs cold*. The look on his face, this flat, barely banked rage…I have no idea what it's about.

"She got married?"

"Um," I say, because what the fuck?

Anderson takes a breath and forces his shoulders down. Every nerve in my body is screaming at me to run but where? "She sullied the bloodline? Slept with some magic-less nobody?"

"Excuse me?" I say through gritted teeth. Magic tingles at my fingertips because boss or not, terrifying angry person or not, I will curse his arse.

He looks at me, his gaze locked on mine, and the air crackles between us. Then he opens the door to Shivam. "You now know the location of the bathroom, Miss Wilson." He spits the name. "Do not go wandering around. The other reapers don't need to be dealing with an amateur when they have so much to be getting on with."

He slams the door shut the moment I'm inside, and my knees nearly buckle. I let my breath out, long and slow, and stretch my fingers, gentling my magic, pulling it back inside me. I'm shaking, the come-down off the adrenaline heavy in my blood.

"What did you do?" Shivam whispers.

"What the fuck is his problem?" I whisper back, furious. "Is he some sort of, I dunno, like, blood purist? I mentioned my half-brother doesn't have magic, and he flipped the fuck out."

"What?" says Shivam, blinking and shaking his head.

I lean on Shivam's desk, my hands still bunched into fists. "Does he have something against non-magic people, or what? Am I working for, like, magic fascists here? Because I'd rather be fucking homeless, do you understand me?" I'll find something to do for Matt, some other way. Nothing good can come of this if they're that furiously magical.

"No," Shivam says. "God, no. Most of my family's non-magical, it's standard. Magic's pretty random, and really rare even within our families. It must've been something else. Tell me exactly what you said."

I slump in relief and pull up my chair. I tell Shivam an edited version of the encounter, make it sound like I accidentally went for the wrong door. Third on the right instead of third on the left, and he happened to find me. When I'm done, I look up to see him chewing on his thumbnail.

"Well?" I ask. "Any suggestions? What did I say wrong?" I hate that it comes out whiny, but now my anger's drained away, I'm upset and confused.

Shivam seems to battle with himself. "I don't know," he says at last, and my heart sinks because I'm the least cynical person I know, and even I can see he's lying. "I'm sorry."

"Shivam," I say.

"No, really, Kitty, I can't. I don't know what it is with him. I'm sorry."

I close my eyes, try to fight back tears. "I just want to learn more," I whisper, the lump in my throat strangling me. "I want to know what my mum couldn't teach me. I thought here…but I'm not even allowed to talk to the others."

I keep my eyes shut a little longer, taking comfort in the darkness. My hands are limp in my lap, and I'm so damn tired. I don't know what to do next.

Something heavy clunks down onto my desk, and I look up. "Here," says Shivam, gesturing to a huge scrapbook. "This is mine. I don't know how much you'll get from it, but, well. That's all my family taught me."

I can't help but stroke at the cover, the soft leather warm

under my hands, the words stamped into the surface calling me. "Is this…"

"It's a grimoire," he says, turning away and sitting at his own desk. He won't look at me. "Stupid old word for it, really."

"Shivam, are you sure?"

He waves an airy hand, but there's tension all up his neck. "Of course. I've got it all memorised, anyway. I had to when I was a kid. My mum was strict. Anyway, I took scans of it years ago."

I wrap my hands around and lift it, cradling it close to me. "Thank you," I say as well as I can around the lump in my throat.

## Chapter Fourteen

### *Talia*

"Does she really treat you like that all the time?"

I frown up at Matt. "What?"

"Your mum." He's sitting on the windowsill again. It's become his place, stolen it from me, the wee shite. "Is she always like that? The swearing and stuff?"

I save my document and turn my chair, pulling one foot up so I can rest my chin on my knee. "Eh, no, I guess. Most of the time, she ignores me, so I can do what I want."

"But you guys don't get on?"

I snort. "No."

He's quiet, and it's unnerving. I'm getting used to his constant monologues on the events in the quad below, and this new silence makes me squirm, like he's annoyed. I've done something wrong, and I don't know what. I don't mind people being annoyed with me, not if I've done something to warrant it. I bite my lip and think harder.

"She probably has depression. Definitely addicted but just to alcohol, so I'm lucky." He snorts, but I'm saying this, so I ignore him. "She had me young. Her own parents were vicious, from what I can tell. I don't know them much. I think they stopped asking after me when I was a bairn." I shrug. "She had her reasons."

"For doing what?" He's sitting with both legs inside the room now, looking intently at me.

I shrug again. "For, I dunno, ignoring me. Yelling, kicking me out—"

"She kicked you out?" He's clearly horrified, and that's a strange reaction. I don't think my home life's that much worse than the norm, surely. Loads of my classmates were kicked out way earlier. Couple of lads slept in the park for most of the summer holidays after S4. Is what it is.

"Aye, she thought I'd stolen some money. I hadn't. Maybe I should've, though." I look at the bare mattress. It's gonna cost half a paycheck just to buy sheets and a pillow.

"Bloody hell, Talia," he says, sitting back and looking away. He sounds angry, and my back prickles.

"Why does it bother you?" I demand. "It's not like it affects you."

"Why does it…bloody hell, because she shouldn't do that. She's your mum, looking after you is her job."

"Well, not like she's good at holding them down either."

"Why doesn't this bother you?" he says, waving his arms at me.

"It's normal for me, you know? Just because your dad is perfect—"

He snorts and turns away, and it dawns on me.

"Matt, are you okay?"

"No," he snaps. "I'm fucking dead. I'm dead, my dad is grieving, he actually bloody cares about me, and it's not fucking fair, okay? Leave me alone."

I'm not sure what he means. I sit as still as I can in my chair, picking at my cuticles, and I hear his words round and round in my head, trying to read between the lines, work out what he wants to say, what's hidden behind the words.

"I'd take your place if I could," I say hesitantly. But now… I'm not sure it's true. I think it might be what he wants to hear.

"Fuck! No, Talia, bloody hell, just no. And don't you dare tell Kitty that either." I bite my lip and watch the sky behind him. At last, he sighs and rubs his face. "I wouldn't want anyone to take my place. It's just not fair."

"Yeah," I say. "I'm sorry this happened to you."

"I wish my dad didn't care," he whispers.

I think if he was corporeal, I would go over there and hug him. I wonder if I would, if I'd be able to. If I'd risk being pushed away. It's pointless anyway. I can only watch him stare out the window and hurt.

"You want to go for a walk?" I ask at last.

The text comes through as I'm walking toward George Street through the fog, numb from the cold, and this *thing* that seems to grab at my ankles and try to pull me under asks me why I bother, what's the point in eating, sleeping, breathing? When I see Kitty's name come up, the thing pulling me down seems to lose its grip on me a little.

*I've been checking this book I got from work. Nothing concrete but maybe a couple of ideas. Want to come over tomorrow?*

I blink sluggishly at the screen and lean against the wall of some bridge or other. Matt is below me, walking along the bottom of the river because, apparently, he can.

*Yeah, I think so, what time?*

*Come for lunch? Any time really, I'm off on Wednesday.*

Wednesday. It's like a punch to the gut, and my eyes widen in horror. I've said yes now. I've said yes to her and yes to Daniel. My mother's voice cuts through the dull of my mind, shouting about how disorganised I am, how useless, how I make everything more difficult for her, I've got to sort this out before anyone finds out, how can I do both how can I—

"Is that Kitty?" Matt says, and I jump so hard, I nearly drop the phone. "Whoa, bloody hell," he says. "Twitchy much?"

"It's…yeah. Uh, yeah, it's Kitty. She wants us to come over tomorrow."

"You've got work tomorrow," he says, as if I hadn't figured that the hell out. "Ask if she can do Thursday instead."

"I've already said yes, and what if she…what if…"

What if what? What can she do? She isn't my mother. She isn't my teacher. I take a deep breath. It doesn't calm me like people say it does. Why does it not calm me? Everyone always says "take a deep breath" when you're panicking, but why?

Matt's looking at me quizzically. "Just say you forgot. Duh."

Duh.

I type again. *I'm sorry, I forgot I have work tomorrow. It's a new job. I'm so sorry I didn't mention it earlier. Can you do Thursday?*

There's a tense moment while Kitty types. Tense for me; Matt seems unconcerned watching the little speech bubble on my screen. I notice I've written "sorry" twice, and it grates at me. I want to take it back, pretend I have my life and my emotions under control.

*Got to go back to the warehouse to pick up my last paycheck that day. You can come after that if it's not too late?*

And that's it. That's how easy it is. Matt's looking at me again, and I scream at myself in the privacy of my own head, do something. Say something. Don't stand there like an idiot. The voice sounds like Ma.

*That's fine. I can pick you up,* I offer, my hands almost shaking with relief.

*Are you sure?*

*Of course.*

*Why don't you stay the night?* she asks, and I have to gulp to swallow my heart, which seems to have beat its way up my throat.

"Makes sense," says Matt, peering over my shoulder. He looks at me, his head to one side. "What're you waiting for?"

"I don't have a sleeping bag," I say stupidly.

"That's okay. Kitty has a duvet she leaves out for me when I stay over." He stops. "Used to stay over."

I'm caught up in my head, and it takes a while for his tone to creep through my mental flailing. When I look up, he's already starting to walk off, his head drooping and his hands shoved into his pocket. *Okay, thanks,* I text back, barely thinking about the exact wording and how to make it perfect. Probably for the best, I've never been good at perfection. Then I shove my phone into my jacket and run to catch up with Matt.

"I'm nervous," he says as I reach him, and he tries to laugh.

"Why?" I frown. It's not like anything she does can hurt him or make him *more dead*. But then, what do I know?

"What if it doesn't work? What if I'm stuck to you for the rest of your life?"

I stare out into the darkening streets. "I don't know."

❖

Matt pretends like he doesn't care about the car journey, but I can tell it bothers him. He jogs his knee, taps his fingers, stares out the window. A bus pulls out on the inside lane, and he shudders and starts jabbing at the radio. "God, don't you have any actually good music? What the hell is this?"

I don't call him on it. This I can do. "Oh, right, what do you consider 'good,' then, Mozart?"

He looks at me with such disdain dripping from his sneer that I can barely hold my laugh back.

"What's so bad about this radio station, then?" I don't even know which one it is.

"Er, only everything. It's crappy generic top forties rubbish, innit? Don't tell me you actually *like* this stuff."

I shrug. "I dunno, just give me something with a beat, and I'm happy." I glance at him. He looks aghast, and it's much better than that raw, blank shell he was before. "I don't really care what it is."

"Come on, you have to have a favourite artist."

"Not really," I say. "It's background noise, that's all."

He throws his hands up. "I can't believe I got stuck with such a total heathen. Seriously, wait till I get you back to Oxford. We are gonna open up my Spotify, and I'm going to give you a proper education. You know, when I'm a producer—"

He stops and bites his lip. It feels like someone's scooping all the manic joy out of the car and leaving us with the grey truth. His hands drop to his lap, and he laughs. "I was gonna be a music producer, you know."

It's silent for too long. When I speak, I have to push the words out of my throat. "Don't say that."

"Say what?"

"Was. Don't say it like you've lost hope."

"What hope, Talia?" he says, and part of me wants to go back to the way we were before, when he was only sharp-tongued and feisty. Before he fell into trusting me with this raw, hollow vulnerability. "I'm dead. We both know this is just delaying the inevitable."

The car eats up miles beneath our tyres. "You're dead," I agree. "But your best friend's a witch who brings people back to life." I turn to hold his gaze at a red light. "Don't lose hope."

He takes a deep breath and smiles. It's sad and broken, but it's there, and the silence feels a little less dark.

Kitty's waiting for us by the side of the road in an industrial estate when we pull up to the pin she dropped on Google Maps. Matt slips backward through the seat to let her take shotgun. He leans forward to kiss her on the cheek as she climbs in. "You look better," he says. "Way less knackered than usual."

"Thanks, darlin'," she says, catching my eye and giving me an amused look. It feels conspiratorial, and I try to concentrate on the drive so I don't blush too hard.

I should have expected someone to be there when Kitty opens the door to her flat, but somehow, I'd forgotten she doesn't live alone. It's not her brother, though, that greets her with a smile. It's Matt's dad.

"Papa," Matt breathes, and Kitty and I glance at each other in horror.

"Everything okay?" Peter says with a confused smile.

"Sorry, Peter," Kitty says, shaking herself. "I forgot to stop at the shop. How's your day been?"

Peter looks thin and drawn, even compared to when I last saw him at Matt's funeral. He's smiling, though, and less manic, at least. I follow him and Kitty into the living area. Sam glances up and nods a greeting to me. I nod back, and he returns to his work, one socked foot tapping against the leg of his chair.

"Peter, this is Talia," Kitty says, and I look up, a rabbit in the headlights.

"Hello," I say awkwardly. *Your son is behind you. He's crying. I'm sorry he's stuck to me instead of to you.*

I swallow.

"Would you two like a cup of tea?" Peter asks.

Kitty nods. She hesitates, then presses forward to wrap her arms around his waist. He's less surprised about the suddenness of it than I am. His long arms cradle her, cupping the back of her skull in one hand, his eyes closing, a window on his grief.

I look away and catch the brother's eye. He gives a sad smile. "Hi again," he says quietly, and I drift over to him. "Kitty says Peter needs more hugs than he thinks he does, so we're to hug him as often as we can," he says with a jerk of his chin toward the kitchenette.

I look up to the depressing tableau. In the harsh fluorescence of the light, they're haloed, the two living people. Matt, though, he's paler. His face is pressed to his father's back as he sobs, clutching his father's shirt, though it makes no imprint on the material. It makes me swallow harder to see him, knowing there's nothing I can do to comfort him. No hugs I can give him, even if I could get over my stubborn reluctance to touch.

Kitty pulls back, and she and Peter give each other a nod and a smile, like they're pretending not to grieve, pretending to be okay. They both know it's not true. Matt continues to cry quietly, whispering something in Polish. The back of my throat stings.

Peter walks around the kitchen, making our tea, and Kitty comes over to give Sam a kiss on the head. Matt follows Peter. I think, distantly, of the sound his shoes should make, shuffling against the lino. Of the way Peter would react.

I try to imagine what it would be like to love my parent so much that it hurt not to be able to hold them in my arms. I don't think I've ever felt that way about anyone. It's always been a good thing. I've relied on myself alone. I've never needed anyone else. I've always known that Morgan and the others at shul were temporary. What would it be like to have deep roots like that? Am I defective? Is Matt?

Peter hands me a mug of tea, and I blink owlishly, reconnecting to my body and reality. "Thanks," I say. He smiles, and the lines around his eyes remind me of Morgan. Matt is no longer crying, but he still stands pressed against his father, his eyes dull and blank. When Kitty tugs my elbow and nods toward her room, Matt doesn't make to follow.

"We can leave the door open," Kitty says softly. "I don't know if shutting it would pull on the bond between you two, but I'd rather not risk it." She straightens the duvet on her bed and sits on the pillow end, gesturing to the foot of the bed, right near the door, for me to join her. "I'm sorry, I should have thought about Peter being here," she sighs. "I just…sometimes I forget, you know?"

"That he's a ghost?"

She nods. "That he's dead at all, really. I didn't think about it when I made him visible. He's here, but he's not here."

I twist my lips and look at my tea. "I think I know what you mean," I say. "He's more real to me than anyone at uni."

She smiles sadly and stares off into space. My mind races for something else to say, something light, something social, something that won't make her think of her dead friend. "So what is it, exactly, that you do? Obviously, I know about the whole exchanging souls thing or whatever, but—"

She sits forward, crossing her legs, a certain animation entering her demeanour. "It's not exchanging a soul. That would be putting the soul of the dead person into the living body. What we do is more like…do you know the story of the Fates in Greek myth?"

"Not beyond what they do in Percy Jackson," I admit.

"That's perfect." She laughs. "The whole threads thing, right? Each person has a thread that relates to their life. It's a common theme in European myths, I suppose, the Norse myths have a…never mind." She smiles ruefully, and I'm shot with a bolt of *she's adorable*. I look at my tea quickly. "Sorry," she says. "I'm a bit of a nerd."

I shrug. "I read books about quantum physics for fun."

Kitty laughs properly, and my head snaps up to watch her. It's like a benediction. I can't convince my gaze to turn away, back to the safety of the tea. "Nerds for the win," she says. "The threads of fate. That's what I, well—we, I guess—all the reapers, swap over."

I nod like I understand. I'm sure that, somehow, the metaphor explains all the changing of the past, and the fact that I'm the only one who knows that *I died*. For a while, I was dead. And nobody will ever really get that except three people in this house.

"Kitty, dinner's ready," Peter calls.

I follow her into the kitchen. Matt's sitting on the counter, swinging his legs. "Dad still can't cook neatly, can he?" he asks Kitty, and he's smiling too, but it's a different kind. You can see the sadness through it, and weirdly, that's less worrying than the alternative.

"Talia, please, have a seat," says Peter, and I feel my scalp tensing up. He's an unknown. He's a parent, a powerful being in comparison to the rest of us. And who am I kidding? I don't know how families have dinner together. It can't really be like it is on the telly, can it?

I slide into my seat with a flash of a smile. I hope they don't try to say grace because I honestly don't know what I'll do. I watch the rest of the room. I try to follow all the social clues, the movements Kitty makes, the way Sam gets off his seat to fetch himself a drink, the way Peter squeezes Kitty's shoulder as he sits. My head already hurts.

"Would you like a drink, Talia?" Sam asks, leaning through the hatch to the kitchen.

"Uh, just water, please," I say. I'm desperately thirsty, I realise as I say it.

"So, Talia," Peter says, and he gives me a social smile. I try to return it. "I think I saw you at the funeral, yes? How did you know my boy?"

I clear my throat and gulp some water. "Uh—"

"Ey, don't panic, Talia," Matt says from his perch. "He's not, like, testing you or anything, chill."

"I met him online," I say. Makes sense to stick to the same lie.

Matt groans. “Ugh, okay, let’s see, you play *Call of Duty*. We met on the Discord server.”

“On the Discord for *Call of Duty*,” I relay dutifully and hope nobody asks me about my stats or anything because I might’ve played once in my life, but I’m pretty sure I only lasted two minutes.

Peter smiles and shakes his head, looking at his food. “The world today is a smaller place. But you are not from England, yes?”

“Yeah, I’m from Glasgow. I moved for uni.”

“In Oxford?” His eyebrows raise. “What are you studying?”

“Physics,” I say. It comes out defensive. I know it shouldn’t, but I expect ridicule. I can’t *possibly* be in Oxford uni. A girl like me can’t possibly know anything about science.

“Talia’s really smart,” says Kitty, and my mind goes blank. I think I’m redder than a tomato. I duck my head and try to be smaller. Don’t look, don’t look, and for God’s sake, don’t test me.

“That’s amazing,” Peter says, and he sounds like he means it. I glance at him. He looks…proud of me? “You must have worked very hard to get there, well done.”

“She’s got a scholarship and everything,” Matt says, and what the hell? He knows Peter can’t hear him. Is he teasing me?

“Yeah, she’s got a scholarship,” Kitty says to Peter, and I think I might implode with how small I’m trying to be. This is too much. Why are they being nice?

“Have you learned about string theory?” Sam says. “I heard about it on a YouTube video once, but I don’t know what it was going on about, something like everything in the world is made of these little strings, and they’re in, like, an infinity shape, and they twist.”

“I…yes, I know it.”

“Tiny strings? How can that be? Is that true, Talia?”

“It’s possible?” I don’t know how to explain string theory to a small child, a pretty girl, and the father of the ghost I have stuck to me. I gulp more water and pray for the strength to survive this meal.

## CHAPTER FIFTEEN

### *Kitty*

I yawn as I help Peter clear the table, my jaw clicking.

"I'll go home now, okay, *kochanie*?" Peter says, dropping a kiss on the top of my head.

"Thanks, Peter, sorry I was late coming back from the warehouse."

"It's no problem, Kitty. I'm sure your old boss was sad to see you go and wanted to hold on to you as long as he could." He holds me by the shoulders and looks at me. "I am proud of you. Your mama would be too, remember that."

I hug him and chuckle. "I know that, Peter, you don't need to tell me."

"Yes, I do," he says, serious enough that it makes that pesky lump rise in my throat again.

I take him to the door and lean against it as I let him out. I try to imagine what the world would look like if it had been me instead of Matt. If I could find some way to swap our threads of fate, like I can with others. If I could find someone to help me.

I'm not stupid. I know nobody would if they knew what I was thinking of doing. And there's absolutely no way Matt would ever let me take his place. He'd be furious I was even thinking it. Doesn't stop me being tempted sometimes, though.

But then again, I've never even met one of the other reapers, let alone got a chance to take them aside to ask for this kind of a favour.

"Kitty?" says Matt, and I turn, forcing a smile. He's so alive. How can he be *so alive* while he's literally a ghost? "You all right?"

"Yeah, fine," I say. "Just tired. Lemme get Sam out of the way, and we'll look at that book."

Talia keeps her eyes on me as I walk past, and I notice even she looks concerned. I flash her a smile and duck my head, tucking my hair behind my ear, and she looks away.

"Sam," I say, sitting on the arm of the sofa next to him. He glances up at me, then goes back to watching *Masterchef*. "I'll let you play on my phone if you sod off to the bedroom."

He looks up at me again with narrowed eyes. "Can I go on TikTok?"

I crinkle my nose up. "Fine," I say at last. "But don't—"

"I know, don't give out any identifying information. You know we have an internet safety class in school every year, right? Since, like, year one."

"Don't care," I say. "I'll still tell you every time."

He rolls his eyes but gives me a cheeky grin. "Whatever, I know you just want me out of the way so you can kiss your *girlfriend*."

"Sam!" I yell, but he winks and runs before I can smack him. I bite my lip and look up at Talia. "Sorry about that," I say. "He's a good kid, but he can be a little shit too. Little brothers, huh?"

"It's fine," she says, sitting across from me. "You said you had some new information."

"Yeah, well, actually, I've got too much new information." I fish the massive book out of my bag behind the sofa and put it gently on the table.

Talia cranes her neck to look at the title on the grimoire and frowns. "*Tax Laws of the Channel Islands*?" she says. "What?"

I laugh. "Is that what it looks like to you?" I say, running my fingers over the embossing. "Most of our books are shrouded to non-magical eyes. They're spelled to appear as the most boring thing possible to the reader. Shivam explained it a little. To me, it's bound in green leather, embossed with the name *Khadem*. I guess it's an old family name because Shivam's surname is

Ahmed. It's all his family's spells. And the reason I asked you to come over is because I found this." I open the book flat on the table. To me, it's a beautifully illustrated double page spread of sigils, ritual movements, and importantly, connections. Talia and Matt look at it blankly, and I laugh. "This might help."

I hand them a piece of paper I've transcribed. Talia's eyebrows shoot up. "This is what you see when you look at that?"

"Yup." I smile.

She shakes her head in wonder as she looks at the paper. "I still can't believe I'm not hallucinating all of this," she murmurs.

"Don't worry," says Matt with a smirk. "I can see it too. You're not going crazy."

She rolls her eyes hard. "Yes, thank you, ghost that nobody else can see."

"I see him too." I grin.

"You don't count either," she says, pouting at me. "Pretty sure you've been part of my hallucination since day one."

God, she's cute with that little crinkle between her eyebrows. I clear my throat and refocus on the spell in front of me. "Anyway, this spell is for breaking a connection. I mean, it's actually a spell for a couple to do to call an end to their relationship. This rune here, it means *to put behind*, and the one above it is *hurt*. Both people repeat it. It's basically like you're agreeing to let bygones be bygones. Kinda healthy, if you think about it."

Talia twists her lip, and there's something sad in her eyes for a moment. She shakes her head. "Matt hasn't hurt me, though."

"Aw, I didn't know you cared," Matt says dryly.

She side-eyes him. "I mean, he's annoying and tried to drive me mad, but…" She snorts. "If I think of people who've hurt me, he doesn't even make the top ten."

I frown. "That's really sad. Are you okay?"

She laughs outright. "Of course, ignore me."

I chew on my lip a bit, but she's already got her blond head bent over the paper. I glance up at Matt. He gives me a sad smile. That doesn't help at all, but I refocus. "Anyway, I used the base of this spell to make a few changes that would suit your situation a lot more."

"Can you do that?" she asks. "Just change the magic around?"

"Sure." I shrug. "Magic is all about intent. I mean, you have to have a bit of a natural aptitude for it, but what really matters is your will. If you don't really mean something, you can't cast a spell. That's why it's actually important here that I change these around, if, like you said, these sigils wouldn't apply to your situation."

Matt's staring at me. "You're actually a genius, aren't you, Kit?"

I blink at him and laugh. "No, don't be silly, I, well, I guess I'm good at cheating."

Talia's shaking her head. "I'm with Matt. You're good at finding new solutions, and that's how true change happens. You can be as clever as anything, but if you don't have that spark of ingenuity, all you'll ever be able to do is copy what's been done."

I realise my mouth is hanging open. Talia glances between Matt and me, then buries her hands in her hair and ducks her face over the work again.

It's all I can do to tear my gaze away from her and back to the work. To point out the new sigils I've chosen. I wasn't planning to, but maybe I point out that one sigil that I made myself, a mish-mash of Norse and cuneiform because I couldn't find another that would work quite so well, to see her look impressed with me again. She's brilliant, and she's impressed with *me*.

"Um," I say, my mind scattered for a moment. I tuck my hair behind my ears again, and it springs loose as always. "Okay, this should—*should*, mind you—break the connection between you and Matt."

"And that'll bring him back?" Talia says.

I grimace. "Ah, no, sorry. It's just to give you guys a bit of separation. Sorry. I should have said that before, shouldn't I?"

"No, it's fine," Talia says, her voice gentle.

"What do you mean, a bit of separation? Could I go wherever I like if we're separated?" Matt frowns. "How would I get anywhere? Would I have to walk?"

I press my lip in with my thumb to get a better grip on it with my worrying teeth. "Um, I don't know. Sorry." I glance between them. "I mean, this is a new spell, to be fair."

"It's worth a try, right?" Talia says to Matt.

He nods. "Oh yeah, of course. I mean, I was leaving it up to you, since, you know, dead and all." He gestures to himself. "Not much can hurt me. You're the one who could end up injured, aren't you?"

"Oh, c'mon, give me some credit," I protest. He winks at me, and I sigh. "You're such a shit-stirrer."

Talia stands. "Well, let's do this. Where do you want me?"

I feel more comfortable in my role as I stand, like something's clicked into place. I stand them opposite each other, lay a mirror at each of their feet. Matt's reflects nothing, and it's like a stab to the heart. Seeing him makes me forget that he's not really here, not the way he should be.

I stand and breathe, putting aside my emotions for now, opening myself up to the magic, allowing it to flow through my veins. Left-handed, I write the first sigil in front of Talia, then in front of Matt with my right hand.

Talia gasps, lifting her hands to her chest, and I blink at the red string that's appeared there. It's more vibrant than before, and clearly, she can see that as well.

I have no idea what that means.

It leads straight to Matt, and I step forward, the spell to sever it on my lips.

But the string seems to sense me or sense my intentions or something because it starts pulling right toward me. The previously straight line bows in between Matt and Talia and curves right toward my own chest. Matt shouts, Talia cries out in pain or shock, and I freak out. "*Sournos!*" I yell, and the three of us are blown backward with a crack.

❖

It feels immediate, opening my eyes. But Sam, Talia, and Matt are crouched over me, Talia's blue eyes wide and scared. She lets out a long breath and slumps back as I focus on her face.

"What the hell, Kitty?" Sam says, throwing up his hands and standing. Matt sinks into the sofa and rubs his temples. "What happened? I heard this bang, and you're both on the floor, and there's this smoke everywhere. What was that?"

"I don't know." I shake my head, which turns out to be a bad idea.

Sam puts his hands on his hips and glares from me to Talia. The urge to giggle swells in my chest. Talia opens and shuts her mouth and looks at me with obvious panic in her eyes, and that's all it takes. I crack up, laughter interspersed with groans of pain as my throbbing head protests.

"Ugh," Sam yells. "I don't know why I bother." He stomps out of the room. Matt laughs with me, soft and exhausted, and even Talia smiles.

"So you really don't know what that was?" she asks.

"No idea, sorry."

"Well, good to know that's not what you were expecting, I guess."

I snort. "Matt, I didn't know what would happen. I've never done this before, have I?"

"What was with the red string?" Talia asks, glancing between me and Matt.

I hesitate to answer. "The bond my mum made, that connected you and Matt? I don't know why it bent like that. I was expecting to break it. Maybe…maybe it reacted to the binding rune I was using. But this is all speculation, and your guess is as good as mine."

"No, it's not. You're the only one of us with experience in magic. Your guess is definitely better than ours," Talia says.

"I've never seen anything like it, though."

"It curved toward you," Matt says slowly, biting his lip and resting his chin on his knee. "What do you think that means? Am I, like, stuck to you now instead of Talia?"

The idea strikes as he says it, and I scramble to my knees, searching through my notes. Bonds, links, connections, this is my *thing*. "Talia, c'mere. Matt, you stay there. Actually, no, move over here a bit. I need to draw another sigil." My mind's crackling with thoughts, with connections, and I feel like I have to run to keep up with it.

When I stand, I realise I'm grinning. The way Talia looks so wary, I must look pretty manic. No time for worrying about that now. I hold my hands out, one to each of them. "Let's see if we can visualise that red string again, yeah?"

They take my hands. Matt's fingers are little more than a cool breeze. Talia's are dry and warm, and I pretend I haven't felt that thrill of skin on skin. I take a deep breath. In my mind, the sigil I've scribbled on the floor is imbibed with power and with my will. "*Achie*," I say.

There's no room for uncertainty in magic. In the rest of my life, I'm gangly, clumsy, awkward, but in this, my mind and my power are in perfect accord. They have to be. The sigil starts to glow white and rise between us, like some sort of Instagram filter. I can see all the links between us.

Matt and I have braided, tangled strands, bright and strong, our whole history of friendship, a family of choice. There are thinner bonds between Matt and Talia, Talia and me.

"This is so freaking cool," Matt murmurs.

Talia's breathing faster, but she shakes her head, and something in her eyes sharpens. "The line between me and Matt, are we still attached?"

"I don't think so," I say. "The red line's gone, for a start. The bonds that are left, that's, well, friendship, I guess."

Her eyebrows shoot up, and she blinks at Matt. "Oh." Her eyes flicker to the space between us, and I try not to think about that.

"I guess you broke the string before it could hurt any of us, huh?" Matt says.

I have no idea. I'm flying blind again, and I can't let the fear cloud my mind or my magic. I release the spell and let their hands fall. "The only thing we can check right now is if you can go farther from Talia."

Matt exchanges a raw glance with Talia. She shrugs and says gently, "Try walking out the front door, yeah?"

He clicks his tongue and shoots finger guns at her. He turns, stiff and awkward. Talia and I shuffle to the living room door and watch him walk, fists clenched, to the door, and through it.

"We did it," I whisper.

Sam's door opens, and he steps out. He stops when he sees us and frowns. "What are you two standing there for?"

"Uh," says Talia, panic widening her eyes again. I burst into giggles.

Sam stamps his foot, actually *stamps* it like a toddler. "You're the worst!" he yells and stomps back into his room, slamming the door.

I don't care. We did it. It worked.

❖

The morning seems to dawn brighter than usual. When I wake up, I'm not as tired as I always am. The weak winter sun coming through my thin curtains is a welcome friend because I did something right yesterday.

I roll out of bed and even manage to get dressed and brush my teeth before making a beeline to the coffee. I have to stop when I reach the door to the living room because Talia's still asleep.

Strands of dark blond hair are falling over her cheek, casting shadows over the little freckles that dust her nose. Her eyelids twitch, skin so fine and pale I wonder if she can see through it even with her eyes shut. She looks like an elf with her fine features, some sort of mythical creature in an enchanted sleep. She's curled up so small under the big duvet. She's taller than me, but right now, she looks vulnerable. Like I could scoop her up and protect her.

"Holy shit," I mutter and force my feet to move. I will not watch her sleep like some sort of creeper. Anyway, Sam needs breakfast.

She wakes up as I flick the kettle on, sitting up dead straight, eyes wide. "Sorry," I call softly. "I didn't think it'd be so loud."

She shakes her head and yawns. "It's fine. Forgot where I was. Can I help?"

"Nothing to do, thanks," I say. She staggers over anyway, and I can't help smiling at the shock of bedhead and the bleary eyes. "Sam doesn't get up till seven. Want some coffee?"

We sit curled at opposite ends of the sofa, leaning against the armrests and facing each other over steaming mugs. "Were you warm enough?" I ask.

She nods. "The duvet's huge."

"Yeah, the heating doesn't last all night so it gets pretty cold in here."

She shrugs. "I sleep with my window open some nights. I like the cold. Or I'm used to it."

"I guess it must be a lot colder up in Scotland," I say. "You're from Glasgow, right?"

She nods.

"You going back for Christmas?"

Her face drops, and she stares at her coffee. "No."

"Oh no, that's sad, why not?"

"Well, for a start, I'm Jewish," she says, still not looking at me.

"Oh, sorry. But isn't Hanukah in December too?"

She sighs. "Hanukah isn't as big of a deal as Christmas, you know."

"Oh, really? I didn't know that." She nods, and I bite my lip. "Sorry. I don't know much about Judaism. I didn't mean to be annoying."

"You're not," she says quickly, her eyes wide as she looks back up at me. "Not at all. Shit." She pinches the bridge of her nose. "Look, I'm a convert. My ma isn't."

"Oh," I say like I understand. I don't.

"Yeah," she says. She stares back at her coffee. "I don't get on with her."

"Oh," I say again. "I'm really sorry."

"Don't be." She shrugs. "I can stay over at uni."

I imagine her all alone in an old, creaky building while everyone else is visiting their family, taking home stories. Bragging about everything they've achieved in the most famous university in the world. Talia's not a people person like me, but even so. I don't like the idea of her being alone in an uncaring place, drifting through like she's a ghost too.

"Will you come stay with us?" I ask, trying to pretend my heart's not beating faster, like I haven't just asked this beautiful girl to spend the holidays with me and my family, to be more a part of my life than she already is.

She looks at me incredulously. "What? What do you mean?"

"Come here for your holiday," I say again, warming to my idea. I sit forward. "It'll be much better than staying in Oxford all alone. You can hang out here, and we can work on bringing Matt back together. If it helps, you'd be doing me a favour, looking after Sam while I'm at work."

"Yeah, right," she says, but she's smiling. "I don't know anything about magic, and Peter looks after Sam when you're at work."

"But he wouldn't have to. I mean, you don't have to either, of course. If you want, you can come over and just do your studying here."

"Spread out all my notes and take over your living room, get under your feet, and annoy you?" she says.

I have an image in my mind. Coming home after work to find her sitting here with her textbooks and a notebook, scribbling equations furiously, that little frown line between her eyes. Something aches deep in my chest. "Yeah," I say and swallow hard. I want her to spread her notes throughout my life and take up space here.

"Why would you want me to do that?" she says.

"Dunno," I admit. "I just do. Come spend the holidays with me."

She blushes right to the tips of her ears and looks at the mug clasped in her hands. "I'll think about it," she says, but I can see the smile curling her cheeks.

I turn my head as Sam's door opens, and I remember my responsibilities. Sam gets free school meals, thankfully, but he'll still need coaxing to have breakfast and get dressed. Somehow, the morning always ends up a rush, no matter how early we get it started.

In the growing chaos, I can almost kid myself that I forget Talia. But she's always there in the periphery of my awareness, finding Sam's novel under the sofa, folding up the duvet neatly, even washing my dishes, all so quietly, I barely notice her move.

"Talia, come with us," Sam says, even as I'm struggling him into a jacket. He's managed to turn the sleeves inside out, and they're still damp from yesterday. "I want you to tell me more about string theory."

"Please," I say automatically.

"Please, will you?"

"Sorry," I say quickly to Talia. "You don't have to, of course. I was only correcting his manners."

"That's fine," she says, and she even smiles at Sam a little shyly, like she thinks she has to impress him. "I can come, if you're okay with that?"

"Of course," I say. "Tell us all about the funky little strings."

She laughs and goes bright pink. "I don't know if I'll be any good at explaining it."

I don't care, but Sam's already off talking about a video he watched with some cute little birds that explained all about gravitons and the theory of everything. Talia tries to explain some of the maths, but Sam picks on anything cool-sounding and weaves it into his own personal little story of strings that make the universe. I understand exactly none of it, but I'm more than happy to wander along beside them, soaking up their enthusiasm.

Talia even gets introduced to a few of Sam's friends. Sam's almost certainly going to tell them something embarrassing about her being my *girlfriend* at some point, but right now, I enjoy watching Talia become a celebrity to a group of ten-year-olds. When the bell goes to call them all in, she visibly slumps.

"Exhausting, aren't they?" I say, nudging her.

"How do you cope with this every day?"

"Oh, I'm not nearly as cool as you, I don't get mobbed quite so badly," I say with a grin, leading her back down the road. "Coffee?"

We stop by a Costa for a bit of a treat, and I lead her back toward the flat. The long way round, though, down the canal path. It's beautiful there, even in the grey of winter. Talia seems to have spent all of her words on her impromptu physics lecture, so we simply walk, our shoulders bumping, by the still water of the canal. For a moment, it feels like spring has come early. There's nothing but fresh air and hope.

Talia crouches and comes back up holding out an ivy leaf, almost all of the green tissue washed away. "Skeleton leaf," I cry, doing a little jump as I take it from her. "I love them."

Talia grins wider than I've seen before. "They're cool, aren't they?"

I nod. "Sam and I tried to make them once, using washing soda. It didn't work. I was gutted. I mean, I love living plants, but it's good to be reminded there's some beauty in death too."

"That makes sense," she says. "Like you."

"Hmm?"

She blushes bright red. "I mean, the whole beauty in death thing."

She mumbles it, her head down and her shoulders hunched, but I hear. I laugh softly. As we leave the canal path to head back, I lean over and brush her hair back behind her ear, tucking the skeleton leaf there.

## CHAPTER SIXTEEN

### *Talia*

Kitty falls asleep on the sofa in the middle of a conversation. One minute we're looking through Shivam's magic book for anything we can use to bring Matt back, and the next, she's snoring gently, her head cricked back at an odd angle. My face feels warm when I smile. It's an involuntary thing that creeps up on me and floods me, and I can't remember the last time I smiled like this.

I lift her feet up onto the sofa, and she mumbles and slides down onto the pile of throw cushions she seems to collect. She tucks her hands together under her cheek like a wee cartoon character. It's adorable.

It strikes me that I can't sit there for the rest of the afternoon watching her sleep. I may be socially inept, but I know that much. I stand like I've been burnt and…now what?

The silence is oppressive. I'm used to paper-thin walls with shouts and fights and laughter, both in Glasgow and Oxford, but here, it's like a ghost town. A door opening and shutting in a flat somewhere else in the block, footsteps on the floor above my head. Nothing more, and I find myself wandering around the flat on tiptoe, freezing at every noise I make, the silence strangely important.

As the boredom grows, I look in every cupboard and shelf that's not in a bedroom. I flick through the books on the shelves, look at the pictures on the walls. I find young Kitty and baby Sam, teenage Kitty and Matt, Sam with a group of kids his age. There are pictures of a beautiful woman with Kitty's high cheekbones and a wide, confident smile, and I recognise her mum, Madeline. She looks exactly like she did in the grey place, a different hippy skirt swishing around her ankles. I think I'd believe she was a witch even if I hadn't seen her materialise a sofa out of thin air.

There's even a framed newspaper clipping, black and white pictures of a group of people leaning over the side of a ship. I can only just read the name, *Empire Windrush*, two names circled in blue biro in the caption below. My eyebrows rise. I wonder if that's Kitty's nan and maybe her grandpa arriving in England. I wonder if Ma's got pictures of her own parents somewhere, black and white photos of post-war Glasgow. Would she have framed them? Displayed them? I don't remember ever seeing any link to my past like this.

I poke at the kitchen cupboards, read the instructions on the back of a packet of noodles, the ingredients of a pot of seasoning. There are spices I've never heard of, and I lean against the counter to pop the lid and smell them.

Matt tuts from the doorway. I jump so hard, I nearly spill the allspice. I'm lucky it's half-empty. I click the lid shut and press my hand against my chest as if it'll somehow slow my racing heart. "You're such a bastard."

He smirks and hops onto the counter. "Says the one sneaking through my best mate's cupboards."

I put the jar back in the cupboard and close it, my blush heating my cheeks. "I was bored," I say, and it sounds defensive even to my ears.

Matt doesn't seem to care anymore. He's staring toward the window, I guess beyond, toward his dad's house. "How was it?" I ask.

"I don't know," he admits. "Dad was asleep when I got there. Then he went to work like ten minutes after waking up."

He falls silent, and I assume that's it. He got bored of being there, made his way back. But he puts his hand up to his face, wipes his cheek. "He looked tired," he says.

I raise my eyebrows, on alert again. What do I know about being comforting?

Matt sniffs and swipes his hand across his nose. "He never sleeps in so late. He works really long hours, but he's always up at the crack of sparrow's fart unless he's sick."

"Maybe he is?"

Matt seems to give up on his posture and slumps with a damp sigh, pressing his hands to his face. "I don't want him to feel like this. I don't want him to be so *sad*."

It takes a lot for me to approach him, put my hand above his knee where I know it would feel the warmth of his body if he were alive. Every moment, I'm expecting to be shoved off, pushed backward, unwelcome in the circle of his vulnerability. "He's sad because he misses you. Because he loves you."

Matt's breath shudders as he inhales. "I wish I could make him forget me."

"He wouldn't want that," I say firmly, and it's funny how the words come so smoothly, like I'm not thinking anymore. "I bet he couldn't bear to not remember you."

"It's not fair."

"No, it's not."

The silence of the house is broken by his soft sobs, and I feel my eyes prickling too. I want to hold him together physically while he falls apart in front of me. Nothing is fucking fair. I hate it all.

"Look, we've just got to hope Kitty can find a way to bring you back—"

"I don't know if I want that anymore," he says, his hands falling from his face, red-rimmed eyes boring into me. "What if she has to exchange someone's life to bring me back? What if…" He swallows, then looks at me, his eyes bleak. "She told me some things back then, when I was alive, you know? The things some of her cases said. How they were so bowed down with grief and how relieved they were when it went right, and they could bring their loved ones home. What if that's my dad? What if my dad wants to exchange his life for me?"

"He would," I say softly.

"I don't want him to," he says, his voice childish and afraid. "I couldn't accept that. I couldn't live knowing my dad had exchanged his life for me. How could I? I don't want *anyone* to die for me."

I bow my head. I can't help it. I can't keep looking at him like an equal right now.

"Shit," he says. "Talia, shit, I'm sorry. I didn't think. I didn't mean that, I was…"

"It's okay," I say.

"No, it's different. It was different for you. It wasn't your dad, was it?"

I laugh and step back, leaning against the opposite counter and crossing my arms, a sorry version of a hug. "I doubt it," I say. "I never knew my da. But he was someone's."

Matt's quiet, chewing his lip. "I'm sorry."

"Me too." I laugh, and it's a sad, bitter sound. "This is all a fucking shit show."

"Yeah, it is." Matt takes a long, deep breath, force of habit, I suppose. "I think I'm coming to terms with it, though. Being dead. I'm not frantic to find some sort of solution to all this. I mean, yeah, it sucks. Fuck, it sucks so bad. But we've looked and looked, and we haven't found any clues that might help, you know? And that's okay." He looks at me and smiles, and it hurts under my ribs with a sort of anger and grief. "I can 'live' like this."

I want to say something. I want to tease him, wind him up. I want to hold on to him and tell him not to give up.

Kitty yawns and shifts on the sofa, her arm appearing as she stretches. Matt grins and jumps down from the counter, vaulting over and landing on her. She squeals and sits up. "You git!"

"Wakey wakey," he says, his grin just this side of manic as he puts his ghostly hands through her face. She shrieks and giggles and flaps at him.

All of a sudden, I'm overwhelmed by the concentration of life and joy in these two people. I feel like the ghost, like I've brought the grey place back with me, cold mist swirling from my feet outward, and I want to run as much as I want to stay and soak up their warmth. "Hey, I'm gonna go," I say. I'm not sure I've said it loud enough, and the thought of saying it again horrifies me, my heart starting to beat faster, my ribs curling in on themselves.

"Oh, really?" Kitty sounds disappointed, or I'm deluding myself. I smile at her anyway. She stands, passing through Matt, who yells at her. "You'll come back, though, right?"

I blink at her.

"You said you'd think about it," she says in a singsong. "C'mon, stay the holidays."

It feels like a trick, too good to be true. She clasps her hands under her chin and makes goofy puppy eyes at me. I laugh. "Yeah. Yeah, okay. You sure?"

"Yes," she says, laughing. "It's definitely totally fine."

I think I walk downstairs on a cloud of confused, fizzing excitement and anxiety. When I get to my car, I realise the skeleton leaf is still behind my ear.

## Chapter Seventeen

### *Kitty*

I'm fidgeting like crazy when I catch the bus to work late that Saturday night. Matt sits beside me and rolls his eyes. "Honestly," he says. "Anyone would think you've got a crush."

I glare daggers at him, but the bus isn't nearly empty enough to talk out loud. Matt knows it. He sits back with a smug smile. "Oh, Talia, I can't *wait* to see you again, won't you come stay with me for the *whole* Christmas holiday?"

"Shut up," I mutter through clenched teeth.

"You're cute when you're annoyed," he says, cackling. "Like a cross little kitten."

I roll my eyes and ignore him. It's much nicer to think of Talia instead. She's back in Oxford now, but she offered to pick me up after work when it's over at stupid-o'clock tomorrow morning. She's getting up early just to drive over and give me a lift home, and then she'll be staying. Yes, *Matt*, for the whole holiday. Because I need all the help I can get to find a spell to bring him back.

That's my excuse, and I'm sticking to it.

Shivam looks flustered when he meets me at the Society entrance, his hair sticking up like he's been running his fingers through it, pulling on it. He glares at Matt. "Oh good. He's here."

Our steps echo on the floor as we walk in, and it takes me a while to realise something's off with the whole place. "Is there something big coming up?" I ask.

"Hmm?" Shivam looks back at me. "Why do you ask?"

I have no answer. Something feels off. The whole place is so new to me, though, that it might not be that obvious to him. It's not until I reach the huge atrium that I realise what it is. It's quiet.

I stop, my hand resting on the railing, and look down. There are no other footsteps than ours, there are no voices, nothing.

"Kitty," Shivam calls from our doorway. "Come on, what're you looking at?"

"Where is everyone, Shiv?"

"Probably working," he huffs. "Come on, we've got a case."

There are little hairs standing up at the back of my neck, but I let my hand fall from the railing. It feels like it crumbles slightly under my fingers, like there's powder there to be brushed off, but I see nothing.

Matt catches my eye. "You okay?" I nod, but I can't help glancing down at the silent atrium. "I'll go take a look," he says. "Anything weird happens, get yourself out. I'll find you."

I nod again and want so badly to hug him right now or say something. Instead, I plaster on my smile and go to work.

"Right," Shivam says, already drawing sigils on the mirror as I shake my coat off. "Your case today is a woman called Bianca. She's looking for her teenage daughter. You ready?"

I nod and straighten my shirt, walk up to the mirror, and start placing my own sigils within the square Shivam's laid out. The final one, the new one I've learned at the Society, is always the hardest. It pulls wrong on my throat, and I wince. I need to work out a way to smooth that one out.

For the first time in days, I think of Mum. I haven't seen her in so long, and it aches worse than any dodgy sigil. I don't exactly wish for the old days of the pull coming whenever it wants, but I wish I'd known this would make it harder to see her. A small but growing voice whispers I might never see her again, and the thought of it is so huge and awful, I almost lose control of the magic.

The world around me takes longer to blur than it should, the glass seeming to speckle and dull for a moment before I break through to the grey place.

"Oh my God," gasps a woman in front of me. "Oh my God, it worked." She claps a hand over her mouth and laughs hysterically, then sobs, harsh, violent sounds that rip themselves out of her.

I reach out to pat her shoulder, a witness to her pain. I know it's important for them to feel this, but part of me always wants to take it away.

"Are you Death?" she asks at last, straightening up and visibly pulling herself together.

I laugh. "Everyone asks that," I admit. "No, or I don't think so, anyway. I certainly don't reap souls or whatever it is."

"So what…" She shakes her head. "Doesn't matter. How does this work, then?"

"You think about the person you want to bring back, and hopefully, they'll appear," I explain, trying to get ahead of her and give her answers before she demands them. "If you're both willing, you'll be able to exchange places."

She closes her eyes, a line appearing between her eyebrows as she concentrates. "And she'll wake up, then?" she asks. "No lasting effects? Scars, that sort of thing?"

"It'll be like you died instead of her. History changes. She'll be the only one to remember, and me, of course."

"How does that work?" she asks, her eyes snapping open.

I shrug, feeling a little stupid.

"It doesn't matter," she says, shaking her head. "As long as she gets another chance, that's all that matters."

She closes her eyes again, and I gaze around the featureless landscape. I should be looking for this woman's daughter, but I have to admit, it's my mum I really want to see.

"Why isn't it working?" she asks, frowning.

"It takes longer for some people than others," I say. "I don't really know why."

"There's a lot you don't know, isn't there?"

"Well, it's not like I signed up to an apprenticeship," I snap before I can hold my tongue. "The magic just sort of happens through me," I say more gently.

"Sorry," she says, to her credit. "I'm…this is my only hope. It's *her* only hope."

"Maybe if you tell me a bit about her, it'll help us to both focus on her."

She nods. "Her name's Eloise. She's my daughter. I had her young. She's just turned nineteen, and she's such a bright girl. She's in her first year of uni, studying biomedical sciences. I think she could have gone for medicine if she'd focused a little harder in her A levels but…" She shrugs. "You know what teenagers are like."

I raise my eyebrows. "Uh, yeah. I hope you don't mind me asking, but how did she die?"

She's silent for a moment, her jaw working. I can see the muscles moving under the skin. "An accident."

Someone snorts, and Bianca spins around like she's ready to fight for her life. A girl a bit taller than me, with cropped hair and lip rings, stands behind Bianca with her head tilted to one side.

"Eloise," Bianca gasps. Then she frowns. "What have you done to your *hair*?"

Eloise runs her hand across the grade-one shave and shrugs. "I can do that here." She marks a line back across the top of her skull with two fingers, and bright green spikes spring up behind, giving her a mohawk. She shakes her head, and it disappears just as quickly. "Cool, huh?"

"That's awesome," I say. "I've never seen anyone except my mum do stuff like that before."

"Who are you?" she asks, frowning at me.

"Oh, I'm Kitty. I bring people back if there's someone willing to take their place."

She leans back slightly, turns to her mum. "Bring me back?"

Bianca's face is flushed with victory. "Yes, you can go back, live the rest of your life. It'll be like none of this ever happened. It's a second chance, El."

"I don't want to go back." She steps backward, looking wide-eyed between me and Bianca.

"What? But you have to. I found a way. I'm…I'm *willing*. Kitty says it'll be as if you never d…never went away. I'll take your place."

Eloise blinks and brings her hands up like she needs to ward us off. "But I don't want to."

"No. No, you can't let this mistake—"

"I *killed* myself, Mum!" she yells, an explosion of pain and truth. "I didn't make a mistake. I planned this, and I thought about it, and I knew what I was doing."

Bianca has her hands over her ears, her eyes shut tight as Eloise rages, just trying to be seen. "No, no, no, you can't," she says, almost childlike. I don't know which of them to step toward, to soothe. "You have to come back, you *have* to."

"Why?" Eloise snaps, and a tear breaks free, running down her cheek, dripping off her chin. "Because you said so? You can't fix everything, Mum, some things are too broken."

"You're not broken," she cries. "Don't say that. You can get through this."

"I tried! I tried so hard, you don't even know. I've tried and tried, and I'm *tired*. I can't do it anymore."

"Then you're a coward!" Bianca screams over sobs.

"Oh, God, no, don't," I beg. My hands are shaking as I reach out for her, try to stop her saying things that she may never be able to take back. She shoves me off and steps forward anyway.

"You are a coward. You're tired? Try being a mum whose only daughter committed suicide. Try walking every day through waist-deep snow because you couldn't save her."

"Oh, here we go again," Eloise says, her voice breaking even as she tries to make it sarcastic and not desperately sad. "This is not about you. You can't *save* everyone."

"It is literally my job. As a mother. This is what I'm meant to do."

Bianca's voice is almost a scream, and I stumble back away from the two of them, blinded with the tears. I can't let them do this. I beg them to stop because they don't get to fix this if they don't fix it now.

I want my mum so bad.

There's a pressure building around my head, like the grey mist is pushing in on me, crushing me. I can barely breathe, and at first, I think it's a panic attack. Then it breaks.

The whole world seems to shatter, and pain blooms through my face. I hear distant shouts and spells. I think one of the voices is my mum, but I can't see anything.

"Kitty!" Shivam's voice is the only clear thing, and it's *so loud*. I groan and try to cover my ears, and I realise I'm on the floor, surrounded by broken glass.

"What the hell?" My voice slurs.

"Fuck," he says, but it sounds more scared than angry. "You tell me what the hell? You were doing the job, standing in front of the mirror, and then it started to vibrate and exploded right as you collapsed. What the hell did you do?"

I push myself up gingerly, wincing as the shards of glass prick my hands. Shivam huffs and comes close enough to help me up. "Jesus, Kitty, your face."

I put my hand up to my face and catch the blood dripping from my nose. "Ugh."

"Go clean up," he says. "Shit. I need to call Anderson."

He scrabbles around on his desk, and I hesitate, dizzy and stupid from the *everything* of it all. "Uh. I'm not allowed to go to the bathroom alone, remember?"

He looks up. I shrug. "Anderson said. He got the hump last time."

Shivam presses his fingertips into his eyes. "Yeah. Okay. Fine. Sorry. Are you all right?"

"Sore," I admit.

"Yeah," he says. "Yeah, I guess you would be. Jeez. You faceplanted that mirror when you fell."

"What, I did all that with my face?" I laugh and regret it.

"I don't know," he admits. "What happened in there?"

"The client and her daughter had a screaming match. I think the girl was magical."

"Maybe so, but she's dead. Her magic shouldn't affect the outside world."

I hum and don't tell him about the bond Mum put on Talia and Matt.

Shivam puts his hand just above my shoulder, guiding me out. Clearly holding my arm to lift me up was enough human contact for one day, I think wryly, but then the wall of the corridor seems to *squirm*, and I groan and close my eyes.

"What? What is it?" he asks. He sounds terrified.

"It's fine. I'm not gonna puke," I say. "My eyes have just gone wonky."

The light in the loo is way too bright for my aching head, and I lean against the paper dispenser for a moment, though I don't need to go. At least the walls have stopped moving in here, the room cool and blessedly alone. No ghosts screaming cruelties at each other that they'll never take back.

Part of me wants to go back and help them. My heart breaks for both mother and daughter. Surely, Bianca will feel absolutely awful for the things that she's said? Surely, Eloise will miss her mum and understand she wants to help?

I think of Talia. I'd say I don't know why, but these days, my mind seems to drift toward her if given half the chance, but now I'm remembering all the little glimpses I've seen of her home life and her relationship with her mum. Would I want to fix them back up? Could I? I can't imagine not loving my own mum, being anything but overjoyed to see her, but I know some parents aren't like her.

It's all irrelevant anyway. Something happened in there, and I don't know what. Something violent and destructive, and it had my mum's voice in the centre, my mum's magic hurling me back out. I open my eyes into a squint and stand to gaze into the mirror like it holds any answers. All it shows is a blood-drenched girl with a swollen lip. I sigh and try to wash up as much as I can.

It's a while before my face looks something approaching normal, and by then, my mind's cleared somewhat. I must've been in here for ages. Shivam will have gotten bored and buggered off by now, surely. But it's Matt I'm worrying about. I feel guilty not thinking of him before. What if he's come back to the office to find me and both of us are gone, with blood and glass all over the floor? He'll be terrified.

Even worse, what if he's been affected by that explosion in the grey place?

I nick the last of the loo roll to wad up against my nose and go to unlock the door. That's when I hear it. Low voices, barely audible without me pressed up against the wood.

"…all smashed up and bleeding like nothing I've ever seen, sir."

There's a pause, and I realise Shivam's on the phone to Anderson. I rest my head against the door. I don't want to interrupt and have that awkward "I was talking about you, but I'm going to have to pretend I wasn't" moment. Anyway, the door is cool and comfortable, and I can rest my eyes here…

"Well, all due respect, sir, but she's your fucking daughter."

My eyes snap open.

I hear Shivam sigh through the roaring of blood in my ears. "Yeah, okay. Yes, I'll do that." My heart is beating so hard, my sore face throbs, and I need to get out of there. I need air and space far away from this bullshit.

On autopilot, I shove the door open and run. Shivam notices me and yells, but I don't even look back.

The walls feel like they're closing in on me, darkening from the stark white into a claustrophobic blood colour, the ceiling lowering. It feels like the Society itself wants to swallow me.

I shove on the doors and burst out into air so cold my lungs howl on it, but I'm free. If I can get away.

Strong arms grab me around the waist, and I scream, kick, bite, scratch.

"Kitty! Kitty, it's me."

"Talia," I breathe, all the fight draining from me. I turn and cling to her. I'm safe.

# Chapter Eighteen

## *Talia*

I check my watch for the twentieth time, but I'm still early. Too early to be cool, that's for sure, but at least Kitty won't notice till she comes out of work. At least I'm not late. I'm picking her up, and I'm gonna stay at hers.

Maybe not the whole holiday. I know she said that, but people say a lot of things. I'm now not sure she said anything about me staying at all. Maybe she was making polite conversation. Maybe I'm putting her in a difficult position by taking her up on her offer. Maybe I've misjudged, maybe she's reconsidered. Maybe, maybe, maybe.

I grit my teeth and push the door open. The rain that has been threatening never came, and the night's cold and crisp. I concentrate hard on the white clouds puffing out of my mouth as I lean against my car. Breath in chills my nostrils. Breath out waterfalls upward in the still air, eddying and twining around itself.

The doors burst open, and a figure throws herself out, almost stumbling, tripping over her own feet. I recognise Kitty as she's almost on me, and without thinking, I reach out, wrap my arms around her, cocoon her from whatever's coming. She screams, and I squeeze my eyes shut against the onslaught. "Kitty! Kitty, it's me."

"Talia." She breathes my name like a benediction, and later, I'll rewind that moment, identify it as another hook in my heart.

She turns in my arms and clings to me, and I want to savour it, but her scream still twangs in the back of my neck.

"C'mon," I say and manhandle her into the passenger seat. Someone appears at the doorway of the Society building and starts running, and I scramble around and have the engine started before my feet are even in, spinning the wheels on gravel as Shivam reaches us.

He slaps the window, and Kitty screams, covers her head. I catch a glimpse of him as I slam us into first gear and get out. He looks terrified.

The skin of my back is prickling as I drive home. I keep checking my mirrors in case he's following us. I have a horrifying image of him running at superhuman speed. He can do magic, so it's not outside the realm of possibility. Nothing is anymore.

Kitty's shaking by the time I get her back to her house. I put my arm around her shoulder and walk her in, and she leans against my side like her legs are going to give up on her. I hold her tight.

She hands me the keys when I ask and flicks the lights on in the dark flat. I guess Sam must be staying at Peter's, but I don't think on it too long because I've just noticed the mess someone's made of her face.

I hiss as I cup her cheeks in both hands, tilting her face here and there. There's dry blood under her nose, a bruise blooming over the bridge of it and under her eye, maybe a bump on her forehead above her left eyebrow. "Who did this?" I ask, and I may have always been a coward, but I'll fight for her.

She laughs. "I headbutted a mirror."

I raise one eyebrow. Pretty sure I've used that exact excuse myself. It's not going to work if she uses it on me.

"Really, I did," she says. She's not pulling away, I realise, and I step back first before I have to feel the rejection of her doing so. She quirks me a little smile, then stumbles into the kitchen, flicking the kettle on.

"What happened?" I ask.

"I don't know."

"Kitty."

"I'm not trying to brush you off," she says and leans back against the counter, pressing gently against parts of her face as if testing it. "I'm really not sure. There was a case, but it went wrong, I guess."

"Wrong how?"

She crinkles up her forehead and winces. I dig in her freezer for some ice and wrap it in the tea towel. She smiles at me as I hand it to her. "Thanks," she says.

I have to swallow hard. "I need to know what it is that made you so scared," I tell her. "I need to know how to protect us."

She nods. "I know, I'm piecing it together. I'm sorry."

"Don't be sorry," I say. She smiles at me again, and it feels like my ribs are cracking outward from the inside, painful and terrifying and brilliant.

"The case, this woman and her daughter. They started arguing," Kitty says, and I focus hard on that, on facts, on information. "It was awful. They were saying such horrible things to each other, I just wanted them to stop. And then I heard other voices yelling at each other, but I couldn't hear what they were saying. One of them was my mum, though, I'm sure of it. She shouted a spell, and I felt like I was being thrown out of the grey place. Next thing I know, the mirror's in pieces, and I've got a bloody nose. Shivam says I faceplanted on it."

I'm suspicious of Shivam, now, but Kitty's not done. "I went to go get cleaned up, and…" She swallows and looks away. "Fuck. I overheard him talking to Anderson."

"What did he say?" I prompt into the silence. She stares into space, biting her lower lip. Tears are welling up in her eyes, and I want to understand. I'm afraid of not understanding.

"He said I'm his daughter," she says in a whisper and starts crying silently, tears falling unimpeded, soundless.

"You're…"

"I'm Anderson's daughter. He and my mum…and he didn't tell me. What am I going to do, Talia?"

She looks up at me like I can fix this, like I have any

suggestions other than stay away from them and that place and any danger ever. I have nothing. I tug her close and wrap my arms around her as she cries into my shoulder.

Her phone rings, and she jumps, her fingertips tightening on my back. Her hands are trembling as she pulls the phone out of her pocket. I think of telling her to leave it because there can't be anything good from a phone call at this time of the morning, and she needs to build her defences back. But by the time I find the words, she's turning away from me, her hand in her hair, pacing. "Yes?"

I don't hear the voice on the other end, but I see her freeze, and every inch of me is on high alert. I step closer, catch her eye in case she needs to signal to me, but she shakes her head and looks away, biting her lip. She glances back at me. "Okay," she says, and hangs up.

"What is it?" I ask. "What do you need?"

"It was Anderson," she says, her voice almost a whisper. "He admitted it. He's my dad. He wants to meet me."

I nod. "Right, so we pick Sam up, and we start driving, yeah? We can stay overnight in my room in uni, then head out and get lost. I'd say Glasgow's a good aim because I know people there, but it might be better to be unpredictable. Maybe go south instead, Cornwall? The moors are supposed to be big and good to hide in, aren't they?"

"Talia."

"You're right, we should stick to what we know. Besides, there's the Cairngorms up past Glasgow. He'll never find us there."

"Talia."

"I'll pack up the food, you get the clothes and toiletries. We can fit quite a lot in the car, but we'll want to streamline."

"Talia, I'm going to meet him."

"What?" My mind's like a train, caught on a rail line I've been planning most of my life, daydreaming of freedom and escape and a life off the grid and out of danger. It takes me a long time to register what she's saying. "Why?"

"Because he's my dad," she says with a shaky laugh. "How can I not?"

"But he's a creepy fucker."

"Still, though," she says. "I mean, he's family, right? You'd do the same, wouldn't you?"

"Honestly, I don't know," I say. "If he's anything like my ma, I'd run as far as I could." She bites her lip, and I take a step toward her, taking her hands. The skin over the backs of her hands is so soft, my thumbs can't help but stroke it. "It doesn't matter if he's your dad or not. You've said yourself he makes your hair stand on end."

"It does matter," she says, and she pulls her hands out of mine. I clench them tight to crush out the rejection. "If he's my father, he's part of me, and I can't let that slip away. Maybe my hair was standing on end because I sensed he was my dad."

I laugh and hate how it sounds. "That's bullshit, and you know it."

She sets her jaw. "Not everyone's like you," she says. Her voice is shaking, but it's sharp and strong. "There's not much left of my family. I've got to make a bit more of an effort to keep us together. I'm sorry if that's too *stupid* and naive for you."

She turns fast and almost runs for the door, slamming it behind her, but I hardly notice. The words hurt too much, like salt poured onto a wound, like everything I think of myself being confirmed: cold heartless bitch. Why would she trust me to care for her anyway? I can't even keep a relationship going with the only person in the world God made to love and protect me from birth. I've run from every home and family I've ever had. I look around the warm living room with its soft cushions and shelves of plants.

Why should now be any different?

## CHAPTER NINETEEN

### *Kitty*

I stomp all the way to the bus stop, angry and hurt. It takes about five seconds once I'm sitting to realise that I went too far. I could have said the same things, explained my reasoning just as well without being mean to someone who only wanted to help me.

I groan and cover my face, scrunching down in my jacket. It's like one of those times when I get cross with Sam and tell him to bugger off because I can't parent properly. There's no relief in it, only shame.

My phone's not in my pocket. It must be back on the kitchen counter, and I could throttle myself for leaving it there. I bite my lip as I consider running back to the flat for it and apologising to Talia, explaining why I've got to do this. I've lost Mum and Nan and Matt, and I can't risk losing my dad too, when I've only just found him. I've got to give him a chance.

The bus arrives, and it feels like a sign from the universe. I jump on before I can think about it anymore, but the ride down to the warehouse is a constant roundabout of *have I made the right choice? Have I fucked everything up?*

I'm grateful for the walk down from the bus stop to the warehouse, concentrating on the rhythm of my feet against the pavement as I argue with myself. "Kitty," Matt hisses, and I just about crap my pants.

"Jesus Christ, Matt! What the hell?"

"What the hell?" he squeaks. "*You* what the hell? Where

were you? What happened to that place? It was like it was falling down. And that's after I wandered around in the atrium trying to find people, and there's *nobody* there, Kit, nobody. And then there was this smashing noise, and the whole place fucking *disappeared*. It just *went*, and there I was standing in a fucking wall."

I scrunch my face up and shake my head, which hurts again. "What?"

"The Society. Fucking. Disappeared. Gone."

I look over to the warehouse. Matt rolls his eyes. "Oh, you know what I mean. The building's still there, but everything inside is gone." He drags shaking fingers through his hair. "It was creepy as hell, finding myself in a wall. I sort of stumbled out the side of the building, spent the next hour or whatever looking for you. I thought you'd disappeared too."

"I'm sorry," I say. I catch him up on the whole deal from my end. "I swear, though, it was all still there when I ran out."

"What, the atrium and everything?"

"Well," I say, frowning. "I guess. I didn't exactly check. I was concentrating on the bleeding."

He seems to deflate a bit. "You're really going back in there?"

I take a deep breath. "I've got to try."

"Anderson, though? Really?"

"Oi, that's my dad you're talking about. Apparently."

He crinkles his nose up. "Fine. Let's do this."

I have to swallow the tears hard as he turns and marches toward the warehouse. I'd never have asked him to come with me on this, but having him with me means the world. I wish Talia had come too. I wish I hadn't pushed her away. I wish she could've trusted me to try this.

"Come on, slowpoke," Matt yells. I put aside my selfishness and run after him.

It feels surreal to be coming back here after I ran away in such a terror just a few hours ago. I half expect Shivam to open the door for me, barely looking up from his phone as he leads me to our office. Has this all been a weird dream?

But when the door swings open with a pained screech, there's a man standing there who looks familiar and strange all at once. "Miss Wilson," he says. "Kitty."

"Anderson?" I frown. Maybe if I squint…

He gives a flicker of a smile. "I thought I would dispense with all illusions. If we're to attempt honesty now."

He's younger than he was, and it's a weird relief that my mum's taste in men isn't *quite* as horrible as I'd been thinking. He's in his fifties, his hair thick and brown, and rather than the Monopoly Man aesthetic he was going for before, he looks a lot more casual now. Not normal. I mean, he's wearing a big brown duster coat, like he's some sort of Jedi, but it's softer. More dad-like. I like it.

I try out a smile. Imagine calling him Dad. Cross my arms because I can't quite make that mental leap yet.

"Come on in," he says. His coat flares as he turns, beckoning with a finger over his shoulder. I follow like a little duckling, and I can't deny the hope swelling in my chest.

Like Matt said, though, the warehouse is no longer the Society building. It's just an old, bare warehouse. All the doors along the main corridor are gone, the atrium is gone—there's a wall where it used to be—and a set of steps are off to one side. I wrap my jacket tighter around me as a cold wind whistles through the boarded-up windows.

"I suppose I owe you an explanation," Anderson says.

"Ya think?" Matt mutters, poking at a mouldering shelf as we pass.

Anderson turns as he reaches the end of the corridor, so suddenly that I think he heard Matt somehow. Instead, he lifts his arms and speaks words I don't recognise, and illusion sweeps from his fingertips. Before my gaze, the Society appears in all its pristine austerity. A woman walks past us, her arms full of files, and simply nods at Anderson. He drops his hands, and it fades.

I stare at him with my mouth open. "It was all an illusion?"

He nods. I feel like he's kicked me right in the chest.

"Why?" I beg.

"For you," he says, and for the first time in my life, my father steps forward and takes my hands. It's sudden, and I startle, almost pulling away. He holds me tight, though. "Kitty, have you any idea how powerful you are? The daughter of two incredibly powerful magic users, I always knew you would be exceptional. If only your mother hadn't stolen you away. I've been looking for you all these years."

"But you never—"

"I could never find you. I had Shivam working on it for so long. I never gave up. I knew I had to keep trying. And then last month, there was a crack in the shield she'd put around you, and I had no time to waste."

"She?"

"Madeline, your mother." He says her name with a curl of his lip. "What did she tell you about me? I imagine all sorts of lies."

"She didn't tell me anything, really." Guilt twists in my stomach when I think of how I never asked.

"What, nothing at all?" He laughs. "Come now, Kitty, we're family. No need for lies between us."

I shrug. "I'm sorry."

His fingers tighten on mine for a moment, then he shakes his head. "No matter. You're mine now. I've found you at last."

I laugh. "That sounds ominous."

He waves a hand. "Well, you have always been mine. My daughter."

His eyes bore into mine. I can barely hold his gaze. I've got an overwhelming urge to giggle hysterically. "Well, I guess we'll get to know each other soon enough," I say. I know I'm babbling, trying to fill a soundless space.

"We are going to achieve so much together," he says. He's still gripping my hands, and I'm shamefully aware of how sweaty my palms are. "Over the past few weeks, I've learned about your power, and I have so many ideas for how we can harness it, take it further. You are going to be incredible, my dear."

"Take it further? What do you mean?"

He releases my hands at last and leads me into a room similar to the one Shivam and I used to use, complete with mirror and computer. "Shivam's told me how flexible your magic is," he says, rummaging through the papers on the desk until he finds a notebook. "How you can make tweaks of your own to the sigils."

I nod. "Mum taught me."

His lips twist slightly. "Well, I suppose she was good for something," he says under his breath.

"Hey," I snap. "That's still my mum you're talking about. I get your relationship was strained at the end—"

"Strained?" he says, his voice pitching high. "Strained would be a divorce or a fit of jealousy. Madeline ran away in the middle of the night with my daughter, hid her from me for most of her life, and then shacked up with some regular magic-less idiot."

"And she also raised me and loved me," I say. "She's my mum, and I don't give a shit if you're the king of England, you don't get to talk badly about her to me. I ain't playing favourites."

His eyes twitch slightly, narrowing, and I swallow hard, very aware of how physically and magically strong he is and how I'm stuck out in a derelict warehouse with him. Matt stands shoulder to shoulder with me, and it's comforting, even though I know he can't do anything.

Anderson turns back to the notebook, dropping the tension like it never existed. "Your flexibility in terms of magic could be the key to almost limitless power," he says.

My head spins at the change in tone. I turn to the mirror, biting my lip. I don't know what I expected. It wasn't this. "What do you want to try?" I ask.

He laughs. It's manic, and now that I'm not looking at him, it's exactly like the old Anderson. "How about teleportation?" he says. "How about flight? Breathing under water? We could have superpowers, Kitty."

I chuckle. "I always did like the X-Men."

"Imagine," he says, walking up to join me at the mirror. "We could go anywhere we wanted. Do anything we wanted. Hell, we could walk into the deepest bank vault and take anything."

I laugh. "I mean, why stop there? We could nick the crown jewels."

He catches my eye in the mirror and smiles, and holy shit, he's serious. "Now you're getting it," he says.

"That's illegal," I say. It sounds pathetic even to me.

He rolls his eyes. "For normal people, of course. Imagine how they'd scurry if we took the Koh-i-Noor diamond. Like ants without their queen."

I force another laugh. "What would we do with the Koh-i-Noor diamond?" Please, please let him show me this is a joke.

"I'm sure I'd think of something," he says. He puts his hand on my shoulder. "With your power, your flexibility, and my creative mind, there would be no limits."

I swallow. The mirror seems to waver like a pool, and I wish it was a door. I wish I could sink into it the way I do when I have a case. Every nerve that would have been twanging before is now going nuts. "What does Shivam think about this?"

He hesitates. "Why don't you ask him yourself?"

I hope my relief doesn't show too clearly. Shivam may be a coward, but he's got a moral compass. I need to know this is all a joke. I need to hear that my father isn't a wannabe criminal. "Where is he?"

Anderson checks his watch. "I'll go see if he's arrived yet. He was terribly worried about you after you ran off. I sent him to get some coffee."

He wanders out the door, and Matt rushes to my side, glancing back. "Kitty, what the fuck is going on? Is he being serious?"

"I don't know," I whisper. "I need to ask Shivam. I mean, I've barely seen Anderson while I was working here."

"Kit, I know he's your dad, but…"

"Yeah," I say. "I know. Shit. I know." I wish he wasn't. I wish he was just my pompous, creepy boss. I could straight up hate him and run far, far away. I wish I'd never come here.

I place my hand on the mirror, wishing again that it would turn to a doorway. I want my mum. I want Talia. She tried to warn me. She tried to save me. My fingers move by themselves over the glass, making the sigils I know so well. I wish they could take me to her.

The door opens, and Matt and I jump violently. "Fuck," Matt says with a little laugh. "You scared the crap out of me, Shivam."

"Hey, Kitty," Shivam says. "I'm sorry about earlier. You were never supposed to hear it like that."

"That's okay," I say, and I can't help smiling at him, at someone familiar.

"You can tell us what's going on with Anderson," Matt says, taking a step toward Shivam. "Is he really planning on using Kitty's magic to rob a bank or whatever? It's a joke, right? He's just got a really fucked-up sense of humour, right?"

Shivam walks right through Matt. He doesn't blink, doesn't make any sign that he's done it to troll him. He holds the notebook that Anderson had. I turn back to the mirror, and my heart hammers so hard, my ears are full of hurricane winds of terror. That's not Shivam. That's not Shivam. The man talking about numbers and sigils and ideas, that's not him.

My hand lands on the mirror again. Tears get shaken loose as I tremble in fear and confusion. My fingers mark the sigils, and I want to be away from here, I want to escape.

So I do.

Arms wrap around my waist. I freak out, screaming and struggling, but I can feel myself being transported, not pulled, just picked up and *moved*. For a split second, I think of Talia, how she held me tight, how she warned me, and how I didn't kiss her every time I had the chance. But mostly, I think of nothing but blinding panic and escape.

"Kitty, Kitty, calm down, you're making shockwaves."

I'm on the floor, a breathless mess, but that's Shivam's voice. That's Shivam, standing over me when he should be in the white room back there, with Matt, with my body, if this has gone the way it usually does. And next to him…shit, next to him is my mum.

"Are you all right?" she asks, crouching, and that's it. I burst into tears.

I can hug her here. I can wrap my arms around her waist and

cry into her shirt. I've turned back into a little girl, lost without her mum and passed around between the social workers, clinging to Sam's hand.

I must cry for hours, but she doesn't make any sort of fuss or try to stop me. She's sitting cross-legged on the floor with me clutching her and smearing snot into her clothes. I don't want to let go. I don't want to go back to the real world. Why would I when I can smell her here and feel her warmth and her fingers stroking my hair?

"Mum," I say. "Mum, I'm scared."

"I know, love," she says. "Me too."

I cry out all my fear and grief, and still, more comes up. When there are no more tears, there's an empty void inside me and still, still, the traces of fear swirling there.

I stay curled on her lap. Mum doesn't make any move to hurry me up or push me, and I luxuriate in it. I wonder if I could fall asleep. When I sit up, I don't feel like I'm being forced by anyone else, which makes me wonder why the hell I bother.

"You're dead," I say to Shivam, wiping my face.

He shrugs. "Anderson. You know he makes illusions, right?"

I nod.

Shivam sighs. "He found me at the train station. Made it look like the platform was a foot longer." He swallows. "He, uh...he took the illusion away a moment before the train hit."

"Fuck." I cover my mouth, feeling sick at the thought. My father did that. My blood. It seems there are more tears to come. "Shivam, fuck, I'm so sorry."

"Bastard," Shivam says viciously. "Not you," he throws at me, though I feel like I'd take it if it was aimed at me. "He's always been such a fucking *bastard*. It's not enough to kill someone, I guess. Got to make them realise just as it's too late."

Mum's nodding. "He's always been that way. I wish I'd realised earlier, before..."

Shivam hums. "He's clever. He comes across as a good guy when you first meet him, and then..."

"By the time you realise, it's too late," says Mum. "It's why I wanted to keep him away from you, I'm so sorry, Kitty. I thought I could do it."

"It's not your fault," I say.

She shakes her head. "It is," she says, and she's crying now too. "I was the adult. I should have seen the red flags. I should have left him way before. I let him get away with so much, and I'm sorry for putting you in this situation. And then the shield broke, and he got there before I could fix it."

"What do you mean?"

She sniffs and wipes her eyes. "I got cocky, started taking risks. When I tried to tie Matt to Talia, to bring him out to you, that was my magic out in the world again. My death was supposed to shield you, put all my magic into hiding you."

"You what?" I say, almost in a whisper. "You did what?"

"I had to," she says, begging me with her eyes. "He was getting closer. And he got Shivam here on his side."

"Blackmailed me," Shivam mutters.

"I couldn't do it by myself," she says. "Not while using my magic for anything else."

I curl up into a ball and break, my heart shattering. I'm the reason my mum died. I might as well have killed her myself. I can barely breathe. Nothing's supposed to hurt here, but living is a fire in every cell of my body. I am the reason my mum died.

She's wrapped around me again, we're sharing tears and this pain, this pain is too much. "I'm sorry," she whispers again and again.

"I'm so sorry," I whisper back.

"You're going to have to go back," says Shivam, and I can't imagine anything worse. "Your body's out there still." With a murderer, he doesn't say. He looks at me, meeting my gaze without the shame and anxiety that's been so much a part of him since I've known him. "You didn't kill her," he says, jerking his thumb toward Mum. "He did. He killed us both. You've got to kill him before he does it again."

"I've got to what?" I say, my jaw dropping. "I can't kill him!"

"You have to." He shrugs.

Mum wipes her eyes and nods. "I'm sorry, love. It's self-defence."

"What am I gonna do?" I ask, despair pulling at my heart, tugging me toward the ground and giving up.

"You've got to get out of that warehouse for a start," Mum says, grabbing my hand and holding it tight. She feels warm, the two of us here like this. "Go and keep driving, get as far away from him as you can. Leave." She swallows hard. "Leave Sam. He'll be safer not knowing any of this. Peter will look after him."

I don't have the heart to remind her I don't have a car. The way she looks right now, she'll probably tell me to steal one. I think of Talia, picking me up from the Society buildings in her old farmer car, and I wish…I wish…

Mum and Shivam are helping me to my feet. "When you get back out there, use this sigil," Mum says, drawing something in the palm of my hand.

"How?" I ask. "Do it again, I didn't see."

"No," she says. "It's already there. You just need to throw it at him. He's not the only one who can tell stories about what's in front of your eyes."

I look at my hand, almost expecting to see something. Maybe the sigil itself glowing, but there's nothing. There's so much about magic that I don't know, so much I'm assuming and guessing, and I feel bereft all over again.

I close my fingers around the invisible sigil and breathe slowly, feeling the knowledge of all I have to do weighing on me again. I don't want to do this. I don't want to fight, not when I feel like I can't possibly win. I put my family in danger by being me, and I'm panicking at the thought of leaving them. Even worse, at *not* leaving them on time. At still being in the flat when Anderson comes to kill all of us. Or to kill Sam and Peter and, I don't know, steal my powers or whatever.

I close my eyes. I don't want this. I don't want any of it, I never have. I wish I was with Talia. I wish I was a normal girl who'd met another normal girl a normal way and could have normal worries, like whether or not she likes me back.

My mum and Shivam are telling me what to do, and I can't focus on any of it. I'm so scared. Mum wraps her arms around me, and I cling to her with my left hand, my right still wrapped tight around the sigil. "Mum," I say, but the rest of the words stick in my throat. *Let me stay. Don't make me face my demons, I can't do this. I'm not strong enough, I never have been.*

She presses her hand against my chest, and I remember the red light that bound me and Talia together. Mum kisses my forehead and steps back. My breathing speeds up, and I squeeze my eyes shut tight. I'm going to return to my body on the other side of the mirror, and Anderson will be there, looking just like Shivam, the guy he murdered.

I want Talia. I want to run away with her. I want her to get mad on my behalf and put her arm around me again, strong and fierce like she did when I first found out about my father. I don't want to fight. I don't want to lose.

I step out of the grey place.

# Chapter Twenty

## *Talia*

I walk into my silent room at uni and drop my bag on the floor inside the door. I flick on the light and stand, empty, staring at the grey dawn out the window.

I'm alone again, and it feels like an inevitability. I can imagine Ma sneering at me or maybe telling me in that sickly sweet voice she sometimes uses when she's trying to be nice, that she's the only person who can ever really love me.

I do what I do best. I push everything that hurts down into a space beneath my chest. For the rest of the day, I bury myself in research and revision, my foot tucked up on the seat of the chair, chin on my knee. I lose myself in numbers and formulae, and for a little while I can tell myself that I don't need any more than this.

I email Daniel, ask him for more work to do over the holiday, which now spreads ahead of me again, empty and hollow. He emails back, asks if I'm okay, if I want to talk. I absolutely don't. I want to work. I want to stop hurting. I want to pretend that hurt doesn't exist. I tell him I'll come over tomorrow. Set an alarm for myself. I will fill my days. Fill this void.

I don't want to go to sleep. I work the hours away, filling my mind with facts and beautiful impossibilities that have rules, that don't mind if I'm brusque or sharp-tongued, that are as cold and heartless and arrogant as I am. The sun sets. I don't know why it ever bothered rising.

I don't want to think about Kitty meeting her father. What

she finds out about him. Whether he's a creeper or a good man, misunderstood. I don't want to think about Matt and how he may never get his wish, never come back to life. Haunt that little town for the rest of eternity.

I don't want to think about what I could have done instead. How I could have said it all instead. How I could have protected her.

I throw my pen down. It's nearly midnight, and work's become impossible. I don't think sleep's going to be any more successful, but it's worth a try. Can't fail at lying down, I guess. I stand and stretch, and that's when Kitty appears out of my mirror.

"What the fuck?" I mutter, already reaching for her. I barely have time to register that she looks frantic and terrified before she flings her hand at me. There's a flash of red light and then darkness.

❖

"What the fuck did you think you were doing?" Ma asks. My chest aches. My stomach aches. My elbows are bruised, and I'm curled on the floor, hand cupped over my throbbing ribs. She must've kicked me at some point. I can hear her, but I can't see her. I can't see anything. I think I've got my eyes shut. Everything hurts so much.

Her footsteps come closer, and I cower, tucking my head in, eyes shut. "Oh, stop being such a pussy," Ma says, spitting hate at me. "I'm the one who should be upset. Who d'ye think you are, not telling me about this? Oxford. Fuck, as if you'd even get in." She laughs, and somehow, that hurts more.

I feel like something's wrong. She never found the letter, this never…I was *in* Oxford. I already did it, didn't I? I've already escaped her, right? But then, how am I back here on the sticky lino in her kitchen? I can hear her pouring another drink, and I stay perfectly still. Sometimes, she forgets if I make myself unnoticeable. Maybe she'll wander into the sitting room, and I can crawl away.

A glass smashes behind me, soaking me and making me

flinch again, hand up over my face. "What the fuck are you still doing down there? Get off your arse and clean up this mess. Fuck me, you're useless."

I stagger to my feet, my hands shaking from pain and fear, though I try to control it and hold them rigid. If I make a fist, she'll hit me for threatening her. If I show weakness, it'll only make her angrier. Because how dare I be afraid of her when she's terrifying me? I retreat from my body, leave it to do the work for me, an automaton. It's a bit like a dream, like I'm seeing with my eyes shut tight, but there's no room in my mind for analysis now. All I can do is pick up the shards of glass one by one. It's almost calming. As long as I'm bent over doing what she wants, she's less likely to notice me.

I can feel flashes of wrong, like a voice calling me home; not here, this isn't home. Morgan and the others taught me what home really means. Sometimes, a strand of my mind reaches out to those flashes, to that voice, wanting to follow it toward the light and crack open this hell, break me out. But every time, the despair and the fear of experience pull me back. I can feel myself walking around the kitchen, I can hear every word my mother says to hurt me because she's not leaving this time. This time, she's incandescent. Some part of me still rebels.

The flashes get stronger. I can hear the words that voice makes. I stop and stand still in the middle of mopping up the mess.

"What are you waiting for, you useless—"

I hold up my hand without thinking what I'm doing, without realising the consequences—she'll kill me, she'll definitely kill me for this—and strain my ears.

"Talia, I'm sorry, please come back, Talia, Talia."

"Kitty?"

There's a gulping, ugly sob and arms around me. I drop the cloth, and it disappears. I open my eyes.

"Talia, oh my God, I'm so sorry, I didn't mean to, I'm sorry."

"Hey," I say, and wrap my arms around Kitty, looking over her shoulder for my mother or other dangers. "It's okay, shh."

She's crying so hard and clutching me like I'm saving her

from drowning. "I never meant to throw the sigil at you. It was meant for Anderson. I don't even know how I got here. I was just thinking about you, and I didn't want to fight, and I was so scared. I never meant to hurt you, I'm so sorry."

Everything's upside down. I barely notice that we've moved to sit on my bed until she's pulling back a bit, hands fluttering over my face and down my arms. "Are you hurt anywhere?" she asks. "You were covering your face."

I look at my hands, the palms free of blood and glass shards. My head is pounding, but the rest of the bruises are gone, and as for the memories, they'll have to go with the rest of them, to the side. To be dealt with never.

I focus on Kitty instead. She wipes tears off her cheeks and sniffs, her face blotchy and swollen from crying and also, the most beautiful thing I've seen. "I'm fine," I say. My voice is gravelly, my mouth dry but still twisting into a smile.

She sniffs again and her lip wobbles. "I didn't mean to hurt you," she whispers.

"I know," I say. I take her hands, and I don't know if my trembling is residual tension from the spell or whatever it was or if I'm as terrified as I should be to be touching her. "It's okay. I'm fine now."

She looks at our joined hands, then up at me. Very slowly, she leans forward and rests her head on my shoulder, her face tucked into my neck. I let out a shaky breath. Without my say-so, my thumbs are stroking the back of her hand.

"I wanted to be with you," Kitty says, so soft it doesn't break the fragile night. "I was terrified."

"You're safe now," I say, though I don't know if it's true.

"Anderson killed Shivam."

Part of my mind fixates on that, circling around and around that new fear. I push it aside and take one hand off hers to wrap it around her back like I can hold her here with me. "Tell me," I say, and she does.

We're silent together when her story comes to an end, the rain outside and our breathing the only sounds in the room. I have no idea how I can help her, so out of my depth in every way.

"What happened to your body?" I say after a while, my voice barely above a whisper. "If you leave your body behind when you go into the grey place, and you came straight here…"

She laughs, shaky. "I would love to know. I imagine it disappeared in front of Anderson's eyes." She sits up, leaving me cold all down my side. "Matt!" she says. "Matt's still there with him."

I bite my lip. I want to suggest going to rescue him. But practicality wins out. "I bet he's left already," I say. "It's not like Anderson can keep him there."

She slumps, holding her face in her hands. "I hope so," she says. "God. Talia, I'm so sorry. I said such mean things."

"It's okay," I say.

"No, it's really not," she says, sitting up. "You were right. It doesn't matter that he's my dad. He's also an evil murderous bastard."

"Well, I didn't predict that, to be fair."

She giggles, turns her face toward me, and smiles. My heart skips a beat and aches in the best way. "Thank you," she says.

"For what?"

"I don't know," she says. She turns so she's sitting angled toward me and links her fingers through mine. "I should go."

It feels like a second chance, and that seems to be my modus operandi. A second chance at life, a second chance at faith, and a second chance at this. I cover her fingers, her skin smooth and warm. "How?" I ask because I'm emotionally constipated, and it's taking all my nerve to make even this much of a step. "There won't be any buses. It's too late." My heart's beating its way out of my throat. "Stay here."

She looks up at me. "Are you sure?"

I think I stop breathing at some point, terror closing up my lungs. Instead, I touch her cheek, feel her chin tilt up. I watch her as I step off the precipice and into freefall, watch her cheeks flush and her eyes flutter shut as she leans toward me, and I kiss her.

❖

When my alarm goes off the following morning, we're curled up together under my duvet, mirrors of each other, our faces pressed close and hands in a tangle between us. I open my eyes, rough with sleep deprivation, and watch her rub her face, press into the pillows, deny the day. I've never felt this warm in my life.

"Mornin'," she says, voice crackling and open. She smiles at me so sweetly, I can't help brushing my fingers over her cheek, the soft round curve rising below her eye. Her skin feels like a peach, flawless and velvet, and even though she's in my bed, even though she ran from her demons to me, I'm still amazed when she shuffles forward to kiss me. This feels like a dream, and I pull her close, pressing my face to her neck, wanting to convince myself she's real.

She giggles and squirms under me. "Tickles," she says. I think the sun must be shining out of my chest. "Have you got uni today?"

I shake my head. "Term ended last week. I've got to do a few hours at the synagogue, though. Do you want to stay here?"

She bites her lip. "Would you mind if I came along? I mean, if that's appropriate. I dunno."

"Of course it is," I say. "It's not a service, anyway, just admin work for Daniel. He's the rabbi. He won't mind, I'm sure."

She lets out a long breath, tension draining from her. "Really? I don't want to be alone, that's all."

"I understand. Of course you don't." I link our fingers, fascinated with being allowed to touch. "How're you feeling?"

"I don't know, honestly. How about you?"

"Me? Fine, why?"

"You didn't have any nightmares?"

I think about it, frowning.

"Only, I think you did. You were twitching, and you looked scared or angry."

"I woke you up?"

"I was barely asleep anyway," she insists, which doesn't make it better. "I'm sorry, it's my fault with that awful spell."

"It's not your fault," I assure her, kissing her firmly. "It's nothing my ma wouldn't've done if she'd had the chance anyway."

She looks horrified, her eyes widening, brown pools of sadness. "Your mother? Your mum hurt you enough to be your worst nightmare?"

I kick myself mentally and look away. "Some families are a bit fucked up."

She's still long enough for me to start drawing back because I should've known I'd be too broken, but then she kisses me and squeezes me tight, her arms wrapped around me, and I realise she's stronger than she looks, caging me in safety. I wrap my arms around her back and huddle into her tentatively. Hopefully. "Yes," she says. "They are, aren't they?"

We never got undressed last night—or early this morning—so when we eventually drag ourselves out of bed, it's just to brush our teeth and share a packet of pastries I bought on clearance the other day. "You want to call your brother?" I ask as I search through my wardrobe for an extra scarf and hoodie. I hold out the warmest to Kitty, and she takes them with a grateful smile.

"I can't," she says, scrunching her face up. "I left my phone at home."

"You remember his number? Or Peter's?"

She bites her lip and shakes her head. "I tried to memorise Peter's, but numbers just don't stick, you know?" She gestures at her head and shrugs.

I hold the door open for her, and as we walk up the street toward the bus stop, she slips her hand into mine, linking our fingers with a little sideways glance. I look down, but that can't hide my smile.

"Sam's at Peter's, right?" I ask as we sit in the bus stop. She's pressed up close to me, shivering, and I wonder if I should put my arm around her. If I may.

She shakes her head. "Yeah, at least he'll get to school okay." She bites her nails. "I still don't know what to do, Talia."

I glance at her, small and hunched and cold, and put my arm around her, tugging her close. It's all I can do.

# CHAPTER TWENTY-ONE

## *Kitty*

Talia's rabbi is tall and thin with a sweet smile and razor-sharp eyes. He shakes my hand and welcomes me in, his eyebrows shooting up when he hears my name. The glance he gives me is short and quickly covered but speaks a hell of a warning. I'm glad she has someone so firmly on her side.

"Is it okay if Kitty waits for me to finish? I won't get distracted, I swear," Talia says to Daniel, and I notice little things, like how hunched her shoulders are, that she's looking up at him through her lashes, how she's fiddling with her fingers. "And, Kitty, I'll be done in three hours, then I'll give you a lift back, yeah?"

"Of course Kitty can stay," Daniel says, putting a hand on her shoulder. I wonder if he does it so slowly deliberately or if it's instinctive, how to calm her. "Talia, you know you can postpone, don't you?"

Talia blinks rapidly. "Oh. Yeah, sure. It's fine, though." She glances between me and Daniel. "Right?"

"Yeah, of course," I say quickly. "I'm already putting you out—"

"You're not putting me out." She smiles and tucks a strand of hair behind her ear, and I flush with pleasure. Now it's me fiddling with my fingers.

"I'll get started," she says, jerking a thumb behind her. She vacillates, puts a hand out as if she's going to take mine, then mutters something to herself and flees.

I glance up at Daniel.

"So," he says, and his smile doesn't meet his eyes. "How do you know Talia?"

"You know, don't you? About the whole death thing?"

His eyebrows rise, and this smile shows a flicker of truth in it. "The whole death thing?"

I sigh. "I don't even know how to explain it," I say, and rub my eyes. I'm so tired. "I don't even know what's going on or what I'm gonna do."

I trail off, and he reaches to pat my shoulder. He's slow when he moves, like he's waiting for a reaction, and I recognise that's how he patted Talia, like he was giving her—and now me—a chance to back away. Every movement is considered. Every word. And I'm relieved to have someone like that around, so careful. So responsible. He reminds me of Peter, and I swallow hard past a lump in my throat.

"How about a cup of tea?" he asks. The smile crinkles his eyes.

## Chapter Twenty-Two

### *Talia*

I peek through the open door into Daniel's office, watching Kitty swing her leg over the side of the armchair as she sips her tea. She's reading a thick book, and hysterical giggles bubble in my chest as I wonder what Daniel might have given her, if she's reading the Tanakh or some of Paul Celan's poems.

She glances up, and I duck away, my back to the wall like a Disney princess, my heart beating fast. I'm still falling; my wings have yet to catch. For the first time, I think maybe I'll be okay with them never catching the wind.

Daniel comes out of the hallway and startles to see me hiding from the girl I think I might love. He simply raises an eyebrow, a slow smile creeping across his face, and I flush bright red and scurry into the office.

"I have been doing work," I say by way of apology when he follows and leans against the desk.

"I don't doubt that," he says. I can't bear to meet his amused, knowing gaze. "Talia." His voice is deep and serious when he speaks again. "Are you happy?"

I look up. I want to hide from it still. I want to close off my heart, hide it back safe in the cage of my ribs, not leave it beating free for everyone to see. I nod.

"Then I'm happy for you," he says.

I can't help it. I smile, the joy bringing tears to my eyes, making it hard to focus on the computer as I input the data from the receipts he's collected. I think my heart's caught the wind, flying, as exhilarating as falling, and as endless.

Then we hear Kitty's voice. "Matt!"

I frown and leap to my feet, rushing into Daniel's office. Kitty's standing face-to-face with Matt. "He's got them, Kit. He's taken them, and I couldn't stop him, I couldn't. I tried to stop him, but he walked through me. He took them."

"What?" I say, fear making me angry. "What's going on, who's taken who?"

"Anderson," says Matt, turning to me. His eyes are wild, and his form seems to vibrate, flickering in and out of view. "When Kitty disappeared, he was swearing, and then he got in his car. I got in because what the hell else was I going to do? I didn't know where you'd gone." He pushes his fingers through his hair, tugging. "He went straight to your place, Kitty, and he magicked the freaking door open and walked in. My dad was there, and he just…he waved his hand, and my dad followed him like a fucking zombie. Has he turned my dad into a fucking zombie?"

"Sam," Kitty says, her voice hoarse with horror. "Matt, what about—"

"Anderson threw him over one shoulder like a sack of potatoes, and I tried—" He sobs or screams, both at once. "I was hitting him and shaking my dad, and he walked right through me. I didn't know what to do."

"It's okay, Matt, you're okay. How did you get here?"

"I ran," he says, and my jaw drops. "I don't get tired, so I ran and kept running, and then there was a bus. I got onto that because it was faster. Fuck, Kitty, what are we going to do? What's he going to do with them?"

She pales. "This is my fault. It's me he wants."

"You're right, Miss Wilson, it is you I want."

Daniel swears and steps backward, clutching at his chest. The rest of us spin around to the window, mirrored by the darkness outside.

"You took some finding," says the man in the glass. Our own

reflections seem to ripple around his image as he paces back and forth. "Even now, I cannot reach you."

"What do you want?" Matt says in a snarl.

Anderson, this different, younger Anderson, ignores him, still blind to him. "What do you want?" I translate for him, my fists bunched around nothing.

"I want Kitty. That's all I've ever wanted."

She shakes her head. "I'm not yours," she says. "I'll always be your daughter, but that don't mean you own me."

He snorts. "Don't be dramatic. I'm talking about family loyalty here."

"I can't let you hurt people. You can't expect me to join you on some crime spree just because I'm your daughter." He looks at her, inspects her, and I can see her hoping, believing in the inherent goodness of people. Particularly her people. "Let them go, please," she begs. "Please, Dad."

"And then you'll join me?" He asks like it's an interesting option, and I want to scream, ready to leap in front of her if he tries anything.

"I won't do anything immoral," she says. "But I'll still be your daughter."

He rolls his eyes. "I don't actually give a shit about your morals, you naive little bitch. Just your power."

I bare my teeth at him.

"Why?" Kitty demands, and I'm so proud of her, that little wobble in her voice holding solid. "What do you want it for?"

"Does it matter?" he asks. "Will it change your decision when you already have to choose between giving me what I want and letting me take my frustrations out on your *chosen* family?" He makes a sweeping gesture with his hand, and behind him, Sam and Peter come into view, silent and bound, their hands behind their backs, unmoving. Daniel looks behind himself, an instinctive move, as if the image in the mirror is only reflecting people in our room. Kitty cries out and clamps her hand over her mouth.

"Let them go," Matt shouts. "How fucking…let them *go*!"

He runs at Anderson. I put my arm out, and he goes straight through it. He'll surely go straight through the window into the street outside, but he doesn't. He's still *there*, still in the reflection, but he can't be, and it's only a second. Anderson frowns, a flash of confusion as the image shudders and fades, and it's just us, just our reflections.

"Matt," Kitty cries. She rushes for the window, and this time, I grab her. I grab her by the shoulders, hold her tight.

"Don't go," I say, desperate, the cage around my heart cracked open and plain for everyone to see.

"I have to," she says, her eyes haunted and already far away.

"No, no you don't have to. You don't have to do anything. Run, run with me. We can get into my car, we can, we can leave the country. Don't do this."

"But Sam, Peter…Matt."

"You can't," I start, and it's a battle to hold my tongue, close my cage. *You can't. It's hopeless. He's too strong. They're already dead, and you will be too if you go after them.*

Her eyes meet mine, and she looks into me, into my soul. "I can," she says, and she's gone.

I gasp, my arms wrapping around the air where she once stood, my breathing rough and strangled to my own ears. She's gone, and I couldn't hold her, I couldn't keep her.

I wasn't enough.

There are rough hands on my biceps, someone's shaking me, and I look up at Daniel.

"Talia!"

"She's gone," I say. My voice is hoarse.

"Where?" he demands. "Talia, where has she gone?"

I feel a flare of bitter anger. "Probably into a mirror." I gesture sharply toward the window.

"But do you have any idea where that man is, where he would have taken her family? Or has he gone into, I don't know, some alternate world?"

I stare at him a moment. "The Society building."

"You know where that is?"

I nod. "In Leithfield. Out near the motorway junction, there's this big industrial building. No windows or anything, it's…" I shudder. I didn't like to think of her being there all alone before, but now…

"Come on," he says.

"Daniel, what?"

"I'm coming with you. You can't think I'd leave you children to go into danger alone."

"And you're not going to talk me out of it? Or tell me to call the police?"

"Will the police believe me? Would I be able to talk you out of it?"

I snort. "No."

"There you go, then. Come on, quickly. Did you drive here?"

"No, took the bus. My car's parked in the college lot."

He nods. "My car's around back. Rabbi privileges. Let's go."

I feel a flare of fierce joy from knowing what to do and having someone along to say *yes, what you want is right*. But just as fast, it turns back to fear because we have no magic. We haven't a clue what we're doing or what we're going to be facing when we get there. Not only have I been left behind, but I may be dragging someone into danger.

"Are you sure about this?" I ask Daniel as he pulls out of the parking spot in his Volvo. A glance in the back shows he's probably got kids, and the guilt intensifies.

He shrugs. "I'm not sure I'm not having a wild dream, honestly." He takes a deep breath. "But this feels like the right thing to do."

"*B'ezrat HaShem*," I say softly. *With God's help.*

He meets my eye. "*B'ezrat HaShem*," he says, with a small smile. "You know, when I say that, I always imagine Him sitting at my shoulder, along for the ride."

I laugh and can't help glancing behind us. "I hope so," I say and like that the humour disappears. I close my eyes and bend all my soul to Him. "Please," I say in my mind. "Please help us save her, save all of them. I can't do this alone. Please help us."

I wish I'd memorised a prayer or a psalm beyond the Shema.

Something to calm my mind and focus on, stop me biting the skin around my nails. Usually I read them, keeping my hand, eyes, and voice completely focused on the same thing, but all I can do now is repeat the Shema again and again under my breath.

Daniel glances over at me and begins to speak. Psalms, passages from the Talmud; he's skipping around, following only his heart, all to make me feel safer. And he doesn't comment when I cry. I let the words carry me through the storm of my fear and grief, a safety line around me leading me to clarity.

I think of her. I want to keep her safe, give her support. Give her all of myself. I think of following her into whatever grey place she's gone, stand at her back, and reinforce her magic any way I can, with my fists or my words. I don't think of how impotent I am. I don't think of how I might be a burden to her, one more magic-less person for her to protect.

My chest tightens, and I put my hand up, clutching at…at a red rope that seems to lead away from me and through the car. "What the hell?" Daniel says, pulling over to the side of the road, his hazard lights clicking. "Talia, what…"

I hold the rope around my heart. A thought rises in my mind, remembering what Kitty's told me about magic and how it works. Willpower. Willpower and mirrors.

"Talia," Daniel says, his voice a forced calm. "You've got a rope sticking out of your chest."

I clench my jaw and concentrate on breathing, once, twice, then pull down the visor, my hands shaking and fumbling. I angle the mirror so I can see my eyes and try not to really *think* about what I'm doing. "Kitty?" I say. My voice sounds weak to my own ears. "Kitty?" I clutch at the rope through my chest, and I know she's on the other side of it, I can feel it. I close my eyes, the hope almost painful. I pray.

"Kitty?"

"Talia McGregor, what are you doing back here?"

I gasp as I open my eyes. "Fuck," I say because I'm standing ankle-deep in fog in the grey place. I was dead last time I was here, and for a moment, panic overwhelms me. What the hell am I doing? What was I thinking? I can't do this. I'm a physicist.

"Talia, what're you doing here?" Shivam's voice seems to ground me, and I wrest control of my breathing.

There's a familiar woman standing in front of me, her head on one side. "Madeline?"

"Well remembered."

I turn to Shivam. "You're dead," I say.

He rolls his eyes and turns away. I follow at a distance, peering around him as he drops to his knees, drawing with his fingertip in the mist. It seems to stay where he wants it to, leaving a swirling mandala on the floor.

"How did you get here?" Kitty's mum asks. She's peering at me with clinical fascination, and I resist the urge to hunch away and snarl.

"I looked into a mirror and followed the red rope," I say and feel like a bloody idiot because what does that even mean?

She looks at my chest. "That's my magic. Or it was until… Kitty must have changed it somehow. May I?"

I shrug and turn to face her properly. She casts some sort of magic around me, signs that appear and disappear in the air around the rope. It sticks out of my chest, parallel to the ground but seems to fade into thin air within a foot of me. Madeline shakes her head. "Incredible."

"What is?"

"My daughter." She smiles up at me, and her eyes crinkle like Kitty's do. "She's a genius. Isn't she, Shivam?"

Shivam pointedly ignores her.

"Where is she?" I ask.

"That's what we were trying to find out when you started to appear. Now." She points down to the rope. "I think we can follow that."

"It'll take me to her?"

"I believe so," she says. "I made it in the first place when Matthew came back with you. I am sorry for that, by the way." She frowns and reaches for it, an aborted motion, to my relief. "Kitty diverted it, though. Or you did. I'm not sure."

"I can't have done it. I'm not magic."

She smirks. "And yet, here you are."

"That's…I just followed the rope."

Shivam sighs and stands. "Most people never realise they've got it unless they're born into a magical family."

"But I don't know how I did it. I don't know all these sigils and spells you guys use."

Kitty's mum waves her hand. "They're just aids to focus your mind."

Shivam nods. "I used to think it was all rigid too, but after Kitty…All the people who found us at the Society and wanted their family back," he says. "They called us with their grief and their willpower. I was just the one listening."

"Yes," Kitty's mum says, her voice ice. "And then you scammed them out of their savings and let Anderson manipulate my daughter into helping."

"I'm helping now, aren't I?" he says, uncowed. He turns to me. "If you want to find Kitty, you will."

"How?"

He shrugs. "What feels right to you?"

I look at the rope. It seems to disappear into nothing, but why? It should give me a direction, show me the way to go.

Kitty's mum nods as if she knows what I'm thinking. "Concentrate," she urges. "Think about her and how you want to find her."

I close my eyes and breathe steadily. How I want to find her! I want to find her as we were this morning, sleepy and warm, cuddled up in my bed. I think of her face inches from mine, her sweet smile, the way she leaned over and touched our noses together, then laughed because my nose was so cold. The way her kisses felt on my lips, the way her heart beat under the palm of my hand. I want her so much. I want her safe and in my arms.

Kitty's mum breathes in sharply, and I open my eyes. The rope leads off into the mist, beyond our sight, and I laugh once, disbelieving. And then I run toward her.

# CHAPTER TWENTY-THREE

## *Kitty*

Leaving Talia is terrifying. It's stepping away from safety into certain death, but she'll live without me. My brother may not. Peter may not.

I don't know how I get there. I think for a moment that I shouldn't be able to do this. I shouldn't be in the grey place at all. I have to be able to go into a mirror and use the sigils. But here I am.

As I walk, terrified, purposeful, I feel others around me. I can't quite see them; it's like the movement in the corner of my eye that disappears when I turn to face it. I don't think on it. It's not like this whole thing can get much scarier. My heart's already beating out of my bloody chest as it is.

I was wrong. Hearing Matt scream is more than scary, and I'm running before I can think it through, my heart breaking. "Leave him alone," I yell.

I don't see them in the distance. I don't run toward them. They appear in front of me. I think fast and jump between Matt and Anderson, holding out my hand. All I think is that I want Matt to be safe, and Anderson is blasted backward on his arse.

"Holy shit," I murmur. Matt groans, and I turn to glance at him. "You okay?"

"Think so."

Anderson is getting up again, leaning on his knee to push himself to his feet. Behind them—my heart hurts—are Peter and Sam, floating in mid-air. They're silent and still, and I'm so fucking terrified that he's already killed them, that it was all a trick to get me here, and he killed them anyway or that I took too long, and he killed them as punishment.

"Ms. Wilson," he says, and I want to be sick. He brushes invisible dust off his coat.

"What do you want?"

"I thought I explained this," he says, and he's like a disappointed teacher. "I want your power."

"What for?"

He actually rolls his eyes, but still, it's genteel, like he's *irked* that I'm bringing him down to such an uncouth level. "Does it matter? We both have something the other wants. Let me complete the ritual to remove your magic, and I'll release your family. It's quite simple."

"How do I know you'll keep your word?"

"What interest do I have in two powerless humans? Of course I'll send them back," he says with an easy shrug.

"Kitty," says Matt, his voice low and warning. I hold up a hand to hush him. We don't have a choice.

"Fine," I say. "Send them back now."

"When you step into this binding ring, I shall."

I look at the floor. The mist rolls away at his gesture, and I see a circle of sigils marked there in dull red. "Shivam's notes were very helpful," he says.

I clench my fists and step into the circle. Matt lets out a wordless shout and rushes to grab me, but the moment he reaches past the line, he disintegrates. "Matt," I scream, but as I turn, the sigils flare, and I'm surrounded by a whirring ring of energy reaching to my knees. "What did you do to him?"

"I did nothing," he says, not even looking at me. "If he's lucky, he'll rematerialize somewhere else, being a ghost already."

I grit my teeth and fight back tears. I can't admit how fucking scared I am, not if I don't want to break down crying. "Let my family go back," I say.

Anderson rolls his eyes and gestures. Peter and Sam move and stretch as if they're in their beds, and I can barely breathe through the lump in my throat. I've been holding this back for so long, but I know there's a chance I won't survive this. I need to know that they will.

Peter blinks as they begin to fade, and his eyes go wide. "Kitty," he says, but just as quickly, he's gone.

"Did you send them back home? They're safe?" I ask. As if the bastard can't lie to me.

"They're back in their beds, none the wiser," says Anderson. "Now, your magic."

"It's going to kill me, isn't it?"

Anderson laughs, once, short and sharp. "I have no idea. Do you really think I go around doing this all the time?"

"I don't know, do I? I thought you were my boss. I thought there were other reapers like me, that we were trying to do something good for people. I thought my father would be better."

"Well," he says as he opens a book. "If it's any consolation, you were doing good for some people."

"What're you really going to do with my magic?" I ask. I don't know why I'm stalling him. There's no help for me. I'm afraid. Something deep inside me tells me it'll hurt, and I'm afraid.

"I'll use it, for God's sake," he snaps, his composure breaking for the first time. "To have the kind of power you do and waste it, mourn over it, there's the real sin. You have no idea how rare it is to be able to simply create in the moment! What *couldn't* I do with your power?"

"So you'll, what, take money from people because they're grieving? Why should you get to do that?"

"Why not?" he says, and it's like he genuinely doesn't understand.

"Because it's not fair. We have this power. How can we not use it to do good?"

He laughs. "Just like a child. People are not born equal. Some have great minds, some have money, and some have other sorts of power. That's how it is."

I grit my teeth. "And me being your daughter. That means nothing?"

He turns back to his notes as if I'm beyond his interest, and I seethe. I clench my fists and jaw as Anderson starts to work around the circle, drawing other sigils. I look past him into the mist, desperate to find something I can work with, some way out of this. I squint to see shapes that seem to be coalescing, but it's hard to tell whether that's my hopeful imagination making patterns out of the ever-changing wisps or if it's really someone coming for me.

And then I cry out and fall to my knees as pain spears through my side. I clutch my waist, and my hand comes away wet, but not with blood. Shaking, I can see a thick, silvery liquid dripping to the floor, running over my fingers, and I'm horrified and captivated. It clings to me, viscous, only falling at the last moment.

Anderson's staring when I look up, and for a moment, I hope wildly that he'll realise how horrible this is and let me go. I catch his eye. He turns away, draws another sigil into the floor, and this time, the pain is all the worse for my expecting it.

I start to panic as the magic drips from me faster. As I search around for some way out, my magic starts to swirl with me, jerky movements, as if it's alive by itself, not just silver blood. It rises up like snakes and seems to beat on our invisible cage, crying out wordlessly, and beyond, the mist seems to writhe in concert with my magic. "Stop this," I cry to Anderson, but he's writing again, writing another one. "Stop, please, stop. Don't do this, Dad!"

Then there's a blast of red light and a roar like a battle cry. Anderson flies across the floor, and Mum appears, her skirt snapping at her heels, her magic a ball of fury in her hands. And Talia. *Talia!*

"What are you doing?" I say, terrified that she's trapped here too, that she's dead again.

"I don't know," Talia yells back. She scuffs at the sigils on the floor with her foot, then the heel of her hand. She stands, tugging both hands through her hair when it doesn't come off, then glances at me.

"Talia, go, it's too dangerous," I beg. Anderson is fighting with Mum and Shivam, but Talia's not magical. The thought of her getting caught in the crossfire is more painful than the magic draining from me slowly.

Talia holds both hands in front of her, staring at her palms. She clasps them into fists, then hurls them toward the sigils at her feet with a shout. It's not magic, not like I've been taught. It's magic like I used to do when I was a kid, when I was just finding out I could bring the dead back to life. It's wild and blue and beautiful, and I think she's swearing to channel it.

The sigil goes up in flames with a shriek, and I fall to my knees, free of the binding circle. "Kitty!" she cries and rushes to lift me.

"No, wait," I beg, reaching to the ground. My magic is streaming back to me, reaching out for my fingers as I reach for it, flowing into me so hard, it makes me dizzy with relief.

"Are you okay?" she asks, half cradling me on the floor.

"Yeah," I say, and I laugh, hysterical. "Yeah, I am. You're *magic*, Talia."

She laughs too and shrugs, and then a blast of magic whips past our heads, and she pulls me to the ground, tucking my head safely under her chin.

I hear Mum scream and fight Talia to let me go. Mum and Shivam are lying on the floor, the mist swirling around them, and Anderson advances on us. "Did you know?" he says, wiping a smudge of blood from under his nose. "That magic weakens when you die?"

Talia and I scramble to our feet, and it's my turn to push her behind me. I crouch and form a sigil of my own in the air over my cupped hand, and Talia snarls her fury until her own untamed magic almost engulfs both of her forearms.

Then Anderson gasps and stumbles. His forehead creases in confusion. "Did you know," says my mum behind him, her arms outstretched to both sides, "that if you use magic to kill, the dead come back for their revenge?"

Anderson looks uncertain for the first time. He glances around him, and the shapes that I've been noticing are looking more solid, more humanoid. I squint into the mist, and my gut swirls because I've been working for him. I'm as much to blame as him, and they'll want me too.

"Kitty, you have to open the doors," Shivam shouts, and I see he's struggling to write sigils in the air. They keep dissolving halfway through. "It's got to be you. Nobody else has the power."

"What do I do?" I ask. I don't know what's going on. I don't even know where to look. I don't know if I'll be a target even if I succeed.

"Matt," Talia says softly.

I turn to where she's looking, and I see him as if through warped glass, pressing up against the boundary, trying to push through. I can only recognise him because he's the closest, and because as he pushes, the mist bends around him, letting us catch glimpses of his contorted face, his black hair.

My fear settles down. Matt's with them, and that's all that matters. I don't care what the other dead want with me, if they'll take their revenge on me as well as Anderson. My best friend is trying to push through, so that door, if you can call it that, *will* open.

I hold my hand up, and my magic flows the way it always did, with just my decision. The grey place bends to my will. There's a ripping sound, and the dead march through. I set my jaw and step forward to stand by Anderson, who's now whimpering and struggling to free himself from whatever bind my mother's put on him.

I expect to see all those I've exchanged. Those I've killed. I'm looking for the teacher who took Talia's place, for the addict who killed someone by accident, for the old man who wanted his wife to live. The people I've exchanged for the Society and those I exchanged by myself, working instinctively with my magic.

I don't see any of them. I don't see anyone I recognise other than Matt, who runs up to wrap me tight and drag me out of the way.

Anderson pleads with them as they surround him, silent and so, so numerous. Talia rushes up to me, and I'm sandwiched between her and Matt as the vast pack of ghosts wrap around

Anderson. His voice continues, begging, and I'm waiting in terror for screams, but they never come. The sound…drifts away, and with it, the dead.

Shivam walks toward the tight huddle of silver forms, and I can see his teeth clenching. Anderson is the reason he's here too. He pauses before he reaches the pack, his gaze catching mine, and he gives me a short nod.

"Why not me?" I can't help but ask. "Why am I forgiven?"

He laughs bitterly. "You know that last sigil you could never get to work quite right?"

I frown. "Yeah."

"That's the one that took their money," he says. "Anderson…" He sighs and stops. "*I* lied. It was never necessary. Your magic always fought it." He holds my gaze one moment longer, then sets his jaw and walks into the pack of the dead, through the other ghosts as if they're no barrier at all. The mass becomes amorphous, and with a crack that makes us all jump, it's gone.

# CHAPTER TWENTY-FOUR

## *Talia*

We breathe for a moment in the silence, then Kitty goes heavy in my arms. I look down in horror, cry out wordlessly as I see her eyes roll back in her head. "Kitty!"

"M'okay," she slurs, her hand lifting to pat my arm, then flopping back down.

"What's wrong with her?" I demand, looking up to Madeline and Matt, begging them mentally to make it all better.

"She's exhausted," Madeline says, kneeling in front of Kitty as I lower her to the floor, my arms still tight around her. "Kitty, love, can you hear me?"

"Yeah," she says, but she doesn't open her eyes, presses her face against my neck instead. I can't help smiling around my relief, tucking my chin over her head.

Madeline strokes her hand, and I wonder if she can touch her here, if she sometimes wishes Kitty could be here more often. The thought tightens my arms around Kitty's shoulders.

"You need to get back," Madeline says softly, looking at me like she's heard my thoughts. She might be able to, fucking magic and all. "Look after her, won't you?"

"Of course," I say.

Madeline stands and holds Matt's shoulders. "You should go back too."

Matt crooks a smile. "Yeah, I've got used to haunting her."

Madeline smiles mischievously. "No, darling. I mean, you should go back."

"What, you mean…"

"There has to be balance, after all," she says. "After they took Anderson. You'd only be putting it right."

Matt's jaw drops. "Are you serious?" I ask, narrowing my eyes at Madeline because magic ghost mother of my girlfriend or not, I will kick her arse for teasing Matt like this. "He can have his life back?"

In answer, Madeline draws sigils in the air. I don't know anything about this stuff, but I think they're the same ones I've seen Kitty draw so long and just a couple of months ago. Kitty blinks in my arms, rubbing her face, and stares up at them in wonder. Madeline pauses at the last one, her finger still in the air, the glow frozen at her fingertip. "Stay safe, my lovelies," she says and *pushes*.

There's a white light in front of my eyes, and I gasp loudly, like I've been pulled out of the water. "Kitty," I say. "Kitty, are you okay?"

"Yeah," she says. "Did she really…is Matt really back?"

"Pinch me," says Matt from the floor. "Someone pinch me right the fuck now."

I kick him instead, and he yelps. "Holy fucking shit I'm alive, I'm alive!"

He bursts into tears, loud, childish, gulping sobs, and Kitty falls to her knees to wrap her arms around him. I pause for a second before I'm there too, rubbing circles on his back and laughing through my own tears.

"Talia! Talia, are you there?"

I blink up in amazement at Daniel's voice echoing in the dark. "Daniel?"

A beam of light blinds me, and I squint and hold up my hand. I realise I haven't a clue where we are.

"There you are! Thank God." To my shock, he grabs me around the shoulders and squeezes me tight, murmuring, "Thank you, thank you," under his breath. I squeeze his shoulder back.

"I'm fine," I say. "I'm fine. Where are we?"

"The warehouse you told me about," he says, pulling back

and shining the torchlight from his phone around. The hollow echo and empty chill of the air suddenly becomes apparent.

"It wasn't like this before," Kitty says with a frown. "Even after I went back. There were still a few rooms and corridors, and now it's just derelict." She stares around at the empty cavern. "Another illusion."

Daniel shrugs. "I don't know about that, but I think we should stop pushing our luck by being here, don't you?" He glances down at Matt and holds out a hand to help him up. "Hi, I'm Daniel."

"Yeah," Matt says, a thread of hysteria in his voice. "I know who you are. I'm Matt."

"The ghost?" Daniel's eyebrows rise so high, I think they might fall off.

"Not anymore, apparently," he says, and bursts into tears again.

It's a slow shuffle getting all of us to Daniel's car, Matt blinded by tears, Kitty exhausted and hanging off me. I don't think any of us would have made it out if Daniel hadn't shown up, and I can imagine the three of us curling up together like abandoned kittens in a corner of the dusty warehouse otherwise.

Kitty and Matt fall asleep tangled in each other's arms as soon as their arses touch the back seat of Daniel's car, and I slump into the front passenger seat, my eyes and mind unfocused. Daniel squeezes my forearm and smiles at me. "Where shall I take you?"

"I don't know," I say. Panic rises in me, and tears come too easily. I know to take Matt and Kitty back to Peter and Sam, but what will they remember? Will it be like my return to life, when I seemed to have been alive the whole time? Will Peter and Sam remember being kidnapped and held like flies in spider silk in the grey place? How much damage could I cause by making a simple decision?

"Oh, you poor thing," Daniel says. "Can I give you a hug? You look like you could use one."

I fall into him and sob on his shoulder, my mind whiting out with relief and shame and the alien, terrifying comfort of a safe place.

"I tell you what," Daniel says as my tears run dry. "I'll take you all to get some food until we decide together. It's dinnertime anyway."

"Really?"

"Yes, you scared the life out of me disappearing like that for hours. At least it gave me time to find my way here, though."

"Thank you, Daniel. I'm sorry to be such a bother."

He laughs. "You're really not, Talia. You know, you're allowed to be helped."

He starts the car and lets me sit in silence, small and drained, until we get to a chip shop. Matt and Kitty stir as soon as he gets back in the car with packets of greasy fried food. "Holy shit, I'm hungry," Matt groans. He hesitates, glancing up at Daniel. "Uh, sorry, blasphemy."

"As long as you're not cursing the name of God, I'm sure we'll be fine," he says, sending an amused glance my way. "We weren't sure where you wanted to go. I assume to your homes, but anywhere between here and Oxford is still on the table if necessary."

"I wasn't sure what Peter would know, if he'd think Matt's been alive this whole time or if he and Sam would remember being kidnapped," I say, twisting around in my seat.

"Shit," sighs Kitty. "I don't know, I'm flying blind." She twists her lips wryly. "Again. But either way, that's where we're going first."

Matt takes a deep breath and blows it out slowly. "How am I going to cope if he doesn't know?" he asks, his voice quiet and young the way he tries to avoid. "I can't…" He trails off and turns his face away, wiping at damp cheeks.

I don't tell him I know how it feels. There's nothing I can say that'll make it better. I leave Kitty to the soft whispers of comfort, turn back to stare out into the darkness behind my reflection in the window. I eat my chips mechanically.

Matt is almost in tears when we knock on Peter's door.

Twitching and shuffling from foot to foot, he's barely able to keep his breath steady.

When the door opens, he falls forward away from our grasp and wraps his arms tight around his dad, burying his face in Peter's neck. Peter blinks, then hugs him back just as tight, murmuring something comforting in Polish as he raises his eyebrows at Kitty.

He's oblivious, then. Kitty has picked that up too. She makes up some story about a date gone wrong, and I notice she carefully leaves the pronouns out.

"You had a fight with Connor? Oh, *kochanie*, I'm sorry," Peter says, and Kitty can't hide the little gasp, the *oh* as she puts her hands up to her mouth. Peter's engrossed in his son, though, and I look away. I'm not jealous, really. It just seems fake to me. Like an American sitcom.

"Come on, Maciek, we'll have some tea, and you can tell me how bad of a person he is," Peter says, tugging Matt inside. "Thank you so much for bringing him home. I'm sorry," he says to Daniel. "I don't know your name."

"Daniel Asiimwe," he says with his blinding smile, shaking Peter's hand.

"Talia's rabbi," Kitty explains, and Peter smiles back.

"Peter Wiśniewski," he says. "I would invite you in, but…" He shrugs.

"No, not at all," says Daniel. "Talia and I are about to head back to Oxford."

Sam squeezes past Peter, who pats him on the shoulder. "See you tomorrow, okay?"

"Thanks, Peter," Sam and Kitty say in concert, and we step back until the door closes. Kitty, Daniel, and I slump.

"You all okay?" says Sam, giving us the side-eye.

"Yes," Kitty says, and I see what an effort it is to straighten her spine and put on a genuine smile. She squeezes Sam's shoulder, and we walk with them up the road to their block of flats.

Daniel and I stop at the pavement. I watch Kitty's back, her shoulders starting to hunch once more as she walks away from me once again. Is this the end? I'd thought it was only a few days ago.

Am I going to let it be?

"Kitty," I say, and my feet are moving me to her. She turns, and I've enough time to spot the deep well of sadness in her eyes and know I don't want to let it stay there. I catch her around the waist, tilt her chin up, and kiss her. "I'll come over tomorrow," I say, and I work hard to keep it a statement, not a question. It doesn't quite work. "If that's okay with you?"

She smiles like the sun coming out, and I feel both her hands tangling in the jumper at my hips. "Yeah," she says, a breath. "To stay?"

"You want me to?"

She nods. "I, uh…I got a menorah." She blushes, and it's the most beautiful thing I've ever seen. I can't help kiss the pink on her cheek. "On the internet. I didn't know if you had one or if you wanted to spend it with us, but I looked it up, and it starts on the twenty-second, right, and I thought I'd…well, I wanted to."

I smile so hard it hurts. "Thank you."

"Awesome," says Sam, clapping his hands once, and I blink up at him. He looks like he's on the verge of laughing or running away. "Cool, so you're staying, that's settled. Kitty will stop moping, and we can try out those latke thingies. Now, can we please go in or something? I'm freezing my butt off here."

Kitty laughs and presses her forehead against my collarbone. I feel something like tears or laughter or fear or joy bubbling up in my throat and hug her tight to me before we pull apart. I think I might run. Not away, just for the joy of movement. "Tomorrow, then," I say as I walk backward to Daniel.

"Tomorrow," Kitty says, walking backward to Sam. He rolls his eyes and shakes his head and drags her into the block of flats. She waves. It's so fucking cute.

Daniel pats me on the shoulder and gives me an amused sideways look. "Sure you don't want me to leave you here?"

I cover my face with both hands, feeling the heat radiating

off me. I'm still smiling. Daniel laughs, but it's with me, and it's in support of me.

"I'm not that daft yet," I promise, rolling my eyes at him. "I need my car and my toothbrush, for a start."

He nods. "I would expect nothing else from you, Talia."

"What's that meant to mean?" I say, torn between laughing and frowning.

"Nothing at all." He grins and turns, trailing me after him like a puppet.

I bug him, and he laughs and pretends he'll never tell, and the bubble in my throat seems to burst, the venom of happiness flooding me. I may never stop smiling.

# Epilogue

## *Talia*

"Kitty," Sam hollers as he opens the door to me. "It's your girlfriend."

"I'm literally right here," she says from behind him, clutching at her ears. I shift my bag on my shoulder and try not to laugh at the two of them. Sam wanders off, his job of small annoying sibling done for now.

"Hi," I say, and resist the urge to wave like a nerd.

"Hi." She walks closer, so she's almost toe to toe with me, and then she looks up at me with a little smile and those big brown eyes, and my face feels like it could catch fire with how hard I'm blushing just from being near her.

I'd hate it, but it seems to be making her smile wider. I'll forgive most things if they make that smile wider.

She clears her throat and steps back, leading me. "Come on in. I've finished sorting out the sofa for you. Uh, did you have a good drive?"

It's so painfully awkward, this politeness, the formal small talk. Sod it, I think, I've never been good at all that social stuff anyway. So I catch her hand, tug her round, and pull her closer. She squeaks as I drop my bag and let the door shut behind me, but her arms come up and around my neck as I pull her in by the waist, and when I glance at her to check that this is real, that it's *welcome*, she cups my cheek and kisses me.

I will never be able to not check. I'll never believe she's

mine, not really, not someone so perfect and sweet and kind wanting to be with *me*. I can't take someone like her for granted.

Luck like this feels stolen.

"Oh, ew," Sam yells from the direction of the living room. Kitty takes one hand away from my face, probably to make a rude gesture at him, but she doesn't break the kiss until we're both giggling, noses pressed together and a bubble of just us formed in the circle of our arms.

"C'mon," Kitty says, her voice softer and more relaxed, no longer the hostess. "I want to show you the menorah we got." She leans in to give me one more peck on the lips, then links our fingers together, tugging me forward. "Sam's been painting the Christmas tree baubles white with blue stars, by the way. I told him that's probably not appropriate."

I laugh to see the kid crouched by the little fake tree, adding the wobbly blue and white baubles to the mishmash of colours already crowding it. He makes a big *ta-da* gesture, and I can't resist giving him a round of applause. "We got the colourful candles too, Talia," he says, pointing. "And I've been reading about Hanukah online. Judith is my favourite. I'm going to paint one of these red baubles to be Holofernes's head."

I blink at him, speechless for a moment, while Kitty facepalms beside me. "I'm sorry," she groans. "Sam, a severed head bauble is definitely not appropriate."

"But it's so cool!"

She looks so embarrassed I can't help but tease her, leaning over to mock whisper, "I'm lowkey judging you for letting him google that stuff. Have you *seen* the Gentileschi painting?"

"What? No, why?"

Sam perks up. "Is that the one with the blood spurting out of his neck? It's awesome, Kitty, you have to see it."

"Oh my God, Sam!"

I can't hold back my laughter anymore and pull her close, kissing her fingers where they're pressed over her eyes. "I'm not really judging you," I say. It's probably obvious that I've been teasing, but I never want there to be any question, not with her. "I think it's great that you're letting him follow his interests."

She snorts but looks less mortified. “It’s only because he thinks you’re cool.”

“Wow, cool enough to inspire research of Baroque art.”

The door bangs open, making me jump. “Matt!” Sam yells and runs down the hallway.

“Clearly, I’m not as cool as Matt,” I say wryly.

Kitty shrugs and takes the opportunity to shuffle closer, tucking her hands around my waist from behind. “He’s trying to be all grown-up with you,” she assures me.

Matt comes in then, and I take a moment to simply wonder. His vitality is no more present now as an actual living person than as a ghost. I’m so grateful to the twists and turns of fate that have brought him back here, where he’s able to duck and pick Sam up and fling him onto the sofa where he shrieks and giggles. He turns to us and nods a greeting. “All right there, Talia?”

“I’ve certainly missed having my name butchered,” I say.

Matt grins and holds out his arms. “Ah, c’mon, you miss me. Give us a hug.”

I roll my eyes but oblige him. It feels strange to be able to feel his shoulders under my palms, and neither of us can resist squeezing just that little bit harder, that little bit longer than normal. He steps back and claps me on the shoulders, glances from me to Kitty. The three of us smile at each other, and there’s a whole history in that, a whole world we may never be able to share with anyone else.

Matt’s the first to break it, clearing his throat and stepping back. “Has Kitty told you about her new job?”

“No.” I turn to her and try not to look too suspicious.

She rolls her eyes. “Don’t worry, it’s legit this time.”

“What, you mean two strange men didn’t find you on the bus to offer you a position in a shady organisation again?”

Matt laughs while Kitty smacks me on the bicep with the back of her hand. “Honestly, if I knew you two were going to gang up on me, I’d have stayed at work where I’m appreciated.”

“No,” I cry, clinging on to her, only half joking. She wraps an arm around my waist again, so I win.

“Peter offered me an apprenticeship,” she explains. “He says he's got more jobs than he can handle, and plumbers are always in demand. If I can pass the apprenticeship, I might not have to worry about money again." She says it in a hush, glancing at Sam as if to make sure he's distracted.

I wrap both arms around her and hold tight. They say money can't buy happiness, but happiness can't buy food. Just knowing she and Sam are going to be okay makes some weight I hadn't noticed lift off my chest. She clings back just as hard, and I know she feels it too.

"Hey," Matt says to me as we pull apart once more. "Dad wants to know if you're coming to Christmas Eve dinner."

"Oh, I…" I glance to Kitty for guidance.

"You're welcome to come or not," she says. "Sam and I will go regardless because we always go to the Wiśniewskis' for Christmas, but you don't have to if it's too Christian."

"I mean, would I be okay going?"

"Yeah, of course," Matt says with a shrug. "There's no pork or anything, Polish Christmas dinner isn't like the usual ham and turkey or whatever. And Dad checked the ingredients for the rest of the food. Everything's kosher."

I can feel my shoulders hunching, I'm not sure what to do with this kindness and effort directed at me. Knowing that Peter extends it to Kitty and Sam is *right*, but me? It's always strange, no matter who's offering. And then I worry I'm being suspicious or ungrateful if I refuse, and it goes round in circles in my head. But I'm trying to trust. "If it's no trouble," I say.

"Great," Matt says. I can't help watching his face closely to catch any tells, but he seems genuine. It really is no problem. "Now, Sam, you still wanna come with me to get Kitty's present?"

Sam claps his hand over Matt's mouth with an indignant squeak. "Matt! You're not supposed to tell her."

"Sorry, mate," he says, muffled by Sam's hand. "I didn't tell her what it was."

"Fine," says Sam, but he narrows his eyes in warning before he releases Matt.

He jumps down to pull his trainers on, and Matt waves to us as he turns. "Don't enjoy yourselves too much," he says with a wink. Kitty groans, and I can feel my face flushing as I roll my eyes.

The flat is plunged into quiet as the door shuts behind the two boys, and still, we don't move. I cover Kitty's hand over my waist, and she leans her cheek on my shoulder. "Thanks for coming, Talia."

"Thanks for inviting me," I say with a soft laugh. Because I really don't feel like I'm the generous one here. I suddenly remember the little keepsake in my pocket. "Oh hey, look what I found."

"A skeleton leaf," she says and laughs in delight, cupping it in her hands. "Aw, is this the same one you found on the canal path that day?"

"No, it's another one," I say, tugging at my hair. I might have developed a habit for looking at the ground as I walk. And the original one might, perhaps, be safe in the back of my optics textbook, but I'll deny that if asked.

Kitty strokes the delicate edges of the leaf, and I'm struck with awe again as she looks up at me. This woman is soft-edged and warm, all smiles and optimism, and yet she's brimming over with magic and a soul of steel. I take the leaf from her and tuck it behind her ear, then dip my head to kiss her. This, I think, maybe this I can trust.

## About the Author

Lyn Hemphill is Kenyan born and bred but now lives in Oxfordshire with her partner and two children, who like to help her come up with some more outlandish plot points. She writes every spare moment she can find, in between teaching science online and developing screenplays with her writing partner Aloïs Castel.

## Books Available From Bold Strokes Books

**Deadly Secrets** by VK Powell. Corporate criminals want whistleblower Jana Elliott permanently silenced, but Rafe Silva will risk everything to keep the woman she loves safe. (978-1-63679-087-9)

**Enchanted Autumn** by Ursula Klein. When Elizabeth comes to Salem, Massachusetts, to study the witch trials, she never expects to find love—or an actual witch…and Hazel might just turn out to be both. (978-1-63679-104-3)

**Escorted** by Renee Roman. When fantasy meets reality, will escort Ryan Lewis be able to walk away from a chance at forever with her new client Dani? (978-1-63679-039-8)

**Her Heart's Desire** by Anne Shade. Two women. One choice. Will Eve and Lynette be able to overcome their doubts and fears to embrace their deepest desire? (978-1-63679-102-9)

**My Secret Valentine** by Julie Cannon, Erin Dutton & Anne Shade. Winning the heart of your secret Valentine? These award-winning authors agree, there is no better way to fall in love. (978-1-63679-071-8)

**Perilous Obsession** by Carsen Taite. When reporter Macy Moran becomes consumed with solving a cold case, will her quest for the truth bring her closer to Detective Beck Ramsey or will her obsession with finding a murderer rob her of a chance at true love? (978-1-63679-009-1)

**Reading Her** by Amanda Radley. Lauren and Allegra learn love and happiness are right where they least expect it. There's just one problem: Lauren has a secret she cannot tell anyone, and Allegra knows she's hiding something. (978-1-63679-075-6)

**The Willing** by Lyn Hemphill. Kitty Wilson doesn't know how, but she can bring people back from the dead as long as someone is willing to take their place and keep the universe in balance. (978-1-63679-083-1)

**Watching Over Her** by Ronica Black. As they face the snowstorm of the century, and the looming threat of a stalker, Riley and Zoey just might find love in the most unexpected of places. (978-1-63679-100-5)

**Always** by Kris Bryant. When a pushy American private investigator shows up demanding to meet the woman in Camila's artwork, instead of introducing her to her great-grandmother, Camila decides to lead her on a wild goose chase all over Italy. (978-1-63679-027-5)

**Exes and O's** by Joy Argento. Ali and Madison really only have one thing in common. The girl who broke their heart may be the only one who can put it back together. (978-1-63679-017-6)

**Paris Rules** by Jaime Maddox. Carly Becker has been searching for the perfect woman all her life, but no one ever seems to be just right until Paige Waterford checks all her boxes, except the most important one—she's married. (978-1-63679-077-0)

**Shadow Dancers** by Suzie Clarke. In this third and final book in the Moon Shadow series, Rachel must find a way to become the hunter and not the hunted, and this time she will meet Eshee Yumiko head-on. (978-1-63555-829-6)

**The Kiss** by C.A. Popovich. When her wife refuses their divorce and begins to stalk her, threatening her life, Kate realizes to protect her new love, Leslie, she has to let her go, even if it breaks her heart. (978-1-63679-079-4)

**The Wedding Setup** by Charlotte Greene. When Ryann, a big-time New York executive, goes to Colorado to help out with her best friend's wedding, she never expects to fall for the maid of honor. (978-1-63679-033-6)

**Velocity** by Gun Brooke. Holly and Claire work toward an uncertain future preparing for an alien space mission, and only one thing is certain—they will have to risk their lives, and their hearts, to discover the truth. (978-1-63555-983-5)

**Wildflower Words** by Sam Ledel. Lida Jones treks west with her father in search of a better life on the rapidly developing American frontier, but finds home when she meets Hazel Thompson. (978-1-63679-055-8)

**A Fairer Tomorrow** by Kathleen Knowles. For Maddie Weeks and Gerry Stern, the Second World War brought them together, but the end of the war might rip them apart. (978-1-63555-874-6)

**Changing Majors** by Ana Hartnett Reichardt. Beyond a love, beyond a coming-out, Bailey Sullivan discovers what lies beyond the shame and self-doubt imposed on her by traditional Southern ideals. (978-1-63679-081-7)

**Highland Whirl** by Anna Larner. Opposites attract in the Scottish Highlands, when feisty Alice Campbell falls for city girl about town Roxanne Barns. (978-1-63555-892-0)

**Holiday Hearts** by Diana Day-Admire and Lyn Cole. Opposites attract during Christmastime chaos in Kansas City. (978-1-63679-128-9)

**Humbug** by Amanda Radley. With the corporate Christmas party in jeopardy, CEO Rosalind Caldwell hires Christmas Girl Ellie Pearce as her personal assistant. The only problem is, Ellie isn't a PA, has never planned a party, and develops a ridiculous crush on her totally intimidating new boss. (978-1-63555-965-1)

**On the Rocks** by Georgia Beers. Schoolteacher Vanessa Martini makes no apologies for her dating checklist, and newly single mom Grace Chapman ticks all Vanessa's Do Not Date boxes. Of course, they're never going to fall in love. (978-1-63555-989-7)

**Song of Serenity** by Brey Willows. Arguing with the Muse of music and justice is complicated, falling in love with her even more so. (978-1-63679-015-2)

**The Christmas Proposal** by Lisa Moreau. Stranded together in a Christmas village on a snowy mountain, Grace and Bridget face their past and question their dreams for the future. (978-1-63555-648-3)

**The Infinite Summer** by Morgan Lee Miller. While spending the summer with her dad in a small beach town, Remi Brenner falls for Harper Hebert and accidentally finds herself tangled up in an intense restaurant rivalry between her famous stepmom and her first love. (978-1-63555-969-9)

**Wisdom** by Jesse J. Thoma. When Sophia and Reggie are chosen for the governor's new community design team and tasked with tackling substance abuse and mental health issues, battle lines are drawn even as sparks fly. (978-1-63555-886-9)

**A Convenient Arrangement** by Aurora Rey and Jaime Clevenger. Cuffing season has come for lesbians, and for Jess Archer and Cody Dawson, their convenient arrangement becomes anything but. (978-1-63555-818-0)

**An Alaskan Wedding** by Nance Sparks. The last thing either Andrea or Riley expects is to bump into the one who broke her heart fifteen years ago, but when they meet at the welcome party, their feelings come rushing back. (978-1-63679-053-4)

**Beulah Lodge** by Cathy Dunnell. It's 1874, and newly betrothed Ruth Mallowes is set on marriage and life as a missionary…until she falls in love with the housemaid at Beulah Lodge. (978-1-63679-007-7)

**Gia's Gems** by Toni Logan. When Lindsey Speyer discovers that popular travel columnist Gia Williams is a complete fake and threatens to expose her, blackmail has never been so sexy. (978-1-63555-917-0)

**Holiday Wishes & Mistletoe Kisses** by M. Ullrich. Four holidays, four couples, four chances to make their wishes come true. (978-1-63555-760-2)

**Love By Proxy** by Dena Blake. Tess has a secret crush on her best friend, Sophie, so the last thing she wants is to help Sophie fall in love with someone else, but how can she stand in the way of her happiness? (978-1-63555-973-6)

**Marry Me** by Melissa Brayden. Allison Hale attempts to plan the wedding of the century to a man who could save her family's business, if only she wasn't falling for her wedding planner, Megan Kinkaid. (978-1-63555-932-3)

**Pathway to Love** by Radclyffe. Courtney Valentine is looking for a woman exactly like Ben—smart, sexy, and not in the market for anything serious. All she has to do is convince Ben that sex-without-strings is the perfect pathway to pleasure. (978-1-63679-110-4)